THE BARTERED SOUL
BOOK 1 OF ANDROMEDA'S ACCOUNT

L.B. BENSON

EMERALD MOON
PRESS

THE BARTERED SOUL
BOOK 1 OF ANDROMEDA'S ACCOUNT

By
L.B. Benson

Cover design by Hampton Lamoureaux/TS95 Studios www.ts95studios.com

Edited by Aimee Vance
www.aimeevancebooks.com

ISBNs
979-8-9861231-0-3 (eBook)
979-8-9861231-1-0 (Paperback)
979-8-9861231-2-7 (Hardback)

Published by Emerald Moon Press
https://lbtheauthor.com

❋ Created with Vellum

To anyone who delayed their dream because you thought you weren't brave enough, or that your idea wasn't good enough.

You are, and it is.

xo, LB

CONTENT WARNING

The Bartered Soul is an adult fantasy/romance that contains content that might be upsetting for some readers. It is intended for readers over the age of 18.

To view detailed content/trigger warnings please visit the author's website: https://lbtheauthor.com

PROLOGUE

E *ight years ago...*

ALTHOUGH NIGHT FELL HOURS AGO, THE FIRES BLAZING ALONG the coastline and through the forest turned the dark skies the orange of a sunset through the haze of smoke. No stars shone through the smog, and the moon hid behind the clouds as though the crackling flames and soldiers' roars frightened her as much as they did the villagers fleeing through the trees. Screams of terrified women and children echoed over the shouts of those who stood to defend them, even if they knew their scythes and axes wouldn't stand against the warhorses and cold steel of the new King's army.

As the homes outside Athene burned, the army turned its attention to the sacred grove and temple on the hill, the same as it had at the Northern point and the Eastern coast. In the month since Queen Adelaide's assassination, the

1

lengthy siege at the castle in Aphros ended, and the troops swept through Selennia.

Dargan Blackwell, a nobleman from the nearby continent, seized the throne, declaring himself the new King. His true desire was always power, but when his attempts to win Queen Adelaide's heart ended in embarrassment and failure, he settled for destroying everything she ever loved. Backed by religious zealots and other men desperate for power, King Dargan pushed his men onward under the guise of revolution to convert the heathen people of Selennia to the true religion and the real God. To *save* them.

His army razed villages, destroyed temples dedicated to the Goddess, conscripted men into military service, and forced women into worse. The new priests who traveled with his forces could be just as cruel as his soldiers, insisting the priestesses in the temples serving the Goddess be cleansed of their sins with holy fire, oftentimes lighting the pyres themselves.

The bells of sorrow rang through Selennia for weeks after the Queen's murder, and those in Athene were no different. But tonight they were frantic, warning the townspeople of the oncoming army, screaming for them to flee.

But the priestesses in the white temple on the hill didn't flee. In the old days, they would have been the ones to defend the town, but over a century of peace lulled them into a sense of security, and they no longer trained in ways of war. Some of the younger novices and initiates – many not even old enough to have taken part in the rites yet, and those not fully trained — cowered in darkened corners, but there was no hiding from the danger lurking at their door. Whether they wore the mark of the Goddess on their brow yet or not, their fates were sealed.

The High Priestess stood in the center of the temple's great entry, her feet grounded on the precious metal sigils that were inlaid on the white marble tiles. She barked orders to the male guards who waited at the oak doors, knowing they would be the first to fall in the name of the Goddess. She knew that she would likely fall shortly after the guards, but held herself straight and proud despite her age — silver hair streaming behind her, the sigil of the Goddess glowing at her brow. She couldn't allow her fear to show; she knew her duty this night.

It was said that the priestesses once *glowed* alongside their sisters, fueled by their hot fury as they walked into battle. But, this night, they stood against the enemy at their doors without their full power to protect them, whispering prayers to the Goddess that one would escape the clutches of the new King. One who would rise again to bring justice to Selennia.

When the sound of hoofbeats became more clear through the open windows high at the front of the temple, and the smell of smoke wafted overhead, the High Priestess knew the time had come.

"Nerissa! Aisling! Layla!" Her strong voice carried through the temple, and three young women stepped from the shadows. Fear showed on their faces, but the girls stood firm. All three worked closely with the High Priestess as they trained to bear the title themselves, she knew they would follow her instructions without fail, even if they trembled in terror. Pride at their courage swelled in the High Priestess' breast as she memorized their faces. Grief gripped her heart that she had not been able to teach them everything they needed to know to keep them safe.

Her voice dipped low, barely above a whisper, and the younger women leaned in to listen. "Goddess be with you all." The High Priestess laid a hand on each of their brows in blessing, then commanded, "Make for the escape ways. Now!"

The three glanced between one another in confusion.

"Go? High Priestess, we can help —" Aisling began. Her quaking voice betrayed fear despite her bold words, but before she could finish her elder stopped her.

"This is not an option. This is a command, straight from the Goddess." Pounding began on the doors of the halls, and every eye in the hall shifted to the wood, groaning loudly under the battering ram that slammed into the doors. "Go now!" the High Priestess roared the command at the three in front of her.

Nerissa, the most solemn of the women, opened her mouth for a moment to protest, but caught herself before any sound passed her lips. Her jaw tightened before she bowed her head deeply in respect, and was the first to turn on her bare feet to take flight. The other two followed, each headed in a different direction, dark hair flying behind them. Their footsteps pounded down the secret passages that would lead to the forest — to freedom — as the battering ram breached the heavy oak doors.

PART ONE
THE BARTERED SOUL

CHAPTER 1

Goddess, I haven't forgotten you. I know I am not the only one who remembers. I can't be the last. I honor you tonight, as I do each night I am here. Give me strength to endure, don't forget me either…

Jingle. Jingle jingle.

The sound breaks through my silent prayer, and my eyes snap to the golden bell hanging next to the door of my room as it sweetly chimes, signaling the start of another evening. I've lain awake for the past hour, absently staring out the window to admire the sky changing colors as the sun slowly sinks behind the buildings that block my view of the distant mountains.

The moon will be full over the city of Artemisia tonight. In what feels like a previous life, my entire day would have been spent in prayer, and I would now be anointing my skin with sacred oils and silks in preparation for the full moon celebration. But that life no longer exists. Instead, I will be anointing myself in the cheap fragrance and tacky clothing Madame Celeste demands we wear.

I assume Celeste isn't her real name; she thinks it a clever choice to play off the blatant celestial theme she chose for the brothel I now call home. Each one of her *girls* must select a constellation for her namesake. I chose Andromeda, but I'm not foolish enough to think a hero is coming to save me.

The bell rings another warning, so I sigh and push myself from the feather bed to begin my evening routine. I wash my body and comb my dark hair, braiding the front portion into a crown with the rest free to tumble down my back. The style, along with the faint crescent sigil on my brow, is a reminder to the world of what I once was. I smear kohl around my eyes and smudge stain on my lips to darken the deep rose hue I was blessed with.

To honor the Goddess, I delicately trace gold dust along my collarbone and the tops of my shoulders. The small jar has barely any dust still clinging to its sides — one of the last remnants of my old life that I smuggled with me when I fled the temple all those nights ago. In the dim lights below no one will realize what shimmers on my skin, but She will know I still honor Her.

My hands graze over the inky blue scrap of fabric I choose to wear this evening, almost the same color as my eyes. Its sheer panels barely hide my breasts and the skirt lands just below the curve of my backside — leaving things to the imagination is not one of the tenets of Madame Celeste's establishment.

Fortunately, she has allowed several concessions for me — I am allowed to pick the colors I wear and I only bed the men of my choosing. I command a higher rate and privilege because of my *talents*, both those I sell to the customers and those I offer to the other girls — challenging me is not worth the hit her profits would take if I left.

With a last glance in the mirror, I stand taller. The proud priestess I once was is a mere phantom staring back at me from behind my kohl-darkened eyes.

Before I make my way down to the main salon, I stop in at one of the girl's rooms. Knocking softly, I push the door open to check on Carina — although she's confided that her given name is Lily — and drift to her bedside.

"How are you feeling today?" I ask. My hand brushes lightly over her arm as she reclines on the bed recovering from a miscarriage.

She smiles politely at me, and I take that as my answer. My hand skims her forehead to feel for fever before I shift to the table in her room, withdrawing a packet of herbs. I mix a tisane for the pain and to soothe her ragged nerves.

She didn't want the babe, but that doesn't change the distress she must feel in her body and heart. She is much younger than I, barely more than a child herself, and I curse the false King and his religion for making this girl's choices harder than they already were.

The door closes softly behind me as I continue down the main staircase, and my bare feet sink into the thick carpet at the bottom — black, woven with silver stars. I nod to Jacob, one of the large men who watch over us for protection, as I do every evening. He rarely speaks to us, but returns the gesture, bowing his bald head to me. The velvet chairs in the main salon are beginning to fill with customers and girls flutter at their elbows like the gulls at the docks flocking to fishermen's boats. The flirtatious giggles from the girls blend with the deeper murmurs from customers and the music from the piano player in the corner.

Madame Celeste reclines against the bar, drink already in hand. In the years I've been with her, I've never actually seen her take a sip. She prefers to always maintain a clear head in case of unruly patrons, but I understand her reasoning — one must keep up appearances.

Tonight she is resplendent in a gold gown that hugs her ample curves, a matching crown of rays on her auburn head like she is the Sun itself. I meet her gaze, and she grants me a smile that's as artificial as her hair color before I scan the men lounging throughout the room.

This early in the night the clientele consists of regulars — merchants, nobles, and other men of means who stop in a few times a week for refreshments and conversation with their favorite girls. Some of them will go upstairs, but many seem to be content with a round ass on their lap while they sip on Celeste's finest whiskeys and wines. They tip the girls handsomely, so no one complains. It's easy money, even if Celeste takes a cut.

Despite being a thorn in my side, I can't fault Celeste. She is usually fair with us, even if we do have to follow her ridiculous rules, and she takes a smaller cut than most of the other brothel owners along the row. It's part of the reason I selected this house. That, and the fact that Celeste allows me to use my healing knowledge to help the other women when I can.

Joining her at the bar, I request the same drink I order every night — a single glass of sparkling wine. I won't allow myself more — like Celeste, I also prefer to keep a firm grip on my faculties, but one drink at the beginning of the night takes the edge off.

"Good evening, Madame," I smirk to my boss, toying with the stem of the glass the bartender passes me.

"Andromeda," Celeste answers as her hazel eyes scan the light dusting of gold on my skin in the candlelight. "You look... *festive* tonight."

"I always try to look my best, Madame," I reply coyly, fluttering my lashes in mock flirtation.

Celeste knows I hold most of the men who pass through the doors of the House of Starlight in contempt, and any flirtation I exhibit in this salon is just another disguise to smother memories of my past. She also knows that I cling tight to the Old Ways. Hell, she might still do so as well. She has never reprimanded me for it, even though, according to the King, she has every right to have me beaten, or worse, for doing so. From what I've gathered she's only a few years older than I am, and as much as I hate to admit it, she feels like a kindred spirit.

At twenty-seven, I am the oldest of the merchandise at Madame Celeste's House of Starlight. I hide my age well. My skin is still milky and smooth due to spending most of my time under the moonlight in service of the Goddess, instead of laboring in the sun or caring for a family.

Some of my fellow girls haven't been so lucky, turning to this life in desperation, but the men here don't seem to care. Most of them are so drunk by the time they reach the rooms upstairs that they can barely remember where to stick their cock, let alone notice a few perceived imperfections.

As I sip my wine, I turn to scan the salon for tonight's

prey. I prefer inexperienced boys with too much money to spend or older gentlemen with refined tastes. They are usually malleable enough for me to seek my own pleasure in honor of the Goddess while lightening their purses in the process.

The rougher visitors, men fresh from long voyages or soldiers from King Dargan's regiments, rarely make it past my threshold. Celeste decided that forcing me to allow such visitors wasn't worth the laundry fees she incurred the first few weeks of my residence — bloodstains, courtesy of the dagger I keep under my mattress, are much harder to remove.

A lonely young man sitting at the corner of the bar snags my attention, and I raise my brow when his gaze meets mine. As I prowl toward him, a hush falls over the salon, as if the air has been sucked from the room on the chill breeze that blows in with the new arrival. With my back to the entry door, I can't see the newcomer, but I already know who has stepped into the room.

Captain William Lennox has arrived.

Shifting my long hair, I sneak a glance to confirm my suspicion and see him settling in at the same booth he has reserved every night for the last week. His hateful eyes sweep the salon and its patrons.

Celeste has already crossed the room to greet him, a bright smile on her face at the thought of him emptying his pockets into her hands. He keeps minimal candles around his table, making his unnaturally black hair almost blend into the midnight sky painted on the wall behind him. Shadows caress the hollows of his sharp cheeks and strong jawline.

I swallow my distaste for the pirate lord and rumored flesh trader, returning my focus to the innocent blond in front of me — the polar opposite of the man in the booth across the room. As I continue around the corner of the golden-edged bar, I feel the Captain's dark gaze prickling between my shoulder blades, the same as I have every night he's held court here. I take a deep breath and smile at the young man sitting in front of me, refusing to look back at the sinister creature.

IT ONLY TAKES A SHORT CONVERSATION WITH MY POTENTIAL customer before he allows me to guide him upstairs to my room.

"Is this your first time?" I ask as the door shuts behind us. Glancing over my shoulder, I see the boy has stopped just inside the door, eyes glancing between me and the bed. The blush on his face is more of an answer than the small bob of his head, but I smile just the same.

His pale skin trembles under my hands as he returns my caresses with gentle, awkward touches. I guide him in the ways of women and it takes less time for him to come than it did to talk him into accompanying me upstairs in the first place.

"Is this enough?" The boy palms several coins as he buttons his breeches, redressing after our quick escapade. The heavy coins clink together as he drops them into my hand, and he blushes before scurrying from the room.

Standing at the washbasin in the corner of the room, I wipe the evidence of our joining from my skin in anticipation of my next visitor. My thoughts drift away from the walls surrounding me as I replenish the water in the ewer, the motions methodical and mindless, landing instead on the moonlit ceremony so many years ago; the night I lost my own innocence in dedication to the Goddess. A smile ghosts across my lips before a quick rap at the door startles me back to the present. My heart races at the sound; no one approaches my door at night.

Customers are required to stay in the main salon unless they are accompanied by one of the girls. Otherwise, someone will ring the bell to request us. Maybe it's just the blond boy coming back for something. I cast my eyes around the room, looking for anything he could have forgotten when the knock comes again, this time louder. Confusion leaks into my expression as I crack open the door, and then step back, surprised to see Madame Celeste herself standing in the hallway.

"Is everything all right?" I glance around the plush hallways for an explanation. The hall is silent except for the moans of pleasure and occasional slap of flesh coming from the neighboring rooms.

My reflection peers back at me in one of the mercury glass mirrors opposite my doorway, and I am ashamed to see a hint of fear in my eyes at the unusual visit. I can only assume one of the other girls is sick or injured for Celeste to leave her post entertaining the customers in the salon.

"Come with me, Andromeda," Celeste commands and turns on her heel, knowing I have no choice but to obey.

I stand straighter as I pull my door shut behind me to follow, padding down the carpeted hallway toward Celeste's office. Jacob has been pulled from his post downstairs and waits at the end of the hallway next to the gilded door that separates our rooms from the Madame's private domain.

I glance up at Jacob in question, but his face is unreadable as he holds the door for us and then steps inside behind me. I'm sure the same cannot be said for my own expression when I stop dead in the center of the doorway staring at the man seated behind Celeste's desk. His boots rest on the top, crushing the papers that litter the surface.

Casually sipping whiskey in the soft leather chair is Captain Lennox.

CHAPTER 2

My heart skips a beat — two — as I stare at the man in front of me. Since he began visiting the brothel years ago, I have avoided this beast's proximity and now he sits only a few feet away from me. His eyes roam my body, matching the wicked grin on his face as if he can read my emotions through my carefully schooled mask. My chin tips towards the moon as I force my legs to propel me into the room after Celeste, who hasn't noticed my hesitation.

"This is who you were requesting, correct, Captain?" Celeste asks, resting her hip against the front of the carved desk. She gives the Captain a sideways glance as she speaks, and her lips purse in irritation at his choice of seat. If I wasn't so concerned with why this man is summoning me I would be surprised at the crack in her pleasant facade.

I stand on display in the center of the room, wishing I could sink beneath the thick rug. My jaw clenches, refusing to show any emotion when the Captain smiles again, flashing his surprisingly straight, white teeth glinting in the lamplight.

Celeste, ever the gracious hostess, never allows anything but her customer's happiness to run the evening. Her hand waves into the air towards me as she encourages him to inspect the goods.

The Captain pushes back from the desk, dropping his feet to the floor. His footsteps slap a loud staccato rhythm in my ears as he prowls toward me, that smile never departing his lips. I grip the edges of my short skirt, wishing it were the hilt of my dagger hidden so far away in my room instead. His steps circle me — fingers grazing my loose hair, rubbing the pad of his thumb across my lower lip. He even has the audacity to casually flip the back of my skirt up to view my bare backside.

Despite willing myself to remain calm, my breaths become uneven at his boldness. I feel like a mare at auction — which, to him, I am — and I'm surprised when he stops short of inspecting my teeth. If he had, it would have taken every ounce of strength in me not to snap them at him. Hopefully, my tremble of rage is mistaken for desire, otherwise, he will know I would love nothing more than to claw his dark emerald eyes from his face.

"Oh, yes," the Captain finally speaks. "This is the one, Madame. I've been admiring this beauty for a while." His voice is deep and melodious, and, dare I say, pleasant. Something I wouldn't associate with the shark circling me like I'm blood in the water.

"She's a bit...older...and significantly more... *experienced*, than your usual preferences, Captain," Celeste delicately states in her soft, breathy voice. "Are you certain she's the one you would like after closer inspection?"

My gaze drops from the ornate gilded lantern above me

to meet her eyes instead, unclear whether she is insulting me or trying to deter what's coming next.

"Oh. I'm very certain, Madame."

The Captain gives me another glance, his lip quirking up on one side as he looks into my eyes, before walking to the desk and dropping a heavy leather pouch on the carved surface. The familiar clink of coins draws my attention and I jerk my eyes from Celeste's to the pouch and back. She has a catlike smile plastered on her face and won't meet my stare.

"Then it's agreed," Celeste replies.

"What is this?" I finally ask, breaking my silence for the first time, looking between the two.

"The Captain has generously offered to purchase your company for entertainment on his next voyage, Andromeda. You should be honored at the opportunity to get away from these walls for a bit," Celeste sharply states, as if I have no say in the matter.

I choke on a bitter laugh.

"Honored....*honored?* To be bought by a madman to do with as he pleases? Celeste! You know what happens to the women he buys for *entertainment*. I will not go! I'm not a slave."

"Andromeda," my name rolls off his tongue as the Captain chuckles to himself. "How fitting. A beautiful princess waiting for a sea monster to gobble her up."

His words unleash my anger. All of my carefully cultivated restraint deserts me as I launch myself toward him, but I'm abruptly caught around the waist by Jacob, who pins me gently to his chest with his massive forearm across my chest.

The Captain seems genuinely amused by my outburst, and he approaches me with a smug smile, running a rough finger down my cheek while my arms are trapped at my sides. He then bites his thumb and continues to smile while he observes me, a few gold rings glinting in the lantern light on his long fingers.

"Oh yes, Celeste. She's a proper she-wolf, indeed. She is *exactly* what I want. I believe the deposit is what we arranged for her... and the younger one." He looks over my bare legs and arms, skirt hiked up around my hips from being restrained. "Of course, she will need more appropriate clothing for the voyage. I will send a trunk of things for her and the girl within the week, on top of the fee arranged."

Knowing I won't be released until I am more composed, I take a few deep breaths, anger still seething through me. As I will myself to calm down, my eyes drift over the Captain.

Up close he radiates authority and control, right down to his simple, finely constructed coat. This man has clearly amassed great wealth through his life of piracy. But unlike some of the other pirate captains who visit the House of Starlight, he isn't ostentatious or a peacock. My eyes slide over the man the same way he has inspected me, before finally returning to meet his stare. A spark of something burns in his dark green gaze. I involuntarily swallow and shrink further into Jacob's chest as Lennox steps closer to me.

"We set sail soon, Andromeda." He bends at the waist and I feel warm, rough hands on my wrist as he focuses on some task. Bound by Jacob's large arms, I cannot see what he is doing — even as cold metal wraps around my skin and I squirm to get a better view. The Captain fiddles about for several moments before he stands and pockets a small metallic object. He then winks at me and bows to Celeste before exiting the room.

WHEN THE DOOR CLICKS SHUT BEHIND ME, I STRUGGLE AGAIN in earnest to escape Jacob's grasp. "If he releases you, will you promise to control yourself?" Celeste asks me. "I don't need you ruining my hair or dress. The night is still young."

My breathing is still ragged as anger courses under my skin, but I give a small nod. Jacob releases me immediately at Celeste's indication and ensures I am steady on my feet before looking to the Madame for a dismissal. Simultaneously, she waves him away and flicks her hand towards the chair in front of me. Although I'm practically vibrating with rage, I know emotions will not win me anything tonight. They haven't in the past.

"Celeste…" I manage to say through clenched teeth, "What have you done? What about my choices?" I demand, trying to rein in my anger. Reminding her of our agreement — that I am not chattel to be sold to the highest bidder.

"Andromeda, be reasonable. You aren't some virginal innocent being sent to sacrifice. The Captain's fee is so handsome you wouldn't have been able to resist the offer if I had given you the choice." Celeste dismisses me as if she doesn't understand that the choice itself is more important to me than the money.

"They don't come back, Celeste," I whisper, fear finally

seeping through me and coating my words. "They *never* come back."

"Don't be silly — a few have come back, Andromeda. There's one at the House of Graces down the row." I know the girl Celeste mentions as she waves her hand dismissively. She acts as a laundress for the pleasure house a few doors down, but no one has heard her speak since she returned from losing her maidenhead for *entertainment* on one of the Captain's voyages. No one knows what happened to her, but it doesn't take much imagination to assume the worst.

Celeste is right: I am no innocent virgin, but the hatred I feel toward the Captain isn't because he exercises the baser needs of humanity by purchasing women's bodies for pleasure. It's because he is known to snap up any of the young girls who have just reached womanhood before their first customers get to them.

Whenever he docks, the brothels know they will have a visit from Captain Lennox shopping for the latest virgin to entertain his crew. The girls know if they step foot on the deck of his ship, they will not return to the city in one piece, if at all. No one is sure if he sells them off at the next port, or if they ever make it to their destination.

"I won't go. Give him the money back."

"Oh, you won't? How will you manage that exactly?" Celeste asks, glancing down at the metal on my wrist. In my fear and fury, I forgot about the cold bite of the bracelet that now hangs from my slender wrist.

I look more closely at the gold band and note that, although it is a delicate piece, it is screwed on securely. Too small to slide over my hand, but not so tight that it's painful. The surface is engraved with various designs representing the sea — waves, reaching tentacles of a Kraken. But in the center, it's clearly marked — *Bartered Soul.*

His ship. I am now marked as his.

There will be no escape from the city if any of the dockworkers or sentries manning the gates see this on me. I would have to cut my hand off and risk bleeding to death to get it off.

"Here." Celeste passes me a glass of honey-colored whiskey. "Drink this."

I grimace at the liquor, but decide to give up my carefully crafted exterior for one moment and swallow the burning liquid in one gulp. It heats my throat and chest immediately and tendrils of fire tickle my senses, ready to numb them entirely with another glass.

"You'll be free, Andromeda." Her voice takes on a wistful tone that catches my attention.

"The amount of money he has offered to pay for your services is more than you could make in several years. You are here of your own accord. Once you make it back, you can leave. Start your own pleasure house, run away from this city. Hell, run away from Selennia altogether."

I look up into Celeste's eyes, and they are gentle for the first time since I stumbled onto her doorstep years ago.

"And you can be there for Lyra," she whispers, clutching my hand. I still and appraise Celeste, the fear and pride warring in her eyes.

So the girl that will be accompanying me is Lyra, her own daughter.

"How could you?" I snatch my hand away, looking at Celeste as if *she* is the sea monster, not Captain Lennox.

"She will command enough to escape this life, too. He promised it will be just one time and then he will give her the fee she is due. Please, Andromeda." Her last words are a plea.

Celeste's reasoning makes painful sense. A woman has few choices without a husband or money in our world. The bastard daughter of a whore, even if she is the Madame of an expensive brothel, won't command either of those options easily. This could be the way for the girl to buy her freedom from the legacy of her mother. If we both survive the voyage.

"Fine," I sigh, holding my glass out for another shot of oblivion. "I'll go. I'll keep watch over Lyra. Without a fight."

CHAPTER 3

The following few days become a blur of flesh and wine as I allow myself to wallow in my misery — the first time I have done so since I first arrived at the House years ago. My usual standards for who I allow into my bed slip so that I only care that they are relatively handsome and clean, and I drink far more than my typical glass of sparkling wine per evening. Anything to distract me from the fact I will be sailing any day now from the relative safety I found at the House of Starlight.

The only standard I cling to is my choice in dark swaths of fabric instead of the bright colors the other girls wear, and I slide into an obsidian silk slip of a dress when a light tapping interrupts my thoughts.

This early in the evening, I have yet to depart my sparse quarters for the opulence of the salon. I wince as the nervous tapping at my door sounds again, echoing in my pounding head.

Tonight I will not drink anything, I tell myself rubbing my temples.

I crack the door open, peering out to see a delivery boy standing next to a large trunk. He's holding his cap in hand and looking everywhere except at me as I stand scantily clad in the doorway. His obvious discomfort causes my lips to quirk at his nervousness.

"May I help you?" I ask the boy who glances up at me briefly before returning his gaze to his shoes.

"I... I was told to deliver this trunk to you, Miss. Um... I mean, Mistress. From the seamstress down the road. On the order of Cap— Captain Lennox, Mistress," he says, stumbling over his words.

I'm not sure who he fears more, me or the Captain.

"I see. Please bring it in and set it near the window." I stand away from the doorway and the boy reddens at the request, clearly nervous to enter a room in such a place. I suppress a chuckle, thinking how many young men only a few years older than him have tried to gain entry into this House, let alone into one of the girls' private rooms.

As he struggles to drag the heavy trunk into the room, I retrieve my coin purse from under my mattress to pull out a few small coins for his troubles. But before I can hand them to him, he holds up his hand.

"Oh no, Mistress! I was specifically told to not accept any coin from you or Miss Lyra. Captain Lennox was very clear that you aren't to part with any money."

"Is that so?" I'm puzzled, but drop the coins back in my purse before dismissing the boy. He bows deeply to me and dashes out the door and down the hallway.

My back presses against the wood of the door as I close it and stare down at the trunk's considerable size; I knew clothing would be sent but hadn't expected something so large. Dread fills me as I inspect the chest, surely full of frothy laces and extravagant corsets to please the Captain's desires, but curiosity takes hold and I can't help but take a peek before I go down to the salon for the night.

When I open the lid, my heart skips. The objects in the trunk are far from what I had imagined I would find. These pieces are neither lewd, nor depraved. At the top, thick, soft fox fur lines an indigo cloak of heavy wool. The cloak is tucked neatly alongside fine dresses in simple, refined styles made from muted neutrals and dark jewel tones. Even tunics and dark-colored breeches cut to my proportions are included in the box.

None of the clothing is in the bright tones women of my station are usually relegated to and I thank the Goddess for the anonymity these colors will grant me. Without a thought, my fingers drift over the fabrics, and just as I suspected, the pieces are as high quality as the clothing the Captain himself wore the night he bought my company from Celeste.

It has been years since I have felt such fine fabrics against my skin and I lovingly run my fingers over the soft materials. Several other lighter items made from linen and cotton for warmer weather lie at the bottom of the stack, as well as a pair of soft leather boots with low heels suitable for walking or riding.

As I continue to look through the selection, my hands still. At the very bottom, I touch a fabric I haven't felt for what seems like a lifetime. My hands move of their own accord, ripping the fine garments out of the trunk and onto the floor next to me so I can see the final piece lying under everything else.

Cloth of silver that looks like liquid moonlight is pooled in the trunk. Golden embroidery is stitched around the edges, showing the moon phases, protective sigils, and healing symbols. A small sob catches in my throat as I sink to my knees next to the trunk, clutching the garment to my chest.

It is a priestess' robe.

When I can breathe again, my eyes drift back to the chest in front of me. A golden choker accompanies the robe with a thin chain dangling down from it to connect to another chain that circles the waist. When worn it glistens on the skin, fully displayed by the low neckline of the robe, matching the hammered gold circlet to place on the brow — both traditionally worn for ceremonies. I haven't seen such things since I fled the temple, when the King's soldiers ripped our garments and adornments from our bodies and burned them to a chorus of our despair.

I have no idea how the Captain came by these, or if he had them made. This delicate fabric is not one you'd find at a seamstress' shop anywhere in Artemisia. Despite the tears gathering in my eyes at the knowledge that I once again own such items, I cannot comprehend the meaning behind them being included in my trunk, or how the Captain obtained them. A knot of anxiety takes shape in my stomach at the possibilities.

After a few moments, I force myself to return the clothing to the chest, carefully hiding the robe and jewelry under the wools and linens. A small compartment on the top contains undergarments and silks, none of which are as scandalous as those most of us wear regularly here in the House of Starlight.

A note sealed with a drop of dark green wax sits amongst the silks. My finger slides under the seal and my eyes scan the document — a note from the Captain himself:

I HOPE YOU FIND THESE ITEMS TO YOUR TASTE AND PROPER SIZE. Should you need any alterations, Mary Ellen at the seamstress shop will visit you at your convenience this evening – send word with the delivery boy. He will wait for an hour outside the House.

I have indicated that you should be provided with a trunk large enough to add any personal effects you choose to bring as well. Have your belongings packed and dress warmly for our departure tomorrow afternoon. – WL

A SHAKY BREATH PASSES MY LIPS.

Tomorrow afternoon.

My mind quickly shifts to all of the many things I must complete before I leave. There will be no time to see clients this evening if I am leaving tomorrow, so I quickly pen a note to Celeste telling her that I will not make an appearance in the salon tonight. I send it with a girl that passes in the hallway and retreat to my quarters. Knowing that Lyra will be leaving with me, I doubt Celeste will make much of an appearance herself.

Striding back to the trunk, my fingers close over the dress from the top of the pile, it's made from lightweight wool in the darkest charcoal. Then I quickly strip out of the gauzy black fabric I'd planned to wear this evening.

Gathering the new dress into my hands, my fingers roam over the fabric again. I'm pleased by how soft the wool is, and despite my hatred toward the Captain and anything he had a hand in, I appreciate the tight weave and fine stitching of the garment and the fact that it will keep me protected in the cool dampness of Artemisia and beyond.

I rarely wear stays or any garments that require assistance to get into, so I slip the dress over my bare skin in trial. As the fabric swishes around my legs, I catch a glimpse of myself in the mirror in the corner and have to suppress a gasp of shock at how perfectly it skims my body. The pleasure I feel from my reflection feels almost shameful.

Curiosity gets the best of me as I slink back to the trunk, removing the buttery soft leather boots. When I slip my feet into them I find they are also a perfect fit. It's been years since I've owned proper shoes – so much of my time is spent barefooted in these carpeted rooms. I twist and turn my feet, wiggling my toes in delight, and am doubly pleased to find that they don't pinch or rub.

Even though I long to run my fingers over the other fabrics again, to feel the textures and inspect the quality of each garment, I assume that there is no need to try on the remainder of the pieces, seeing as how these are all a perfect fit. With a contented sigh, I quickly undress and throw on a loose robe before dashing down the stairs to dismiss the delivery boy. Unless Miss Lyra needs alterations, my pieces are fine, and he may go.

When I return to my quarters, I take inventory of the meager assortment of personal effects I possess. My dagger is the first, and most important, item I gather. It's placed with the cloak, grey dress, and boots to wear for the journey. Next, I carefully package my sparse collection of herbs and journal of remedies to lay on top of the clothing.

Chewing on the inside of my cheek in contemplation, I quickly decide to separate several blends to leave for the girls in case of cramps or other feminine ailments while I am away. On each one, I write a brief recipe and leave it with the teas, in case I don't return. The thought brings goosebumps to my flesh, but I push it aside and continue to pack.

The small compartment in the trunk I fill with the almost empty jar of gold dust from the temple and a few select silks, jewelry, and hairpins that favored clients have gifted me over the years. Hopefully, the lock holds to keep out prying eyes or sly fingers.

From my vanity, I pack the small number of cosmetics I keep — kohl for my eyes, stain for my lips and cheeks, and the cheap brush and hand mirror provided by Celeste to all her girls. I am still not certain what form of entertainment the Captain expects me to provide, but these will help me keep the mask I wear firmly intact for the voyage.

My eyes scan the room as I check to make sure I haven't missed anything vital, but nothing stands out, anything that remains are pieces of a life I am content to leave behind.

Packing done, I slip into a simple shift and ghost down the hallway to check on the few girls that have needed my aid in the past week. Lily has recovered from the worst of her loss, although she is still low in spirits, and I cannot leave in good conscience until I am certain of her mindset. My worry for the girl eases when she smiles up at me, clutching my hand in thanks. I can only hope she will pull through this without me guiding her.

One of the other women has delivered a new babe. Both appear healthy, but the new mother is struggling with pain when she nurses the child, so I offer her an extra jar of salve for her nipples to aid in pain relief and healing the cracks in her skin. If she can keep her milk flowing, she will have the option of working as a wet nurse for a noblewoman, and that could help her leave this place.

The rest of the herbal mixtures I prepared I leave with the cook and explain to her how to steep them in the boiled water like she has seen me do. Worry eats at me — I hope she will remember the details while I'm gone — but there is no more I can do.

As I walk back to my room cocooned in the din of soft voices and piano notes drifting from the salon, I glance around one last time at the House of Starlight, illuminated by the candles and oil lamps burning dimly. The gilded trims, plush carpets, and silver stars are everywhere, as if I am supposed to feel like I'm outside instead of trapped within four walls. Emotions war in my breast — I'm torn between the fear of the unknown duties Lennox has planned for me, and the kernel of excitement blossoming in my chest at the idea of being free again. Soon, I will be back under real stars.

When I pass by Lyra's room, soft female voices intermixed with the sound of crying drift through the door — Celeste must be in with her daughter, then. My eyes drift closed for a moment as I say a silent prayer for the girl, asking the Goddess for a safe passage for us both as I pad back to my room. After one last rummage through my chest of drawers, I close the lid of the chest over my belongings — new and old — and curl up in my feather bed for the last time.

CHAPTER 4

Huddled under my blankets to protect me from the crisp air, I watch the early morning light seep through the transparent curtains on my window. They blow lightly in the chill breeze as the odor of fish and sea mist wafts in from the docks while the gulls cry for their breakfast. The knot in my stomach has tightened since I finished packing last night. Sleep did not come easily knowing today is the day I might escape this place and start a new life, or I might be walking headfirst to a watery grave.

Unable to stand making small talk with the other girls over the rough wooden table downstairs, I requested to have my breakfast brought to my room. I said my goodbyes to the ones who matter last night; I don't need to draw out my departure this morning. When the kitchen girl knocks, I let her in and she carefully places my tray on the vanity before curtseying and running back out. She is one of the ones who are still afraid of me, or of what I once was.

I choke down the boiled egg and dry toast and wash it down with too strong tea, then begin to dress. Once I slip into the charcoal dress, I admire it anew in the light of day, running my hands over the skirt to smooth it. Thick warm stockings and the new leather boots chase away any remaining chill before I comb through the dark waves of my hair. Today, I braid it all back into a tight plait at my crown, wrapping the ends into a tidy chignon at my neck.

Forgoing any cosmetics, I stare at my wan reflection in the mirror. Dark blue eyes framed by thick lashes look back at me without emotion – a mask I have mastered over these past years. A faint crescent moon with the horns pointing upwards still rests between and just above my dark brows — the last outwardly visible sign of my life at the temple.

A small amount of balm for my full lips is all I add, only enough to enhance their natural color, but not to add any other shade than what the Goddess gave me. I am a study of contrasts, vivid features painted on pale parchment. My cheekbones are more pronounced than in my youth and I know I am thinner than I was when I lived at the temple, but I stand straight and remind myself that even now, I will bow to no one.

As the bells toll noon in the distance, wagon wheels and the beat of hooves stop outside my open window over-looking the street below. A small wagon with a large man driving a team of two mules stands on the cobblestones when I peek outside. A younger man, a wiry boy halfway through his teens from the looks of it, hops lightly from the passenger seat and rings the front bell. Our carriage awaits.

By the time someone knocks at my door, I am wrapped in the dark blue cloak, so close in color to my eyes that it cannot be a coincidence. My dagger is secured in one of the

deep pockets of my skirt and I don soft kid gloves in anticipation of the crisp air outside.

Celeste awaits me at the door when I open it, Lyra at her
side. The girl is more beautiful than I remember, dressed in
a cloak similar to my own, hers a bold saffron compared to
my deep sapphire. She is a beam of sunshine in the darkness of the hallway. Her hazel eyes show only a brief flicker
of fear when they meet mine before she smiles and reaches
out for my hand. A bracelet similar to mine wraps her wrist,
stamping her as Captain Lennox's property.

From what I've heard, her father was a sailor from one
of the Southern continents and she has a beautiful warm,
brown skin tone, a wide, full mouth, and thick, tight curls
that I know reflect red and gold tones in the sunlight. I take
a deep breath and, despite not being very affectionate,
allow her to clasp my hand as I look at Celeste. The
Madame gives me the barest of smiles before turning to
lead us down the stairway to our waiting transport.

It only takes a few minutes for our trunks to be loaded
into the wagon. Lyra's is similar in style and size to my
own, and I wonder if it holds similar pieces in different
shades like our cloaks. The young man offers me a hand to
step into the back portion of the wagon where a bench lines
one side while Lyra hugs her mother goodbye. As I settle in
and arrange my skirts, the boy helps Lyra up with a
crooked smile.

Celeste walks to my side and whispers so softly only I
can hear, "Goddess be with you, Andromeda. Thank you."

I'm stunned at the statement — Celeste has never
mentioned the Goddess directly to me before. Before I can
reply, the driver cracks the reins and the mules have walked

on. Lyra and I both stare back at Celeste who wipes her eyes, squares her shoulders, and walks back into the House of Starlight.

LYRA IS SILENT THE ENTIRE WAY TO THE DOCKS, LOOKING around and taking in the sights of the city. Although I rarely step into the streets unless I have to visit the apothecary, Celeste kept Lyra sequestered in the House of Starlight for most of her life and despite the fear in her eyes, I can feel excitement ripple off her, as though this has the potential to be a grand adventure.

The boy in the passenger seat of the wagon has been chattering away to the driver who answers in noncommittal grunts, but I tune them out, my heart beating faster with each hoofbeat closer to the ship. For distraction, I admire the different vessels in their berths and examine their figureheads: mermaids, unicorns, dragons, and other fantastical beasts.

When the wagon stops abruptly, the cheerful young man continues to prattle away about nothing in particular as he helps us down from our perch.

"Oy! You two! Get these trunks to the ship!" he calls out to two men loading barrels, indicating they do the heavy lifting in his place. Then he gestures with a wave that we should follow him down the quay to our awaiting vessel. I avoid the eyes of the sailors along the docks and read the names of different ships as we pass. A shiver crawls along my flesh when the words *Bartered Soul* comes into view.

The ship is a large brigantine with numerous men

carrying crates and barrels up the gangplank in preparation for our impending departure. I stop completely as we near the bow, my eyes drift upwards, transfixed on the figurehead of the ship — a woman with her breasts bared to appease the sea; full red lips smiling, hair a deep black, the mark of the Goddess on her brow, and... *they can't be real...* sapphires for eyes. She wears an ornately carved black lace mask around her eyes.

A priestess of the Goddess.

And, despite the mask, she looks just like... me.

"Missus? Are you well?" the boy from the wagon asks when he realizes I am no longer trailing his steps. The question snaps me from my reverie and I walk swiftly to catch up as my heart races in my chest. He leads us up the gangplank and onto the deck, making us pause before stepping aboard to make sure we step on with our right foot first.

"For luck!" he explains cheerfully when I furrow my brow at the hand he has thrust in front of me to hinder my steps.

As I set foot onto the mist-soaked deck, I meet the eyes of several crewmembers who either give a small nod or avert their gaze quickly. Most don't heed us at all. I expected the men aboard to leer or make lewd comments, but no one speaks.

It's common knowledge that most seafaring men believe a woman on board is unlucky unless she is topless at the front of the boat, so I am a bit surprised, albeit relieved, at their casual acceptance of our presence.

I hope that's not what the Captain has planned for us, I think, remembering the superstition, my eyes drifting back to the black-haired figurehead. Several of the men look to be very young, barely edging into manhood, our present company included. I wonder what sort of predilections the other crewmen lean toward for so many young members to be chosen to man the ship.

The boy leads us down steps into the hold and to a small room with two beds. "This is your room Missus, Miss," he gestures as he holds the door for us, giving a slight inclination of his mousy brown head in respect. The top portion of his hair is longer than the sides and it flops over his forehead as he dips his head. We will share a room, then. This will make it easier for me to keep an eye on Lyra at least, even if it doesn't afford me the privacy I'm used to.

"Thank you, Mister... ?" I trail off, realizing he hasn't given his name.

"Oh! Charlie, Missus, just Charlie. I'm one of the cabin boys and I can help with anything you might need. Cap'n said you're to want for nothing, so just let me know how I can be of assistance!"

"Thank you, Charlie. We should be fine with some water to wash with for now," I advise and glance over to Lyra who is rotating in a circle to admire the tiny space.

"Yes, Missus, right away. Your trunks should be here shortly!" With that, he slaps his cap back on his head and darts up the stairs to do my bidding. A few moments later, grunts carry through the air as two men lug each of our trunks down to the room. By the time they have them tucked into corners for us, Charlie is back.

"Cap'n asks that you dine with him tonight, Missus, um, Andromeda. He said you can pick whatever you like to wear and I am to bring you to his quarters at eight o'clock."

So it begins.

"And where is Miss Lyra to dine, Charlie?" I ask, not wanting the girl to be cast to the wolves.

"Oh, Cook will bring her dinner here in the room, Missus. No one will bother her. Cap'n's orders." Charlie smiles at me and indicates that the small table in one corner will be Lyra's dining room for the night. He then smiles wider at Lyra. She has still not spoken, but returns the look with a broad grin of her own, a ray of sunlight in our dim confines. Charlie blushes and bows once more before departing, leaving us to prepare for the first night of many aboard the *Bartered Soul*.

"Are you all right?" I ask Lyra once Charlie has shut the cabin door. There is one small porthole in our room that she is staring out wistfully.

"Oh, Andromeda, I don't know. I am so excited to leave the House, but... I miss my mother already and I'm so nervous. I don't know how to feel," Lyra blurts out, more words than she has ever spoken to me. "I've never been farther than a few streets over from the House. I can't begin to comprehend being on a ship going to other lands."

"It will be fine," I tell her, realizing that perhaps she isn't afraid of the situation she is in at all, that she is just nervous about the journey. "Just please be careful onboard, and don't leave the room unless I am with you, if you can help it."

What has Celeste told her? I wonder. *Surely she knows her maidenhead has been sold to the Captain.*

Soon the gentle swaying of the ship at anchor gives way to deeper undulation, and I peer out the small window to confirm that we have set sail. The din of men's shouts and footsteps overhead blend with the creak of the hull and crash of waves as we leave the safety of the harbor.

I breathe deeply and watch the docks get smaller from our porthole, the city that was never truly a home disappearing on the horizon. The mountains outside the walls of the city look like hills as we continue to drift out to sea. I have traded one prison for an even smaller one, with less privacy, for the time being.

At least at the House of Starlight, I had an idea of what to anticipate each day. Now I am at the mercy of the unknown and the desires of a sea monster. I roll my eyes, the irony is not lost on me. Perhaps if I had chosen a name with a different legend attached I wouldn't be in this position – though maybe the Fates have a sense of humor after all.

With a sigh, I glance out the window one more time before laying down on my small bed to rest before I must steel myself for dinner. Curled up on her bunk, Lyra is sleeping — the day's excitement, and her nervous fluttering at the window, finally tired her out. Sleep clutches at me, reminding me how poorly I rested last night. I relent and drift off to restless sleep as the ship drifts through the waves.

CHAPTER 5

The smell of vomit and the sound of retching pulls me from my doze. When I roll toward Lyra's bed, it's abundantly clear that the poor girl has most certainly not found her sea legs yet. Her normally dewy skin is sallow and covered in a sheen of sweat as she clutches a chamber pot and heaves again. She can't possibly have anything left to bring up, but I know the nausea won't release its grip.

Although I had little notice to do so, I curse myself for not going to the apothecary for ginger to aid with seasickness before I left shore. Thankfully, the pitcher of fresh water Charlie fetched for me is here. I gather it and a cloth, then sit by the girl, rubbing her back and gently blotting her forehead and face with the cool rag. Words of comfort are lost to me, but I hope my steady presence eases her discomfort. Eventually, she stops vomiting long enough for me to sneak from the cabin to look for the cabin boy.

The mist from the sea washes over me as I step out onto the deck, a refreshing respite from the acidic smell of our cabin. Breathing deeply, I stare at the sea over the railing. I really should drag Lyra up here for the fresh air, but she doesn't seem inclined to move from her bed. The men continue to ignore or avoid me, so I take my time examining them from my post.

Some are older, with weather-worn faces and hard eyes; others are in the prime of life, attractive with tan skin and sinewy muscles; but many are youthful like Charlie. A motley crew of men as one might expect from sailors on a pirate vessel, they wear mismatched clothing and, what I can only assume is stolen, jewelry — probably trophies and mementos from prior expeditions.

One brute of a man at the rigging makes me uneasy. His eyes roving over me feels as if he is looking straight through my fine wool dress to the naked flesh below. I meet his gaze with a tightening of my lips and stare him down until he finally relents and averts his eyes. I need to find out who this man is and keep a close watch on him for this voyage, lest those looks turn into unpleasant actions.

After standing at the rail for a quarter of an hour, Charlie appears at my elbow. "D'ye need something, Missus?" he queries, cocking his head. I smile involuntarily as it dawns on me — he reminds me of a sparrow with his dark brown eyes, light brown hair, and boundless energy. He seems to hop about at all times.

"Does the ship have a barber-surgeon, Charlie? Or any herbs in the kitchen, perhaps?" I ask. At his look of confusion, I explain, "Miss Lyra is suffering terribly from seasickness and ginger tea would be a welcome remedy for her."

"Of course! But I thought... well, I will go see what I can find and bring it to you with hot water for tea, Missus," he replies and trots off on my errand.

"He's a good boy, Charlie," a deep voice rumbles next to me. I was so enchanted by Charlie's sprightly nature that I didn't realize I'd been joined at the rail. The voice sends a shiver through me and I turn to meet the hard gaze of Captain Lennox himself as he leans his hip against the railing. I haven't seen him since boarding the ship and didn't expect to encounter him until our dinner in a few hours.

"It seems so, Captain," I reply, holding his gaze.

"How do you and Lyra find your room?" he asks as he admires my dress, raking his eyes along my figure, not bothering to hide the boldness of his gaze. I wait, holding my breath under his scrutiny, expecting him to take the fabric between his fingers, but he places his hands on the railing and stands at my side so that we both face the open water.

"It's satisfactory. Thank you," I reply succinctly. From the corner of my eye, I discreetly look him up and down. A pistol is tucked into the waistband of his tailored trousers and a gleaming cutlass swings at his side. His coat is deep green and I can't help but think about how it accents his dark emerald eyes.

"And your trunk?" he prods, smiling at my — apparently not so discreet — inspection. Perhaps he is a bit of a peacock after all. As he looks out at the horizon, I cut my eyes in his direction to admire his profile in spite of myself. His nose is straight and refined, his cheekbones high and sharp, and his lips are full with a permanent smirk. He is not difficult to look at, but I know a pleasant exterior serves a predator well as they lure in their prey.

"I am pleased with the items you sent. I am sure Lyra is as well. They seem very suitable for the journey." I refuse to admit how the pieces are some of the finest I have touched in years, or that the colors he chose are the same as I would have selected for myself. I will not give him the pleasure of thinking I am happy about my situation, even if I do love the collection of finery he has provided.

"Very good. I look forward to seeing what you choose for dinner tonight." He gives a wry smile and curt nod as he departs toward the stern of the ship.

As he walks away, I watch his graceful movements and admire the fine cut of his coat across his broad shoulders. Even if I dislike the man, I must admit he has a decidedly attractive frame to go with his handsome face.

In the sunlight, his hair isn't entirely as black as I thought. In fact, it isn't even as dark as my own. He wears it in a shorter style than many of the men on the ship and has always been clean-shaven instead of covered in days-old stubble like the older men in his crew. The younger men probably can't grow facial hair even if they wished to. I wonder if he keeps this image to distinguish himself from the crew or if he has other reasons.

After my encounter with the Captain, I make my way back downstairs to check on Lyra. A pair of teacups and a teapot of hot water sit atop our small table awaiting my return. Steeping inside the pot are slices of ginger root and an additional piece is wrapped in a cloth on the table. The poor girl is still groaning on her bed when I step through the door. I give the root a few more minutes to steep while I open my trunk to make my decisions on what to wear to dinner this evening.

Unsure if I should simply anticipate a meal, or if I should be prepared for him to want to indulge *other* appetites, I pull all the dresses out of the trunk and lay them across the chairs and my small bed to decide. I should just continue to wear the same grey gown I'm already wearing – what is it to me if he is pleased by my appearance? But the hedonist in me wants to touch the beautiful fabrics and make the one choice I can control for the evening, so I inspect my options.

Finally, I settle on a midnight blue gown that shows my collarbones and skims my hips before pooling at my feet. It shows my curves, but not in an overt way – a refreshing change from the House. I allow my hair to fall from the braids I have worn all day and it flows in tight waves down my back, the salty air making them hold the style well. I run my fingers through the waves and leave it all down, foregoing my usual crown braid in favor of the less formal look to ease the tension I feel taking root in my head.

As I sit on my bed, I inhale deeply, letting it back out slowly to steady myself. I will not show fear of the Captain tonight, regardless of his actions. I will survive whatever he asks of me and collect my freedom at the end of this journey.

With that reminder repeating in my head, I prop the mirror I brought on my knees and line my eyes in kohl, but leave my lips bare. I will be just enough of the woman he saw in the brothel, but on my own terms. Satisfied with my reflection, I glance at the small clock that is tacked to the wall of the cabin — it's almost time.

Before I leave the room, I give Lyra a steaming cup of ginger tea to sip and instruct her to drink more from the pot when she's finished if she can stomach it. She nods that she understands, but is still a sickly shade of green when she smells the spicy aroma of the ginger. Charlie — the sparrow — is flitting about outside our door when I step into the hallway, just as I expected he would be.

"Ready for dinner, Missus?" Charlie asks as I close the door behind me.

"Yes, Charlie. Please lead the way."

We walk silently along the deck and to the door of the great cabin. A few members of the crew still man the deck, though I assume the majority are below for their meal. They watch me as I pass, but I keep my eyes focused on the backlit windows of the cabin ahead of me where candles flicker behind the wavy panes. Charlie doffs his hat and gives his little bow to me when we reach the doors.

Before he can bound off, I ask, "Can you please ask the cook to send broth, and only broth, down to Lyra? She is still quite sick and I am afraid anything more will make her vomit again."

"Oh! Of course! I'll make sure of it myself, Missus," he responds and heads to what I presume is the galley to relay my message.

I'm alone at the precipice. I know I have no option but to go inside to dinner, but I still hesitate. No one *willingly* walks into a lion's den. Resigned to my fate, I take a deep breath and knock on the door.

CHAPTER 6

Captain Lennox opens the door himself and a small black cat darts from the room, startling me. I certainly didn't expect to be greeted by a *pet*.

I hardly recognize the Captain without his overcoat. Much more relaxed than I've ever seen him, he wears a fitted white linen shirt with dark trousers tucked into knee-high leather boots. His sleeves are rolled up to reveal well-muscled forearms with tattoos covering tan flesh.

Hesitant to look too closely for fear he will think I am admiring him again, I only allow myself a quick glance at the inkwork which disappears under his sleeves. Some appear to be nautical symbols like I've seen on most seafarers, but I am confused to see other symbols closely associated with the Goddess intermingled. His pistol and cutlass are laid aside for the meal and Lennox welcomes me with a sweep of his arm as he steps aside from the doorway.

I step through like a queen — shoulders back and chin high to view the large great cabin. The back of the room is covered in windows overlooking the dark water and starry skies beyond. There is a table that can seat six to one side and an ornately carved desk perpendicular to it covered in maps and stacks of books.

On the opposite side of the room is a large bed, neatly made with a dark coverlet and plush pillows. I glance toward it briefly, but refocus on the table set for dinner. Carpets woven with exotic designs decorate the floor and I pretend to be overly interested in them as I slowly walk toward the table. Everything in his cabin is opulent, which I suppose makes sense for a pirate captain.

The seat to the right of the captain holds a second place setting, next to the head of the table where I assume he sits. An elaborate silver candelabra illuminates our meal of roasted chicken with potatoes and carrots laid out alongside a decanter of red wine and various fruits and hard cheeses. I haven't eaten anything since my meager breakfast and my mouth waters at the sight of such rich dishes.

I can feel his eyes on me, the Captain inspecting his purchase as closely as I inspect the food. I wonder if he's salivating as much as I am. He steps closer, moving behind me, his breath tickling my hair, causing my breath to catch momentarily. Then, he lightly brushes against my arm as he reaches past me to pull my chair out to sit. I fear my legs might buckle and I'm relieved to have a place to land, hoping he doesn't notice the thrill I feel at his touch. He moves to his own chair and sits before taking a sip from his wine goblet. My eyes remain focused on the candelabra in front of me until he speaks.

"Would you like wine, Andromeda? May I serve you?"

I nod slightly in response and within a few moments my glass and plate are full and he is eating his meal with finer manners than I anticipated. I don't know why I expected him to be unrefined; his grooming and fastidious dress should have been more of an indication of his manners. After the rumors that followed him through the Houses, I half expected him to rip my clothing from me and take me like an animal the moment I stepped through the door. Instead, it feels like I am the uncivilized beast accompanying a gentleman for a meal.

I delicately sip my wine and start in on the food, barely containing a moan at the taste. Such a simple meal takes no elaborate skill, but I am so hungry that I devour the entire serving. His eyes remain on me as I eat, but I refuse to look up.

Once I finish, I dab my lips with the linen napkin and sip my wine again, casting my eyes around the room. They linger on his sleeping area, noting a wardrobe that I can only assume holds his fine clothing, and a trunk at the foot of the bed. A small table with an oil lamp stands next to the bed with more books stacked on its surface.

As my eyes drift around the room I see a cat-of-nine-tails hanging from a nail on the wall near the door. My heart skips at the sight — I don't know whether it is something he plans to use on me or if it is used for doling out punishment to his crew.

Finally, I allow myself a glance at the Captain who has a look of amusement dancing across his face, clearly tracking my eyes in their examination. His dark hair is messy from where I assume he has run his fingers through it, even if I have never actually seen him make the nervous gesture. It's the only part of him that is rumpled. He leans back in his chair, holding his goblet leisurely, and smiles when my eyes meet his, hooded and unreadable.

"So…" The word does nothing to cut through the tension that surrounds us.

"So…" he replies, eyes glittering in the candlelight.

"Perhaps you can tell me your… expectations?" I venture, hoping my emotions are not written across my face. I cannot seem to rein them in in his presence as easily as I am used to, and I have to strive to maintain a blank expression.

"Tonight, I'd like to talk, Andromeda. No expectations."

I take another drink of my wine to hide my shock, toying with the silver adornment on the stem of the glass. This is definitely not what I anticipated when I entered the great cabin this evening.

"All right. What would you like to talk about?" I ask, boldly meeting his gaze.

"I understand you were a priestess of the Goddess."

I bark a harsh laugh. "Judging from the items in my trunk, I think you know that to be true. Where did you get the robe?"

"I have many connections, as you will learn." His answer is vague and evasive, but he continues, "How long were you at your temple?"

"From the time I was fourteen until the King's men arrived at our gates." I finish my goblet of wine and hold it out for another, pursing my lips. My eyes remain focused on the glass to keep the sadness of the memory hidden.

"And do you have healing gifts, or only the other skills the priestesses are renowned for?"

I look up at his face expecting derision, but find only

curiosity. He refills my goblet and I drink deeply before responding.

"I have *many* gifts, Captain," I retort, earning a chuckle. "But yes, I know herblore and some healing. I'm not a physician by any means, but I can ease discomfort and prevent infections."

"Did you participate in the rites?"

"I did. When I was sixteen I chose to dedicate myself fully, and gave myself in the rites."

"I see. And when was that?" he studies my face as he asks casually.

"A lifetime ago," I whisper, looking into my glass. "You seem very interested in my skills and my past, Captain Lennox. What do you know of the Goddess and her priestesses?"

"My mother was a believer; I know more than you'd think," he answers curtly, his smile faltering. I'm surprised, but the robe in my trunk has told me as much and the figurehead of his ship should have solidified my suspicions.

"Why am I here?" I ask directly. If he can ask me so many questions he can damn well answer some of mine.

"Because I wanted you to be, my pretty priestess." His words are a caress as he pours himself another glass of wine. "I saw you at the House of Starlight and knew I had to have you. It just took time to negotiate with Celeste."

Finally, the man I anticipated shows himself, and I find myself almost relieved to be back on even footing after so many of his disarming comments.

"Why?" I press.

"Because the sight of you pleases me. Tell me," he pauses, eyes raking over me as he leans forward over the table. "The last time I saw you in that color, you weren't wearing anything underneath your skirt. Are you tonight?" He smiles wickedly and takes another sip as he raises a brow.

The memory of his inspection in Celeste's office, of him flipping up my skirt to admire his purchase, grates on me. My pulse quickens and I swallow my irritation, but don't answer his question.

At my silence he continues, "Celeste told me you're a challenging one." He smiles again, further instigating my ire.

"I don't want to disappoint. It would be terrible if I was falsely advertised," I try to say sweetly, but sarcasm laces my tone as I speak through my teeth. "I thought we were talking tonight, Captain. If you'd prefer, you can tell me what you'd like me to do, and I can take care of it for you."

"Oh, Andromeda," he practically purrs. "I'll tell you exactly what I'd like you to do to me. And what I would like to do to you, as well. But that will wait for another night, I think."

He stands and walks behind me, brushing my hair away from the side of my neck with his long fingers. A gasp leaves me as he runs one finger down the side of my neck and across my collarbone, my body trembling slightly at the sensation. I have to fight the urge to lean into his touch, to bare my neck further, my muscles betraying my brain as a heated flush covers my skin.

I half expect him to pull me from my seat and bend me over the table, but he steps back and assists me in pulling my chair out. As I stand and face him, my gaze reaches to his chest, forcing me to look up into his eyes. He runs his fingers down the side of my face and touches the ends of my hair once more before quietly dismissing me.

"Goodnight, Andromeda. Sleep well."

The Captain's gentle caresses still radiate on my skin as I walk back to my cabin in a haze of confusion. My flesh feels hot and flushed, my breath uneven. The mist from the sea cools my burning cheeks as I travel over the deck. He had done none of the depraved things I anticipated — merely fed me, observed me, and asked a few questions. To make matters worse, I'm not sure if I am more confused over his behavior, his questions about my previous life, or the reaction my body had to him.

I wish I wasn't sharing a room with Lyra this evening because the ache I feel between my legs after the Captain's touch will keep me awake tonight without satisfaction. When I creep into our room, the dim candlelight outlines Lyra's sleeping form in her bunk. Silently as possible, I undress and crawl into my bed before blowing out the candle and turning my back to my cabin mate to will myself to sleep.

CHAPTER 7

I'm sixteen again. The spring evening air is warm, and a soft breeze wraps itself around me and the other initiates as we await the start of the rites. Sheer panels of fabric that look like sea foam wrap my body, matching the other girls around me. Each of us wears a coordinating mask, hiding enough of our identity to make it hard to know who we are to untrained eyes, but we know one another closely and chatter nervously while we await the signal.

I know that boys from the nearby villages will devote themselves to the Goddess on this night too, and my only concern is that my partner is handsome and gentle. It will be the first time for both of us, and I am anxious and excited for the experience. I've lived in the temple for the past two years, learning the secrets of the Goddess and the ways of pleasure. I am ready to test my education.

The priestesses told us what to expect, and provided us the teas necessary to prevent us from getting with child — we are taught that bearing a child should be a choice to be made between two people who wish to commit to the babe and each other, not a punishment for a night of pleasure and merriment. I know, that as long as we take our time, the pain will be minimal and the potential pleasure great, so I am practically alight with anticipation.

The drums begin. My fellow initiates and I grasp hands in a line and proceed down the hill through the sacred grove of trees to the clearing, stifling our nervous giggles as we approach. A great fire lights the open center of the grove and the High Priestess has already addressed the ring of boys awaiting our arrival. As we enter the circle, we face the outer ring of young men and begin our dance.

We rotate through the circle once, twice, thrice, making eye contact with potential partners, admiring their bare chests and arms. Our loose hair flows around lithe bodies as we twirl. Some of the boys look to be barely old enough to partake, but each boy in the outer circle and girl in the inner ring are here by their own choice. The Goddess does not demand participation to worship Her, nor is there a required age one must join.

The drumming reaches its crescendo — our signal to mingle with the boys to choose our partner. If no one pleases our eyes, we can wait until the next rites. Several suitors have caught my attention, but one stands out. His eyes have been locked on mine since the dance began and I feel my chest tighten under his gaze.

I can only see full lips beneath his mask, but I can tell he is handsome. The firelight shimmers on his golden hair, hanging in loose waves almost to his shoulders. Those shoulders are broad, and even though he still needs time to fill out his frame, he is already taller than many of the other suitors. As he approaches me near the firelight, I see his dark eyes are green, not brown like I expected. They're the color of the forest canopy we dance beneath. When he reaches out to stroke my arm, heat rushes through my body and pools at my core. This is him.

I take his hand and pull him outside the ring, asking as I tug him along, "Do you choose me?"

"I do," he replies in a deep murmur.

Once we reach the trees, he pulls me to him and kisses me softly at first, then more deeply, our masks rubbing, but never removed. The sheer fabric that covers me slips between the skin of our chests. Even though we are inexperienced, instinct takes over and we know what to do: clothing is stripped away, warm skin lays flush with one another, needy kisses deepen in the darkness.

My lessons return to me and I giggle as I roll him onto his back, straddling his hips. He runs his hands over my small breasts and stomach as I rub my wetness against him. Soon, teasing isn't enough for either of us and I gasp at the sting when he enters me. However, he is gentle, and I lower myself on him slowly until the pain is gone — until only the ache of wanting remains.

We move our hips together, stealing kisses, until I cry out with pleasure. As I clench him between my thighs, he follows me into oblivion and we lay together, sated under the starry skies.

I WAKE ABRUPTLY, FILLED WITH A LONGING I HAVEN'T FELT IN years. My inner thighs are slippery with desire at the memory of the long-ago rites relived in my dream. It's been years since I dreamed this vividly of that night and the sweet memory leaves me aching in my chest and core, forcing me to curl into myself in the bed.

I can still remember watching the priestesses from the temple when they visited my village as a child. They were ethereal, powerful, and feared. Men both trembled at their feet and sought their guidance on everything from livestock and crops to healing and divination.

These holy women prayed for blessings and taught knowledge from ancient texts. They cared for the people and the natural world. To lay with a priestess was a sacred act, one that was saved for rituals, or holy days, to ask for great blessings from the Goddess.

From the moment I saw them I knew I would be one, even if it hadn't been expected of me by my mother. They accepted daughters from peasants and nobility alike, all treated as sisters under the Great Goddess.

But that was then. This is my reality now.

For a moment, in the haze of sleep, nervousness threatens to overwhelm me at finding myself in a strange room. The confusion briefly overpowers the lust and longing I feel before I remember... I'm on a ship.

Lennox's ship.

Lyra rustles nearby, using the chamber pot — the sound of liquid hitting the side of the basin rather than the sound of retching. *Thank the Goddess.*

"Your stomach has settled?" I ask, propping my head on my hand.

"I'm feeling much better, thank you," Lyra answers. She looks refreshed and has some color back in her cheeks.

She is sixteen — the same age I was when I participated in the rites, which seems somewhat shocking to me. I drop my feet to the floor and pull myself up to prepare for the day. Catching my reflection in my small mirror while I braid my hair, hard planes and feral eyes look back at me, no traces of the soft cheeks and wide eyes of youth. Was I ever as innocent and lovely as Lyra is now?

Hair done, I don the charcoal dress I wore yesterday, and Lyra removes a beautiful cobalt option from her trunk. Curiosity gets the best of me as I peek inside at the items she was given — bold colors that bring out her darker complexion and warm coloring. The Captain certainly has good taste.

As I clasp the last few buttons on my bodice, a knock sounds at our cabin door. Gesturing for Lyra to open it, I expect it to be our ever-present cabin boy, but am surprised to find a large man hovering a respectful distance outside the open frame.

"Oh, um, good morning to you, sir!" Lyra brightly greets the man before looking to me for guidance.

He stands back from the cabin door, but I quickly realize it is not merely out of respect. The man is enormous, at least a half a head taller than the Captain, and would have to duck were he to enter our cabin. Although he's a giant of a man, he doesn't seem to have an ounce of fat on his intimidating frame. Long, dark hair is braided down the center of his head and hangs down his back, but the sides are shaved, revealing tattoos on his scalp. This style, plus the heavy torcs of gold and silver he wears at his neck and wrists, and thick facial hair covering his chin and cheeks suggests he must be a Northman, known to be fierce warriors and excellent sailors.

The faint accent when he speaks confirms my suspicions. "Good morning, ladies. The Captain would like me to escort you to the quarter deck before breakfast. He has an announcement."

"And you are...?" I study his face at my question,

expecting him to respond with harshness at my reluctance to take him at his word obediently.

"I am Erik Varangr. Quartermaster for the *Bartered Soul*, Mistress. I will wait outside until you are ready," he answers without hesitation, then turns to stand sentry outside our door, giving us privacy to finish our preparations. Lyra and I glance at each other before smoothing our skirts and making any last-minute adjustments.

Within moments, we follow behind the hulking man and up to the fresh air on deck. As the crisp sea air cuts into my cheeks, I pull the fabric of my cloak closed, thankful I chose to wear it. Lyra and I both huddle in our woolen shelters as the ocean mist blows past us. All members of the crew, including the cook, were pulled from their places to attend this *announcement*. I should be nervous — this kind of attention cannot bode well for two lone women aboard a pirate's vessel — but I stand tall and secretly clutch the dagger I always keep hidden in my skirt pocket.

Captain Lennox steps from his cabin and climbs the steps to the quarter deck to stand next to us. Lyra and I are now flanked by the two highest-ranking men on board. Erik crosses his large arms over his chest again, his biceps bulging under rolled sleeves, the pose as intimidating as the scowl on his face. This must be his usual stance, while the Captain appears relaxed and amenable.

"Gentlemen," Lennox's deep voice rumbles, carrying over the waves crashing against the hull of the ship. "There have been whispers reaching me about our recent guests that I wish to address.

"These ladies," I hear a few snickers at the word and his lips flatten into a tight line, silencing the murmurs before he continues, "are *my* guests and are here at my behest. Anything that they need or desire is to be granted. However, should any of you find yourself with desires of your own…"

My breath catches as I wait for the words I am dreading — that I am to be used to fulfill those desires, that I am here for their pleasure. My hand tightens and I swallow back any emotion as I lift my chin, my expression a challenge to any man who might approach me.

The Captain finishes, "…know that you have two hands to use at your leisure." A few men chuckle at the insinuation.

As he continues his speech, his tone shifts to a growl. "These women are *mine*. Should any of you offend them in any way, they have my permission to retaliate. If that retaliation proves ineffective, you will face my swift retribution. If any of you have a problem with this, you can speak with me immediately or depart the ship — whether we are at a port or not. You are dismissed."

Years of practice in hiding my reactions is all that keep my jaw from hitting the boards of the deck. Did he just give us permission to say *no* to these men? To mete out punishment for their unwanted behavior? I have not had outright permission to do such a thing since my life in the temple.

The sound of the sea drowns any responses the men utter, but most nod and return to their work — this is not a new edict on board, it seems. A few stand together with red faces, and I catch the eye of the same distasteful man who tried to stare me down yesterday. He has a thick beard liberally salted with white and a knit cap covering his head. His eyes are cold when he sneers at me with missing teeth. I swallow and continue to wear my mask — no man will frighten me, here or elsewhere. Not again.

"Ladies, you may join me in my cabin for breakfast, if you'd like." I almost jump at the Captain's voice as he brings me back to the present and out of my own thoughts. Lennox has snuck up on me again, and I feel a small rush of anxiety at the ease with which he does so.

"Afterwards, I can have Varangr show you around." I cast a wary eye at the Captain, unsure of what breakfast might be like following the tenor of our dinner last night, but Lyra happily accepts the invitation and I trail them to the great cabin.

Breakfast is a simple meal of porridge, and I keep my thoughts to myself as Lyra chats easily with the Captain. She behaves as if we are ladies entertaining a gentleman caller, not whores purchased for his desires. Lennox is relaxed in her presence. Indulgent, even.

His gaze rests on me several times throughout the meal. Each time my eyes flick to his, he gives me a wicked grin, but continues to drink his tea and listen to Lyra's chatter. The little black cat that escaped the room last night prowls around the edges of the room until Lyra coaxes her into her lap, completely enamored by the little beast.

"Who is this adorable creature?" she asks, scratching the animal's chin and eliciting a warm purr in appreciation.

"She doesn't really have a name. She's the ship's mouser, but she's become spoiled sneaking in here at night," the Captain says.

His voice hints displeasure, but his lips quirk at the little cat. He doesn't strike me as the type who would tolerate something in his presence if he didn't want it to be. Lyra smiles down at the ball of fur curled in her lap and continues petting her.

"How long will it take to reach the islands?" Lyra questions between petting the cat and delicately eating her porridge. My interest is piqued, as I have yet to be told exactly where we are traveling to.

"It's usually a six-week voyage to Delosia, barring any unfortunate events," Lennox replies. I look up in surprise, my spoon held aloft on its way to my mouth. *Six weeks?*

"What sort of *unfortunate events*?" I wonder aloud before I can stop myself.

"Storms, raids, illnesses. All would be inconvenient," he replies to me succinctly, taking a sip of tea. "We will stop at one last port before fully departing the Selennian coast to add any last-minute supplies, then continue west."

I wrack my brain to remember maps I've seen of the world, vaguely aware of tropical islands across the sea where valuable fruits and sugar are grown and shipped at exorbitant prices to Selennia and the nearby continent. Where the water is clear and the climate is warm. Is that where we are bound? The reason for the lightweight clothing in my trunk?

I haven't traveled beyond the borders of Selennia before, and a part of me welcomes the idea of a completely new land, even if the unknown feels daunting. I have survived so far — surely I can make it another six weeks before starting a new life in a new place.

Once we have finished our breakfast, Lennox walks us to the door where Erik is indeed waiting for us to emerge. Despite my earlier reservations about the meal, I find comfort in my new knowledge — at least I now have some idea of where we are sailing and how long I will be trapped on this ship. The Captain's announcement — and his kind treatment of Lyra — hasn't quite made me trust him yet, but I relax slightly for the first time since the night I was brought to him in Celeste's office.

Lyra excuses herself, she's still feeling a bit weak after the previous day and wishes to lay down in our room. We follow Erik down the stairs to the hold and Lyra departs to our cabin under the Captain's quarters, while I continue to follow Erik toward the bow of the ship. We pass the storage hold, filled with crates and barrels of various items for trade and several cannons with ammunition and powder laying in wait. The guns remind me that this is, in fact, a pirate's vessel, prone to a different sort of violence beyond that which I have been preoccupied with.

"Do you often use the cannons while out to sea?" I ask my guide.

"When needed. We try to avoid damaging the other ship in case it has valuable cargo or might be of use to us. Many times the Captain's name is enough to encourage surrender," Erik smiles down at me, clearly proud to be a member of this crew.

"He's quite well known, then?"

"Yes, around Selennia, the continent, and across the sea. No one wishes to cross the Captain."

"I see. Have you sailed with him long?" I inquire. Despite being laconic, Erik has a warm demeanor, so I allow myself to pry.

"For around seven years now, Mistress. He's a fierce fighter and a fair captain to the men. You can't ask for much more in this line of work. Here we are," he points to a small door on the side of the hold. The crew's berths are a bit farther forward, so I am unsure what I will find beyond this door. Erik pushes the door open and hands me an oil lamp to illuminate the space. My eyes scan the space, but words are lost to me.

"What is this?" I breathe, stepping through the door frame. He stands outside giving me space to take in my surroundings.

"Captain said you are a healer of sorts. He thought this space might be suitable for you to assist the men with any illness or injuries they might have," Erik explains.

The room is small with a plain wooden table and chair against one wall, complete with a stack of parchment and a small inkwell and quill. There is another chair across the way for a patient to sit. Herbs hang drying from the ceiling and a small shelf contains vials of oils and tinctures useful for treating a variety of ailments. The shelf has a smart little lip around the edge to keep the bottles from falling during rough seas and I bite my lip as I reach up to take a peek at some of the labels.

"Is it to your liking?" Eriks asks, blue eyes studying my expression. "Do you have any other needs?"

"It's... well... it's wonderful," I whisper, tears threatening to fall as I turn to him.

"I will tell the Captain you are pleased. Do you need assistance finding your room when you're finished here?"

"Yes. I am pleased. And no, I can find it myself. Thank you."

As Erik departs, I quietly shut the door and sit in my new surgery, tears flowing freely for the first time in years. To have these items on hand, Lennox must have known of my healing work in the House. These things would not have been laying around on the ship to be rounded up after our dinner conversation about my *gifts*. There is a small spark of... gratitude... forming toward the Captain that I don't wish to inspect closely.

One kind act, if that is even what this is, does not cancel out his true desires for me and Lyra. This is to benefit his crew, not me. But, that does not mean I can't feel pleased with the opportunity to distract myself on this voyage with the herbs and tonics in this room. I wipe my tears roughly with the back of my hand and move to inspect my supplies.

CHAPTER 8

The next few days run together as I refresh my memory of herbs and tonics other than those for women's troubles so I can be helpful to the men on the ship. Surprisingly, a few have already come to see me with rope burns, cuts, and other minor injuries associated with life as a sailor. Most who enter my surgery have a sense of reverence, and for the first time, I feel like I did at the temple — respected and valued. Even still, I sense the wary gaze of several of the other sailors when they see me on deck.

The sea is relatively calm one afternoon and I spend the day curled in my bunk reviewing notes and drawings in one of my journals. A sound in the hallway draws my attention away from the papers, and I find Charlie hopping into the room with another note sealed with emerald wax. The seal pops as I slide my finger under it and find another invitation to dinner in the Captain's cabin that evening. A sigh escapes me as I read the dark lines of ink on the crisp paper, his handwriting bold and elegant. I know this is an invitation in name only. I don't truly have a choice in my attendance.

Dropping the letter to the bed beneath me, I rise, leaving the cabin and heading for the main deck. My walk is brisk, and the deep breaths I take of the crisp sea air as the sun sinks clear my mind. As I turn to head back to my cabin to dress for dinner, a derisive whisper from the shadows reaches me.

"Heathen whore," the voice hisses.

I stop and look toward the group of men standing near the mast, the only ones who are close enough for their voices to carry to me. In their midst, the same hard stare I felt when I boarded the ship and during the Captain's announcement finds me. His rotten sneer sends a shiver down my spine, but I do not falter. My eyes travel over him from head to toe, and I frown at his paunch, knowing my distaste is evident on my face, then continue walking. Nevertheless, my hand stays on the dagger in my pocket and I keep a prayer on my lips as I descend the stairs and reach our cabin.

Except for a few brief glimpses when I pace the deck, I have not seen much of the Captain recently. I spend much of my time sequestered below deck in my surgery, inventorying herbs and reading my healing journal, so we haven't spoken since the breakfast we shared with Lyra. Even though it pains me to show this weakness, I decide I must mention the sailor's words to him tonight. I do not want this stranger to involve Lyra in any potential conflict.

Tonight I don an emerald gown that gathers at the shoulders, leaving my arms and shoulders bare, with a neckline cut low to reveal my chest. It still covers more than anything I wore at the House of Starlight, but is revealing enough to make it provocative. I haven't forgotten the kindness the Captain has shown me in allowing me to practice my healing arts here, and appreciation for the opportunity to show my value — besides what's in between my legs — drives me to dress with care for his enjoyment tonight. Plus, the silky fabric feels decadent and I know his cabin will be warm enough to keep the chill off me. With my cloak wrapped around me, I walk along the bridge and stride confidently to knock at the great cabin door.

The door swings open almost immediately as if he has been standing nearby awaiting my arrival. Lennox steps back to allow me entry, then takes an appraising glance at my ensemble, asking me with a twist of his index finger to turn for a full view. When I am facing him again, a devastating grin graces his face and he reaches toward me. I hold my breath, unsure where his fingers will rest when they connect with my skin.

The gentle touch against my shoulder runs down the length of my bare arm and stops at the gold shackle I wear at my wrist, toying with the cold metal. If it wasn't part of what chains me to this ship and this man, I could admit it's beautiful with the engravings depicting the swirling sea, but I cannot bring myself to admire it with any charity.

"You look lovely tonight, my pretty priestess," the Captain whispers, his lips close to my ear so I feel his breath wisp through my hair. A shiver of anticipation courses through my body involuntarily at the breathy compliment.

"Please, eat." He waves an arm toward the waiting food on the table as he steps back and shuts the cabin door firmly.

The fare tonight is another simple dish of potatoes and carrots, this time with white fish. I can tell the food will grow more plain the longer we are at sea; it is hard to keep the number of men on board fed with fresh produce and meat without it spoiling on the voyage. Thankfully, I have seen fresh fish hauled over the sides on the ends of sailor's rods and nets while we are still in shallower waters near the coastline. I fear this may not be the case in more open waters.

The Captain's manners are as polite as before, and he pulls my seat out and serves me before himself.

"I haven't seen you on deck much lately," I open the conversation, more because of my curiosity at his absence than because I care about his affairs.

"Oh, I've been around. Dealing with ship's business, but I've been keeping an eye on things," he answers vaguely, cutting his eyes to me before changing the subject. "I hear you are settling in with your herbs and potions. Is the room suitable?"

"Yes, thank you. Some of the crew have come by to visit for minor ailments already," I reply, still savoring the potatoes as I clear my plate. Lennox smiles at me and refills my glass without prompting as he watches me eat.

"I'm sure they are more interested in safely looking at you than they are in having their injuries treated," he smirks, a small huff of laughter escaping his lips.

"That may be, but your warning seemed to tell them where they stand on that front. Although," I pause, "I do have a… concern…," I cannot decide how to address the situation. I do not want him to think I am afraid of the men in general, but I also want to know more about the hostile crewman. Lennox watches me expectantly, prompting me to continue with a raise of his brows.

I dab my lips with my napkin, then take another sip of wine before elaborating, "One of your crew — an older man, with a salt and pepper beard, missing teeth?"

"Round gut and short stature?" Lennox finishes the description for me, lips pursing in distaste.

"Yes. He's… disrespectful." I don't mince words. The man has not done anything to me physically, but he has certainly not upheld the Captain's decree.

"Jon Crewes. He's a bastard, new to the crew," the Captain names the man, his eyes narrowing. "I only took him on because one of the others vouched for him and I needed a few replacement men. What has he done?"

"Nothing directly. I just get the impression he would… like to. He's made remarks. No worse than I've heard a hundred times before, but it's a sensation I get in his presence."

"I'll have Erik speak with him tomorrow. He will be removed from the crew at the next port. No man will disobey my orders on this ship." His jaw clenches briefly before he relaxes and takes a sip of wine.

My wine stops midway to my mouth as I reel in shock. *He will dismiss a crewman for simply making me feel uncomfortable?*

My comfort has been the least of anyone's concern for many years, let alone one of the men who has bought my body for his own use. I recover and sip my wine, nodding as if I expected nothing less. Lennox is watching me like I'm the dessert course though, and I return his heated gaze boldly.

"So Captain, I've been aboard your ship for over a week now. Do you plan on telling me what exactly you plan to do with me, or Lyra for that matter?" The wine loosens my tongue and I am direct, looking for a hint at his intentions.

"Lyra is special and will come to no harm on this voyage. You have my word on that. *You*," his eyes gutter, and that wicked smile returns. "I plan on giving great pleasure — whenever you request."

I almost spit out my wine at this declaration. I will *not* be requesting this man to give me any such thing.

"Is that what happened to the other girls you've bought from the Houses on the row? You gave them such *pleasure* that they combusted and couldn't return to shore?" My face is hard and my words bitter. No matter how well fed I am, or how fine the wine, I will not allow myself to forget those girls. Nor will I let him forget that they're not far from my thoughts.

Lennox pushes his chair away and stands abruptly, shocking me at his sudden reaction. He steps around the table and yanks my chair out, rotating it so I am seated in front of him. I'm forced to stare up at him, my hands fisted in my lap, teeth gritted at his behavior. He jerks me upright to standing, strong fingers gripping my upper arm, and tilts my chin up with his other hand forcing me to look into his deep green eyes.

"You don't know anything about what happened to those girls," he snarls, gripping my chin harder. *This is it, he's going to take me now because I've offended him.*

I swallow and accept his challenge, knowing my eyes are blue flames with my anger. I continue to clench my teeth until his grip softens and he runs his long fingers along my jaw, down my neck, and then down the open front of my gown barely grazing the skin on my breastbone.

My body breaks rank from my mind and trembles under the touch, my stomach fluttering at the sensation. He pulls me even closer to him, and I gasp as my breasts press against his muscular chest, the thin fabric of my dress and fine linen of his shirt the only thing separating our warm flesh. His hand continues its light touch down my side and over one of my hip bones while his other presses lightly against my lower back, testing to see if I will fight him.

My core ignites with his touch. There's no denying that, despite the anger I feel toward him, I find him physically attractive, and I catch myself gazing at his full lips. My mouth parts at our close proximity, our breath mingling in the space between us. He gives a ghost of a smile and I'm not sure if I rise up or he leans down, but our lips meet.

It's been an age since I have felt such heat in a kiss, and my body presses against him involuntarily as the kiss deepens. Despite everything, I long for him to touch me everywhere, so I wrap my arms around his neck to encourage him. My fingers run through his disheveled dark hair and pull lightly, causing me to smile internally when he breathes a moan against my mouth. He cups my face as he pulls away and breaks free from my arms. I can't read the expression on his face as he inspects my countenance; surely my wantonness is clear in my eyes.

"I think that will be all for tonight, Andromeda. Sweet dreams," Lennox whispers before planting a kiss on my brow, right where my faded sigil rests. He straightens his shirt and smoothes his hair before walking to the cabin door to let me back out into the night air.

I am stunned. Never before have I had a customer resist me, especially one who has already paid. I can see clearly that he desires me; his trousers fit tightly enough for me to view proof of his arousal as he stands straight at the door. The longing I have felt since I woke from my dreams earlier in the week combines with the ache of desire from the Captain's hot kisses. I brush my hair back and make sure my dress is lying properly before tucking into my cloak and breezing from the room.

"Goodnight, Captain," I declare coldly, hoping my tone masks my frustration as I march to my cabin below deck.

CHAPTER 9

When the door swings open to our cabin, my angry footsteps falter as I'm taken aback to find Lyra enjoying a cup of tea with Charlie. I'm not the only one startled; the cabin boy stands so quickly from his seat at the small table that he knocks his chair over.

"Oh! Andromeda! You're back so soon! Charlie was just keeping me company," Lyra explains as though this is a tea party with a porcelain doll instead of a young man.

My anger at the Captain shifts to the scene in front of me. Lyra continues to view this entire excursion as a grand adventure. For someone raised by a Madame in a brothel, she is wildly innocent and acts as if my evening meals with the Captain are part of a romantic tryst instead of comprehending the reality of our situation. My hands fist in the folds of my skirt to prevent me from shaking the girl in my frustration at her carelessness, while I bite my tongue to keep myself from lashing out at the two of them.

"Missus, good evening, I...um..." Charlie twists his knit cap in his hands, bracing as if he expects me to strike him with lightning. He doesn't meet my eyes while he struggles for words, brown hair falling across his forehead as he stares at his hands.

"Good evening. Leave. Now."

"Good night, Missus, Miss Lyra," Charlie ducks his messy head and disappears quickly down the hall, and I slam the door behind him.

"Lyra. This isn't a game," I warn, struggling to keep my words civil. "Didn't you hear Lennox? If anyone does anything to you the Captain doesn't like, he will likely be removed from the ship, if not worse."

"Oh, Andromeda — Charlie is different." Lyra's pretty eyes sparkle and her tawny cheeks flush with happiness. "There's nothing to worry about!"

Oh, Goddess, she's in love with that boy.

Closing my eyes on a long inhale, then another, I mentally wash my hands of the situation. I promised her mother I would keep her safe. Charlie hasn't shown any sign he would harm her, and the girl is free to make her own decisions. But I am not responsible for protecting *him* from Lennox, too.

"How was your dinner with the Captain? He seems to really admire you. I see him watching you whenever you walk on the decks." Lyra's brow raises as excitement shines on her face, hoping for a story of a grand romance with a handsome Captain. But, there is no redemption tale tonight to appease the girl.

"I'm sure he's just keeping watch over his property." My answer is curt, and her hopeful look falters. "Dinner was fine. Goodnight, Lyra."

Turning my back, I change into a simple shift to sleep in

before rubbing my face with a damp cloth and rinsing my mouth out, effectively ending the conversation. Following my lead, she quickly changes as well and settles on her bed. My breath is heavy as I blow out the candle, the smoke rising into the room from the wick as I pull my coverlet over me.

Despite the darkness of the room, sleep does not come easily. The sound of Lyra's steady breath and the gentle rock of the ship on the calm sea should relax me, but I am wound tight with the memory of Lennox's kiss mingling with yesterday's dream of my participation in the rites years ago. Finally, I give in and cup myself with my hand, holding my breath and hoping Lyra doesn't hear me.

Memories of the young man with green eyes and a masked face who made love to me gently so many years ago fill my mind as I rock against my hand, rubbing against the bundle of nerves between my thighs. It only takes a few moments of caressing between my legs before I feel my climax approach. I bite my lip to hold in my whimpers as the ripples of pleasure run over my body. After, I curl up on my side, catching my breath for a few more moments before the waves and Lyra's breathing finally lull me to sleep.

OVER THE NEXT FEW DAYS, SEVERAL CREWMEN STOP BY MY little surgery. The cook has a burn that I can soothe, and another young man, barely past boyhood, has complaints of upset bowels. I give him a mixture of herbs to brew into a tea and instruct him to drink fresh water as much as possible to help him stay hydrated. Hopefully, it isn't something contagious; the thought of an illness like that impacting the entire crew makes me grimace.

As I tidy up after a particularly slow morning, I jot down a list of items to purchase at the next port, our only stop before crossing the ocean, and tuck it into one of the pockets of my grey dress. I've worn it often since leaving the shore; it's my favorite of the ones the Captain provided me — simple, comfortable, and unassuming. My hair is tightly bound when I work in this space, intentionally maintaining the air of a priestess, not a whore, lest any of the men have a misunderstanding as to why I am secluded down here. Patting my pocket, I check to make sure my dagger is stowed away as usual and smooth down my skirts, appreciating that all of the simple gowns have useful pockets built in. The weight of the steel blade satisfies me, and I close the door, walking toward my cabin.

Bright sunlight streams through the lattice above where I walk amongst the stores. It's always dim below deck between my surgery area and the cabin I share with Lyra, but the cheery sunbeams light my path, in contrast to the dark spaces along the sides of the hull. Footsteps sound from behind me as I approach our cabin, and I pause, looking around. Familiar, hateful eyes meet mine as Jon Crewes steps from the shadows. Two other men lurk in the darkness at his sides as he runs his eyes over me.

Although he isn't much taller than I am, and has a paunch from age and too much ale, Crewes is stout with thick muscles and broad shoulders. The thick fingers that grip a leather coin pouch are most likely calloused from years of handling rigging, like the rough men I refused to entertain at the House, and I know he can easily overpower me. His companions are equally intimidating as they watch me.

"May I help you?" I ask, standing as straight as my spine allows. He and his companions continue to leer, silent.

"The surgery is closed for now, but you may come by tomorrow if you have an ailment," I advise and turn to walk away, a chill spreading over me.

The sound of coins clinking together gives me pause and I turn once more, the hairs on my neck rising at the implication.

"I have money to pay you, *whore*," Crewes sneers and clinks the pouch of coins he holds toward me again. The other men's eyes glitter with malice as I meet their gazes.

"Clever," I reply, not hiding my disdain. "Let me make this clear. Even if I weren't the Captain's — and if you had three times that paltry amount in solid gold — I wouldn't allow you within arm's reach of me or in my bed."

Foolishly, I spin on my heel to retreat to my cabin, hoping the solid door between me and the men will make a difference. But my hand never makes it to the knob, and I know I am mistaken. Fingers latch onto the neck of my gown, dragging me back.

The door of our cabin is so close that I scream for Lyra. The girl can do nothing to stop them, but no one else is below deck. The crew's berth is at the other end of the storage space, and doubt fills me wondering if they would stop the attack, even on the off chance some of the men were there during this hour of the day. Nevertheless, I thrash and scream, but whoever holds my dress drags me backward. Our cabin door swings open with a slam, and Lyra and Charlie burst into the hallway.

"Get Lennox! Lyra, run!" I shriek and fight the men.

This will not happen.

Not here.

Not again.

At the sight of my struggle, Charlie dashes forward to my aid, but the smaller man is knocked into the barrels lining the hallway by a blow from one of Crewes' companions. Lyra's shrill screams reverberate in the hold as she stumbles up the stairs to the deck above.

"Get the little bitch!" Crewes orders, and the man who hit Charlie starts up the stairs after Lyra. Boots pound overhead as they drag me back into the shadows.

These last movements cause me to lose my footing, and my back slams onto the wood beneath me, my left arm ineffective against Crewes' weight crushing me against the floor. Dirty fingers clasp onto my hair, his tight grip pulling strands loose from the tightly coiled plait at my nape. With his other hand, he rips the front of my gown open, exposing my breasts. My lungs burn as I still scream and struggle beneath him until he slaps me across the face with an open palm and my lip splits where it hits my teeth. Rotten teeth and foul breath make me gag, his face inches from mine as he drags my legs toward him. I spit blood in his face, and Crewes rears back, wiping it from his cheek before hitting me across the face again with the back of his hand.

"You should have just taken the coin and enjoyed it, you stupid cunt," he snarls. I blink my eyes rapidly, waiting for my ears to stop ringing and my vision to clear, trying to regain my senses from the impact of his blows.

His wiry companion stands to the side, laughing and watching. My struggling grows weaker as I continue to fight back, but neither man realizes my true goal — my right pocket. Finally, I feel the hilt of my dagger in my palm, cold steel centering me. As Crewes yanks my head back by my hair and hoists my skirts up, I strike. Slamming my dagger down into his shoulder and back, over and over.

Screaming. Always screaming.

Crewes' blood drips down onto my cheek and coats my hand and chest. I bring my hand back to strike again, and the other man catches my wrist, pinning my hand over my head against the hard wooden floor. A sob escapes my lips as fear settles into my chest, pulse racing wildly — my last attempt to free myself has come and gone.

Suddenly, the tight grip on my wrist is gone. Crewes no longer crushes me with his weight. Men's angry shouts reach me through my terror-filled haze, followed by the thump of a fist hitting flesh. Through the tears that fall involuntarily, I recognize the massive form that has pulled Crewes from me — Erik, the quartermaster. I whimper and kick out at the hands reaching for me through the shadows until my vision clears, focusing on the emerald gaze of the Captain. Lyra rushes to my side, her fine lavender dress now soiled with blood as she kneels at my side, seizing the fabric of my torn bodice to cover my naked breasts.

Two additional crew members I don't recognize, their faces filled with rage, hold Crewes and the other man who aided in his attack. Crewes' other accomplice is restrained near the stairs where Charlie sits, holding a hand on his red cheek where he took the punch trying to help me. My trembling hand still clutches my dagger, and I cannot will my fingers to relax their grip as I push myself further into the shadows, away from the happy sunlight and gentle hands that reach for me. When my back bumps against one of the barrels I finally release the weapon to the long fingers that carefully cover my hand and remove the blade.

"You're all right, Andromeda. We have them. You are safe." Captain Lennox smoothes my wild hair back from my face and lifts me from my hiding place. Lyra wrings her hands, desperate to help, but she is also trembling, likely frightened by witnessing the attack.

"Oh, Andromeda! Let me help you get cleaned up." Lyra tries again to pull my damaged gown to hide my naked flesh from the crew members' stares.

"No," my voice is cold. Emotionless. The men are silent.

"What do you need, Andromeda?" Lennox asks me as I curl into his chest, the blood seeping from my clothing and body onto his fine coat.

"My retaliation," I whisper.

"As you wish. Would you like Lyra to help get you changed first? To tend to your injuries?" He doesn't coddle me, he doesn't demean me, he simply asks.

"No. I want it now."

CHAPTER 10

All three attackers are marched up the stairs to the deck, followed by Erik, then Captain Lennox with me cradled in his arms. He grips me firmly, one arm under my knees and the other carefully supporting my back while avoiding any of the skin bared by my torn dress. Instinctively, I wrap my arms around his neck and allow my cheek to press against his chest, listening to the steady beat of his heart for comfort. Even if it does beat more quickly than it should, the sound helps me calm my own racing pulse. Lyra moves up the stairs to follow, but I shoot Charlie a look and a slight shake of my head, which has the desired effect — he takes her elbow and gently coaxes her back below deck. She doesn't need to see this.

The remainder of the crew must have heard Lyra screaming for the Captain before he and Erik rushed below; they stand in silence along the railing of the deck, their eyes watching as we move to the middle of the ship. The only sounds are the sails flapping in the wind and the waves lapping against the hull.

My attackers stand before us now, Crewes is bloodied and holding his shoulder askew where I stabbed him. Even now, he doesn't look remorseful as anger wars with his pain. The older, wiry sailor who held me down drips blood from his nose, he makes no move to staunch the flow as his eyes flit over his crewmates. If he is seeking reassurance from them he receives none. The younger, bulky man who hit Charlie looks defeated as he stands silently staring at his boots, rather than meeting the harsh glares of the others. After making sure I am stable enough to stand, the Captain sets me on my feet. Dark crimson stains the front of my charcoal dress, and my breasts remain bare where Crewes tore it from my body. The blood on my face has dried into a crust that cracks on my chin and lips, its copper taste lingering on my teeth and tongue. Loose strands of my dark hair float on the breeze from where they were pulled from their tidy chignon.

I do not hide my nakedness or my injuries. I am not the one who should be ashamed of what has occurred.

From the looks on the faces that stare back at me, I can tell that the men are disturbed. Sailors' superstitions run deep — any vengeful goddess they hope to appease will now haunt their dreams wearing my visage.

"The first full day aboard I made it clear — the women on this vessel are *mine.* I also made it clear what would happen should the order to leave them alone be violated. As you can all see, that has happened." Lennox's deep voice is a snarl that carries over the waves as he makes eye contact with each of his crew. He then swings his fierce gaze to the three men in front of him. They do not raise their faces to meet his eyes.

"Andromeda has requested that I honor my promise. She will have her retaliation for this attack." His voice rings loud and deep on the breeze. "If I think it's fitting, I will leave it as is. If not, I will seek vengeance for her."

"She's a whore, and a heathen witch on top of it!" Crewes spits in my direction. "I didn't do anything that hasn't been done before."

The Captain doesn't deign to look at him.

"Andromeda, do you need anything?" Lennox asks me, placing his hand on my hip with his back to the crew.

"No," I answer, and prowl toward the three men.

Crewes stands in the center of the three, and I meet his gaze directly before lowering myself to my knees in front of him, glancing upwards through my dark lashes to see his face. He sneers at me — seeing me on my knees with my breasts bared is probably what his dreams are made of. I reach up and unbutton his breeches the remainder of the way, never taking my eyes from his.

Once I have them loosened, I pull out his flaccid manhood and chuckle to myself at the pathetic sight. His expression transforms from one of lust to anger as I smirk at him. My laughs have distracted him from my right hand, which has again reached into the pocket of my dress, gripping tight to the dagger Lennox slipped back in its place when he touched my hip. Crewes' anger soon turns to fear when he sees my feral smile.

My dagger is sharp, but I make sure to take my time.

His screams rend through the silence of the deck as I cut him; he will never dream of taking a woman by force, or otherwise, again. In the distance, the sound of someone retching blends with the waves as I continue my work.

Erik's huge arms hold Crewes upright when he passes out.

I stand when I am finished, fresh blood joining the stains on my white breasts and arms. Some of the men have turned away, pale at witnessing my brutality, but many of the fresh-faced boys bow their heads to me as I walk to the rail and throw Crewes' bloody cock and balls into the sea.

The men who helped Crewes on his errand against me are aghast, still held tightly by their fellow sailors. When my gaze returns to the Captain, our eyes lock. His emerald stare sparkles with savage pride and his lips turn up in a vicious grin — his approval at my choice of punishment evident to everyone on deck.

Then, he turns to Erik and commands, "Cut their hands off since they dared to touch my property. Then throw their bodies into the waves. If anyone has an issue with this sentence, they can join them."

Erik says nothing, just gives a curt nod of acknowledgment before pulling a small axe from where it was tucked at his lower back.

Lennox strides to my side and scoops me back into his arms, carrying me toward his cabin. The pleading of the two men combines with Crewes' moans as he bleeds out on the deck until the great cabin's door closes, blocking out the sounds of death.

THE TREMBLING BEGINS BEFORE I CAN MASK MY DISTRESS. I HAD tucked myself against the Captain's chest as he carried me to his cabin, but I manage to push away from him and stand on my own before crouching and emptying my stomach on the beautiful rug under my feet. The violence I've experienced — and that which I've inflicted — in the past hour, is more than I can process as I kneel on the floor next to my vomit.

A knock at the door sounds behind me as I stare at my bloodied hands. I vaguely hear the Captain's voice, quiet and soothing, tell the visitor, "Thank you, I will send for you if she needs anything else," before sending them away and closing the door again.

He sits something down on the table with a clink, and then his boots appear in my peripheral vision, but I remain motionless on the floor.

"There is hot water to wash with, Andromeda. Lyra has brought you a change of clothes. Do you require privacy, or may I assist you?"

For the first time, the Captain's voice is soft. There is no hint of the growl he uses with his crew, or the teasing tone of the cad from our dinners and at the brothel. My own words are lost to me though, and after several moments without a response, he turns to leave. Before he takes a full step, my hand shoots out, almost of its own volition, to grab his boot.

"Thank you," I whisper.

"Do not thank me. It should not have happened. You warned me about Crewes, and I didn't take care of it soon enough," he replies, disgust coloring his words. "I'm sorry."

"Thank you," I repeat quietly. "For stopping him before he could...for letting me have my vengeance. He wasn't wrong; it wouldn't have been anything that hasn't been done before, but...thank you."

Lennox crouches next to me and places his hand under my chin, raising it so I meet his eyes. His touch is gentle on my bruised skin. His lashes appear damp, but surely this man cannot feel sadness for my plight.

"No one should ever touch you without your permission, whether it has been done before or not. No one on this ship will touch you unless you ask them to, Andromeda. You have my word."

"What about you?" I ask, my voice wary.

"Including me," he assures me, releasing my chin. He stands and makes his way toward the door. "I will be on deck should you need me. I'll leave the water and clothing for you. Take as long as you need."

"Lennox." I stop him before he can reach the door.

I don't know why, but I want him to stay. Despite the stories and the missing girls, despite the reason I am on this ship in the first place, he feels safe, and I don't want to be alone.

"Please, help me."

His body tenses at my words, but he returns to my side and extends his hand to help me stand. I take it and he pulls me to my feet, making sure I am steady before releasing his grip.

He removes his blood-stained coat, laying it over a chair, then rolls his sleeves up to his elbows before turning to me. My heart flutters as he pulls a sharp knife from his boot, uncertain as to its purpose. Since the majority of my bodice is ripped, he delicately inserts the knife under the fabric and cuts the remainder from my body, dropping the ruined garment to the floor.

Even though I stand before him in the nude, I feel no fear. He walks me to the table where a bucket of warmed fresh water is waiting and instructs me to sit on a towel that's laid across one of the chairs. Then, he wets the wash-cloth and gently washes the blood from my chin, breasts, and arms.

Gathering the shift Lyra brought for me, he pulls it over my head before removing the pins that remain in my hair. A tremble runs through me as he stands behind me and care-fully begins to comb my hair. When he runs his fingers through the thick locks, I realize it has been years since someone cared for me like this. Has touched me with kind-ness, with no expectations. The tears I have held a tight grip on slip down my cheeks while he continues to smooth the knots from my hair, and I try to remain silent and hide the shaking of my body with each sob that escapes.

Lennox doesn't mention my tears when he finishes with his ministrations, but he does pour a liberal glass of brandy from the decanter on his desk for me, offering it along with a linen handkerchief. The warm liquid is a balm to my nerves, and I finally allow myself to relax fully.

When my eyes meet his, there is no hiding the way he clutches the edge of the table, nor the color high in his sculpted cheeks. He clenches his strong jaw, and there is a look in his eyes I cannot name. Something almost akin to fear. Although, perhaps fear is the correct emotion for a man to feel next to a woman that just mutilated someone on the deck of his ship.

"Would you like to rest?" He asks as I finish the glass of liquor.

My adrenaline has fully worn off, and I am hollow and exhausted. My lip is swollen and my cheek feels bruised from Crewes' blows. I would like nothing more than to curl up in a feather bed and sleep, but I don't want to return to the small cabin with Lyra and face the questions she will inevitably have waiting for me.

"Yes, I would." I start to rise, but he steps forward and sweeps me into his strong arms again. Before I can protest or panic, he carries me to his large bed and tucks me under the warm coverlet.

"Rest here. No one will bother you. I'll make sure of it." He steps away to grab one of the chairs at the table and returns to my side.

For reasons I cannot identify clearly at the moment, I desperately want him in the bed with me, not in a chair at my side.

"Lennox, will you... will you lay next to me?" The words come out barely above a whisper.

His eyes snap to mine in surprise, but he promptly pulls his boots off and places his cutlass on the chair seat. He walks around the other side of the bed and I feel the stuffed mattress sink behind me as he crawls to my side. I remain on my side, still facing the chair, when I feel him curl behind me, our bodies fitted together with the coverlet between us.

"Thank you," I whisper and sink into his protective warmth.

As the haze from the brandy washes over me, I begin to

drift to sleep. I am on the edge of wakefulness, so I can't be certain, but I swear I hear a whisper against my hair.

"I knew you would be fierce the first night I saw you. Rest, my she-wolf." Gentle fingers caress my hair as I fall asleep.

CHAPTER II

The smoke from the ruined temple chokes me as I run through the narrow hidden passage. Stones bruise my bare feet as I flee in the darkness, too afraid to carry a lamp or candle in case I am followed. Angry voices drift through the air, a mixture of soldiers bellowing commands and my sister priestesses crying out in desperate sobs.

Guilt swells in my chest that I'm leaving them behind, but the only thing I can think of is escape. Refugees that pass through the temple have spoken of what awaits if the King's men capture me; we are no longer sacred beings who honor the divine. We are whores and heathens to be used as they wish, or burned for heresy. Those are the options left to me if I stay behind.

I will not be captured.

Heavy footsteps echo in the darkness behind me and I run faster on bloodied feet. A hand reaches out to grasp my hair...

I SIT UP IN ALARM. SWEAT COATS MY FLESH AND THE LIGHT shift I wear is stuck to me. My chest tightens as my eyes dart around the dim space, pushing the warm coverlet off. A lantern burns on the table on the other side of the bed, illuminating the space enough to spark recognition of my location as it reflects off the now familiar furniture and the form resting at my side, allowing my breathing to slow. I'm in the Captain's cabin. I'm safe.

Captain Lennox is still at my side, but his body is relaxed in sleep, his right hand resting across his stomach as he lays on his back. I'm relieved to see he is still fully clothed on top of the coverlet. A book rests face down on the mattress next to him, so he must have moved at some point once I fell asleep, but returned to me.

His face is calm, the furrow normally present on his brow softened. Glancing up at his eyes again to make sure he is still asleep, I take a moment to admire his full lips, parted slightly. His lashes are lighter than I expect, as is the barest amount of stubble along his strong jaw — time spent in the amplified sunlight off the sea must have lightened it like it has his dark hair as our voyage continues.

It's easy to see his life hasn't been peaceful; the scar on his right brow and across his knuckles are indicative of a life full of violence. With his forearms bare and his eyes closed, I can openly admire the different tattoos that mark his tan flesh. Many are the usual nautical symbols common amongst sailors and pirates — birds and stars symbolizing luck, safe journeys home, and miles traveled. But I was correct before; there *are* symbols of the Goddess — moon phases, sigils, and stars woven into constellations on his skin.

Who is this man and what does he know of the Goddess?

When I look toward the windows lining the back of the cabin, a hint of starlight shines through the wavy glass. I've slept so long that it's already night. Carefully, so I don't disturb Lennox, I climb down from the bed and walk quietly to retrieve a glass of water, swishing it around my sore mouth before drinking. Then, I sit on the bench that lines the windows and gaze out at the stars and the thick slice of moon in the sky.

My heartbeat slows, and my nerves calm after my sudden awakening, the twinkling sky soothing the ache in my soul. I know we are traveling down the coast, but I have no idea which of the port cities we will stop at before crossing the sea. I've only traveled long-distance once, but it was overland, and I was in such a panic that I've tried to forget most of the journey.

My thoughts are arrested by movement on the bed as the Captain stirs. From my vantage point, I watch him reach for where my body should be. His eyes fly open when he finds the space is empty, and he sits up suddenly, looking around the room before locking eyes with me on the bench.

"Are you well?" he asks, standing and approaching me, running his fingers through his hair. Although I trust that I am safe in his presence, my heart stutters a bit as he nears, eyes roving across my body in the dim light of the lantern burning low.

"I am. Thank you. I'll retire to my own cabin now. I don't wish to trouble you further." I stand and move to return my water glass to the table when he reaches for my empty hand.

"You don't have to leave. Stay as long as you like. I won't... " Lennox pauses. "I have no expectations," he says, delicately stroking my palm. Unbidden, heat pools in my belly as warmth spreads from his touch and I find myself allowing him to entwine my fingers with his, my smaller hand swallowed by his rough palm.

"I know, I just..." I stumble over my words and unlace our hands. "I should check on Lyra."

Lennox clears his throat with a nod. "Of course." He straightens and hands me one of his coats to wear over my light shift, then walks me to the door. Before he opens it, and before I can reconsider what I'm doing, I stand on my tiptoes and brush a chaste kiss on his mouth. A stunned look crosses his face, but he doesn't have a chance to speak before I am out the door and rushing to my cabin.

None of the men on deck pay me any mind as I walk quickly toward the stairs that lead below to my shared cabin. Either they are unconcerned, or are avoiding me after the display earlier. Pausing at the top of the stairs, I take a deep breath, the sea breeze soothing my nerves while the bright stars above ground me.

I am whole, I am strong, I have survived worse than this.

Fortified by my own words, I descend into the damp lower decks.

As I approach the door, the sound of muffled voices and a light groan seep through the wood. I still, trying to listen more closely, the sound comes through the door again and panic for Lyra seizes me.

Is she ill? Surely, no one would dare harm her after today's show of punishment from the Captain.

Without pausing to even consider what I will do if

someone *is* hurting her — I don't even know where my dagger is from earlier — I push the door open quietly and step inside.

Our candle resting on the small table has burned low, wax pooling at the base. Lyra's dress lies discarded on the floor, a pair of men's breeches and a dirty shirt alongside it. Two bodies writhe under the sheets on Lyra's bed and I blink rapidly in the dim lighting, trying to focus. Lyra's tight curls peek from under her partner, but I can't make out who has joined her. The sound of muffled giggles and moans of pleasure mingle with the creak of the ship. I have clearly walked in on a consensual romantic embrace, but it's too late for me to retreat. As soon as the door scrapes in closure the bodies freeze on the bed.

"Lyra — what is this?" I ask in a hushed tone. I'm in no place to scold the girl for seeking pleasure with someone, but I *am* fearful of what the Captain will do if he discovers the jewel he has purchased has been tarnished by another.

"Oh! Oh, Andromeda, um... well..." Lyra stumbles for words as she pulls the shoulders of her shift up to cover her breasts. Her partner has still not turned to face me so I move closer, holding the candle I've now pulled loose from the table close to view his face.

Shocked at the sight of familiar messy, mousy brown hair, I gasp, "Charlie!" The boy turns toward me, eyes downcast, holding his hands across his – *breasts*?

"You're —?" I start. "You're a girl!" I exclaim in confusion, looking between the two young women.

The gleam in both their eyes almost makes me laugh. They look both chastened as well as thrilled that they have fooled me for this long, like a joke shared between children hiding things from an oblivious parent.

"Aye, Missus. I am. It's not so easy to find work on the ships as a girl though, so I have to keep up appearances, you see." Charlie gives me a wry smile, ever the little sparrow.

"And the Captain? Does he know?" I ask, still looking between them.

"Oh yes, Andromeda. Of course! Captain Lennox assigned Charlie to be our cabin...um, attendant... specifically because of her sex. To make sure no one would harass us," Lyra explains.

"I see. How... thoughtful... of him." I truly don't know what to make of this revelation. I stoop to retrieve Charlie's shirt and toss it to her while I return the candle to the table. "I'm sorry to have... interrupted... "

"Don't be silly! This is your room, too, Andromeda. We just thought, since you were with the Captain and all, that you might not come back tonight, you see. Oh, Andromeda, are you all right? Truly?" Lyra asks, looking over me.

Lennox's oversized coat still hangs from my shoulders as I sit down on my bunk. Lyra climbs out of bed to sit by my side, sweetly holding my hand.

"Yes, Lyra. I am." I grasp her hand tighter and smile at her and Charlie in turn. "He didn't... he wasn't able to succeed in his attempts. Thanks to you and Charlie. Thank you both for helping me."

"I'm so sorry it happened, Missus. But I'm glad you took care of the bastard," Charlie replies, her normally upbeat tone cold. A bruise darkens her cheek from the attack to match my split lip.

"So am I, Charlie. Now if you both don't mind, I'd like to go to sleep."

Shrugging out of the Captain's coat, I lay it across one of the chairs and adjust my coverlet while Lyra says goodbye to her lover. She floats back to her bed and snuggles in without another word. Once she settles, I blow out the dwindling candle, my mind racing over all of the new revelations.

CHAPTER 12

The next day is spent cocooned in my cabin, curled under the coverlet and Lennox's heavy coat with my journals and thoughts. But as the night comes and goes, I refuse to allow myself any more time to retreat inward. I will not be broken by the actions of the foul men whose bodies now drift in the sea.

The following morning I'm informed by the boatswain, Pike — an older, dark-skinned sailor with rings climbing his ears and one in his nostril — that we are pulling into port today before setting sail across the ocean. He hands me a note with familiar green wax sealing it, explaining that the Captain has a few requests for me to pick up from the apothecary in addition to my own needs. He also hands me my dagger with a smile. It has been sharpened and shined to a brilliant gleam, and its weight in my hand once more is a relief.

Once I have securely pocketed the weapon, Pike reminds me to be sure to visit the apothecary on the street where the brothels are located. As if I could forget the danger of selecting one of the shops in the more respectable part of town, even in an unfamiliar city. The King has all but outlawed women from utilizing healing herbs and knowledge, so the only places we can purchase these items, without being questioned by Blackwell's men patrolling the streets, are the less lawful areas.

Instructions delivered, Pike hands me a pouch full of coins to use for my purchases before he resumes his work, inspecting the ship for any last-minute repairs before we return to sea. The purse feels much heavier than I will need for the errand, but I tuck it in my other pocket for safe-keeping.

The wax seal pops as I slide my finger beneath it, and a stained page falls from the center to land at my feet. Before reading the list written in the Captain's script, I pick up the page from the floor. The list I had stashed in my dress pocket before Crewes accosted me is smeared and crumpled from the struggle, but gratitude swells in my chest that the Captain thought to retrieve it for me — I won't have to waste time taking inventory again. His list is short, but includes an odd request: black walnut hulls. Climbing the stairs to the main deck as we prepare to dock, my mind races through the uses for these items until I recognize where we are.

Sweat prickles across my skin as my heart skips erratically in my chest, and my breaths become shallow when I view a newly erected cathedral on a hill. Mountains topped in light snow and pines rise in the North behind the construction. The land around it is scorched; all the trees that once stood here have been either cut down for the cathedral's construction or burned to ash. My mouth is bitter as I hold back tears at the sight of the scarred city of Athene. My home.

The remains of the temple I called home for years have been razed to make way for the King's new religion. The sacred grove where I participated in the rites and numerous other ceremonies over the years is char.

Breathe. No one knows you here anymore, I tell myself over and over as we inch closer to the town.

Sooner than I wish, the gangplank is lowered and men begin to gather chests and barrels to carry down, ready to sell or trade for new cargo.

"Do you need assistance finding your way, Mistress?" Erik asks me as he towers above me, watching over the men working. He must have confused my hesitation to disembark as fear of getting lost in the streets. He doesn't realize I am afraid of being lost in my memories instead.

"No, um, can you please just point the way? I am sure I can find it," I say, knowing full well where I am going. He points to the right of the ship and tells me directions that I can't hear over the pounding of my heart. Slowly, I step down the plank, nervous sweat seeping from my every pore when my feet hit the solid ground at the bottom. I take a deep breath, square my shoulders, and head in the direction Erik indicated.

It takes me only a few minutes to reach the correct street — brothels and taverns are never located too far from the docks, after all. Tucked into the middle of the street between two infamous Houses is a small apothecary. With the lists in hand, I step through the door into the dim interior. A short man behind the counter glances up as the bell rings over my head, and his eyes widen at my fine attire. I don't look like the usual customers he sees on this street.

"Good afternoon, my dear," he greets me, fiddling with the spectacles he wears over cloudy eyes as I approach the counter. He is balding and his clothes are shabby and patched. "How may I help you?"

"I need these items, please." I pass the two pages across the counter to him. He looks vaguely discomfited by the stains on my list, but begins to pull jars from the shelves and fill labeled bags and bottles at once. I wipe my sweaty palms down the front of my dark dress and try not to fidget while he readies my order, but I can't stop myself from nervously glancing out the front glass as I wait. I haven't been to this town since I fled, and I hope to avoid seeing any other reminders of my life here. Through the cloudy glass, a familiar shape retreats into one of the larger Houses across the way.

Captain Lennox.

At the sight of his familiar form, all nervousness vanishes, replaced with jealousy and anger at the sight. The Captain has yet to take advantage of my services, for which I am grateful, so why do I feel jealous of the idea that someone else might service him? Perhaps I *am* too old for his tastes, and he merely needed a healer on board. But then, the amount he paid for me is entirely too high compared to what he could have hired an actual physician for. The mild shopkeep snaps me out of my disordered thoughts when he clears his throat.

"Anything else, my dear?" he asks me kindly, handing me my lists and a package full of herbs. I am not used to being spoken to in gentle tones like this and catch myself smiling at the man as I hand him his coin.

"No, thank you, sir," I reply as I take my change and turn toward the door.

"Watch yourself alone on these streets, Miss. Even though it's been a while, it's still not safe for your kind," he says softly behind me. I turn to look over my shoulder at him and find him smiling sadly.

He raises his gnarled index finger and taps lightly between his eyebrows, indicating the place where my sigil rests, before he bows his head to me. My lips tighten into the barest of a smile in thanks as I nod and pull up the hood of my cloak in response to his warning. I take a calming breath, deeply inhaling the comforting herbal aroma of the shop before I reach the door and step onto the cobblestones beyond.

A part of me — the irrational part — wants to enter the dark door of the brothel I saw Captain Lennox walk through earlier. Curiosity to find out who he has decided is worth his coin, and his body, mixes with fury, but I know I'm being a fool, and turn to head back to the docks. I can sort the new herbs into their containers before we set sail again.

Passing one of the many dark alleys along the street, a faint whisper brings me up short and my blood runs cold.

"Nerissa?"

It can't be. It's this town messing with your mind, keep walking.

But the faint voice comes once more, and I cannot make my feet move. I turn toward the alley, toward the whisper of the past.

"Nerissa? Is that you, sweet girl?"

An older woman huddles in a pile of rags in the mouth of the alley. I wouldn't have even noticed she was a human at the clip I was walking without looking closely. As I look down at her, I swallow back the bile that rises in my throat. Her hair is brittle and streaked with grey, bruises mar her lined face, and she is missing several teeth. But the faded sigil on her brow is unmistakable. This is the face of the fate I ran from years ago; the promised future that drove me to the House of Starlight instead of staying in the streets.

"Priestess Amaya." I choke on my tears as I crouch down and reach to touch the woman's familiar face. Tears cloud her eyes as she clutches my hand to her damaged cheek.

"Oh, I knew it was you, child! I knew it wasn't a vision," she cries to me. I have no words. Nothing to say that will ease her suffering. "Have you wed, then? Found someone to save you from this fate?"

"I… no… not exactly." Shame and sorrow wash over me. I can't tell my elder truth. That I am a whore that just happened to run to the right doorway instead of suffering in the streets as she has. That I fled instead of standing with my sisters when the soldiers ransacked our temple. "Oh, Amaya. Are you all right? How can I help you?"

"Seeing you, and knowing there is hope for some of us, is enough." She glances up at me with her broken smile, and I remember the purse of coins I still have, retrieving it from my pocket and pressing it into her hand.

"Here, Amaya. Please, take this and find a place to

stay... to get warm for the evening." I still clutch her hand when heavy footsteps approach from behind me.

"Is this creature bothering you, Mistress?" the stranger's rough voice asks, and I freeze. I haven't shown my face, but I realize that my clothes mask who, and what, I am. This man thinks I am a respectable woman who stumbled onto the wrong street. I barely turn to look over my shoulder and see the uniform of one of the King's soldiers. I can't control the trembling that begins immediately.

I can't breathe.

I can't think.

If he sees my brow he will know what I am.

I whisper over my shoulder, "No, sir. Thank you. I was just offering comfort to the less fortunate." I stand, praying that he doesn't see the distress written in the tension of my body, and keep my back to him.

"Do you require assistance, Mistress? To find your way to a safer part of town?" He continues to speak to me, even though I have not turned to face him.

"No, thank you. I see where I am going."

I force my feet to move, roughly brushing the tears that have escaped off my cheeks. If I look back and see the man, I am done. When I pass another shop, then two, I allow myself to look behind me. The soldier stands confused near the entrance of the alley, staring at my retreating form. I round the corner and begin to run. I don't know where I am running to, but I cannot be here.

I can't breathe.

I can't think.

My lungs ache with the exertion, and my heart nears bursting. I only slow when I arrive back at the docks, sinking to a crouch behind a shipping crate, trying to pull any air at all into my lungs. Black boots suddenly stand in my field of vision and terror shoots through me.

He's followed me, he knows.

I can't get away; there will be no escape this time. My back rests against the hard wood of the crate and my path to escape is blocked by a man.

"Andromeda," I hear my name, but can't look up. "Andromeda, look at me."

It's Lennox.

He is breathing hard as if he has been running as well, and I look up at his face. His cheeks are ruddy from the cool air, and his eyes glitter as he asks, "Are you well?"

"Distract me," I answer abruptly.

"Excuse me?" he answers furrowing his brow slightly, head cocked to the side.

"I can't breathe. Distract me." I look him in the eye with a challenge. I will him to understand what I want. What I need him to do.

His lips curl into a wicked grin. "As you command."

Before I can regain any composure, he reaches down and roughly pulls me to my feet, scoops me up, and tosses me over his shoulder. His steps are hurried as he walks toward the gangplank and I bounce against him.

"Out of the way," he commands gruffly to the men loading new goods on the ship, and carries me up to the deck. To all the dockworkers and onlookers, I look like a disobedient harlot about to receive my punishment, but the entire walk he whispers softly so only I can hear, "Breathe, Andromeda. Breathe."

I am carried thus all the way to the Captain's cabin

before he gently sets me on my feet. My breath comes easier, and my thoughts are forming coherently, the cloud of fear and confusion from the docks fading into a memory. The jealousy I felt at seeing the Captain entering the brothel returns when I look at him and see that devilish smile. His hair is mussed, the color is still high in his cheeks, and I find myself wanting to either slap him or kiss him. Or both.

"So, Andromeda, was that distracting enough? Or do you require additional aid?" he huffs a laugh, crossing his arms over his chest. The attitude of the rakish pirate is back to hide his gentle whispers of moments before.

"I don't know, Captain. I'm not sure of your abilities. You may have tired yourself out at the brothel in town." I barely recognize the sarcasm in my voice; these feelings are not something I am used to.

Who am I to get jealous?

"Oh, do you doubt my virility, my pretty priestess?" He takes a step closer to me, and heat courses through my blood. "You know you only have to say the words, and I will prove to you what I am capable of."

The familiar ache of longing throbs between my thighs, and I can sense the wetness building there. Lennox looks at me with a cruel smirk, yet I take a step in his direction, closing the space between us further.

"Distract me, Captain," I challenge him again, recklessly staring into his eyes. I can see desire ignite there, and I know I was wrong to doubt whether he found me appealing before.

I want to drown out the fear that I've been running from. I want to dissolve the bitter taste of jealousy I felt seeing him enter the brothel in Athene. I want *him*.

"Are you sure, Andromeda?" he asks huskily, studying my face as he uncrosses his arms and leans closer. "This is what you want?"

"Yes."

Before the word is fully out of my mouth, I'm in his arms. His mouth crashes against mine as our bodies urgently press together, the heat I felt during our first kiss flames hotter this time as we cling to one another. I pull at the clasp of my cloak and let it fall to the floor before pushing the Captain's coat to the ground behind him. Lennox walks me backward, still pressing kisses against my lips until I lean against the table we shared our meals on. He lifts me so that I sit on the wooden surface, and I wrap my legs around him, pulling him closer.

My fingers tug at his soft hair and he moans against my mouth as he runs his hands over my breasts and sides. I want to be closer, to touch his bare skin, so I reach to pull his shirt from his trousers. He stops me for a moment, breath hitching as he pulls back abruptly from my kiss to meet my eyes, and the muscles in his jaw flex. Then, he sighs heavily and allows me to pull his shirt off, revealing tan flesh covering the lean hard lines of his body, the barest glimpse of paler skin showing where his trousers hang lower on his waist. His tattoos travel up his arms and across the expanse of his broad chest. I can't help but run my hands over them before pulling his face back down to mine for another desperate kiss.

I move to hike my skirt around my hips to allow him to have his way, but he pulls me from the table and spins me in his arms. My palms press into the hard surface of the table as I lean forward, waiting for his hands to grab the edge of my skirt. Surprise fills me as his long fingers begin unbuttoning my dress, achingly slow. He grazes the bare skin of my back with his lips as it's revealed with each button opening, and my arms tremble, barely able to hold myself upright, under his gentle touch. Each whisper soft caress feels like a spark against my heated flesh. Once the buttons are undone, he pushes the wool from my shoulders, and the dress falls to the ground, only an underskirt covering me.

Lennox's hands drift down from my shoulders, over my naked back, and onto my hips as he slides the underskirt from my body, baring me before him. Still bent over the table in front of him, I turn, glancing over my shoulder to see his heated gaze on my body. I press back against his hardness and gasp at the delicious friction of him, his ragged breath matching mine. Instead of removing his own clothing, as I expect, he again begins to kiss my naked skin, traveling from my shoulder blades, down my spine, and over my backside, rough palms skimming my curves as he moves. I arch my back, biting my lip to stifle a moan, as he kneels and kisses up the backs of my thighs. The sensation of his touch almost overwhelms me, and I reach between my legs, eager for relief from his teasing. With a chuckle, he replaces my hand with his own, sliding against the wetness at my core as he stands behind me. Slowly, he inches one finger inside of me, and I rock back on him.

"More, please, more..." I moan as he slides a second digit into my warm flesh. "Captain," I gasp. "Take me to bed, please."

With another masculine chuckle, he slides his fingers out, turning me roughly toward him. I reach up on my toes to claim his mouth with mine again, and he grips under my thighs, lifting me so I can wrap my legs around his waist. His steps are sure as he carries me to the bed and lays me down gently. I inch back on the mattress, watching as he kicks off his boots and removes his trousers. When his cock is freed from his pants, I clench my thighs in anticipation, reaching for him.

"Patience, Andromeda. I told you I would make sure you find your pleasure. Would you like me to tell you what I want to do to you?"

"Yes," I pant through my longing, running my hands over my body, clutching my breasts.

"I'm going to tease every inch of you until you are begging me for more." He kneels on the bed, leaning his body across mine while I recline beneath him. His tongue trails up the sensitive side of my neck until he is breathing against the shell of my ear. "Then, I'm going to make you come so loudly that every man on this ship hears your screams, and knows that you're mine," he whispers, pressing his nakedness against me. His words are a dark promise, and I part my legs in wantonness, whimpering with desire.

Lennox slides his length between my thighs, teasing me again, and I arch my hips in response, desperate for the feel of him inside me. But instead, he leaves a trail of kisses along my neck, sucking at the tender spot where it meets my shoulder.

"Lennox. Oh, Goddess," I gasp, as heat surges through me under his touch.

Then, he cups my breast in his rough hand and takes my nipple in his mouth, sucking and nipping it until I writhe beneath him. Trying to rub against him. I can feel his smile as he treats my other breast to the same attention and continues to kiss down my belly, stopping just below my navel. I clutch his hair in my hands and raise my hips again, begging with my body for him to take me.

He slides his hot mouth against me, kissing and licking back up to my breasts, where he nips at me again before smiling up at me with a wicked gleam in his emerald eyes. When he slides one long finger through my slick core I buck beneath him, unable to control my reactions to this delicious torture. As he slowly slides his finger inside of me, he whispers against my neck, "Is this the kind of distraction you desired, my pretty priestess?"

I'm so engulfed in the pleasure he is wringing from me that I can't form words as he presses the heel of his hand against my aching core, sliding a second finger inside of me, so I pull his mouth to mine in answer, fisting his hair between my fingers.

"That's right. Come for me," Lennox murmurs against my lips. My climax coils as he claims my mouth, sliding in and out of me while rubbing against the sensitive bundle of nerves until I come undone.

"Oh, Goddess!" I pant, still gripping his hair in my hands as I bury my face against his shoulder. Once my waves of pleasure stop, he smirks in satisfaction, biting his lip with his brow raised in question.

"Are you distracted enough, Andromeda? Or do you need more?"

I raise my hips to rub against his arousal in answer, reaching my arms up to clasp the back of his head, and bring his mouth back to mine.

"I want you inside me, *now*."

"Thank fuck." He smirks as he teases my entrance, slippery and ready for him.

Slowly, he slides inside of me, and I gasp at the sensation of him filling me. He smiles against my mouth in a gentle kiss, before it shifts to something deeper, needier, as he moves his hips against me.

When I run my hands down his back, my fingers trace over thick scars running along his skin. He stills for a moment, pulling away from my lips as he stares down at me. His jaw is tightly clenched as his eyes meet mine, but he resumes his motion once my hands reach his hips. I pull him closer, clutching him as our bodies move together. I found my pleasure, and now I want him to have his.

"Take me from behind," I murmur, bringing my mouth back against his as he thrusts. He pauses, pulling out for a moment, while I roll over. His hands grip tightly on my hips as he yanks them into the air, and I gasp when he thrusts into me.

"*Fuck*, Andromeda," Lennox groans while I moan into the pillows, clenching his length. His fingers wind into my hair, tugging it firmly while he keeps up a punishing pace. It isn't long before he finds his release, growling a moan as he finishes.

A few moments pass, his body draped over my back while we are still joined, before he slowly slides out of me. I collapse onto the feather bed, and he turns to lay beside me. His fingers gently skim my spine, then over the smooth skin of my backside and thighs. I cannot help but smile to myself at the gentle caress. When I turn my head to look at him, he is smiling at me — not the wicked grin I am used to, but a small, genuine smile of contentment. I can't help but return the look and lean over to kiss him gently.

"Was that distracting enough?" his chest rumbles with a laugh when we break apart.

"I believe it will be sufficient, Captain. Thank you," I reply coyly, a blush creeping over my pale flesh.

He settles onto his back, a hand behind his head, almost as relaxed as when he slept beside me after my attack. I swallow hesitantly, but can't help but ask, "What happened to your back?"

Any sense of relaxation is gone at my inquiry. His body tenses, the lines on his face deepening, and I instantly regret my decision to question him. Surely such injuries bring back terrible memories.

"I'll tell you," he says finally, "if you tell me why you ran down the streets and hid like a rabbit being chased by hounds."

My breath is ragged, but I nod. "Deal."

CHAPTER 13

LENNOX

A long exhale fortifies me before I begin. This isn't what I thought we would discuss immediately after she begged me to bed her. But then again, I hadn't expected her to be the one begging. I imagined I would be spending far more time seducing her than I have, so nothing is going to plan. But, a deal is a deal.

Rehashing this history is made only slightly better by having her naked body next to mine, where I can admire her round backside, and freely touch her soft hair as she lays on her stomach waiting for me to speak.

"When I was twenty-one, I was pressed into service aboard one of Blackwell's ships. They ambushed me on the docks when I was visiting town from my village. I was not an obedient sailor, and I was rewarded with the cat. Often. The only good thing that happened on that ship was that I learned to sail and to be cruel."

My eyes flicker to the nail where the cat-of-nine-tails still hangs. The sting of saltwater in bloody wounds is memorable enough to make me grit my teeth, even years later. I don't confide that it was these very docks I was taken from. Or that my home was only a few hours north of here on horseback. Or that the captain and quartermaster who beat me felt the bite of that same cat plenty of times before I ended them. Crewes would have welcomed her choice of punishment if he knew what I had in mind for him before she took her vengeance.

"When the opportunity for desertion was presented, I took it and went on the account. I sailed upon a pirate's vessel for a year before they returned to the port near my home. By that time, Blackwell's men had been through the village. I told you my mother was a believer in the Goddess. When I made it home, when I found her, they had…" The words stick in my throat, and I squeeze my eyes tightly at the memory of what I found. My mother and brother-in-law had been left to the scavengers.

Andromeda's breath catches before she whispers, "I know what they did…"

She rolled to her side facing me while I spoke, and now tears fall from her dark blue eyes as they meet mine. My tears are barely contained as she trembles from her own memories.

"My brother-in-law was killed defending my mother. Thankfully, my sister had already fled with their small daughter before the soldiers arrived. I found her in one of the Houses in a nearby town, making money the only way she knew how. She's lucky she had a place to go where she trusted the proprietor." My voice is barely above a whisper, the memories washing over me as I recount those horrible days.

"I'm sorry." She reaches out to stroke my cheek. We lay

facing one another, and I can't keep myself from leaning into her soft touch, placing my hand over hers. I have wanted to touch her gently like this all those nights in the House of Starlight.

"I am, too. I didn't know you would react to this town as you did." I had my suspicions, but assumed she wouldn't be honest with me if I asked outright. But, now I know. Her next words confirm it.

"I…" she begins hesitantly. "I didn't know we were coming here. But, I knew where we were as soon as we arrived in the bay. The temple… where I studied… where I worshiped… my home… is gone." She stumbles over the words, her low voice cracking from the pain of seeing the destruction outside the port. Her eyes leave my face for a moment, glancing in the direction of the new cathedral before she continues.

"We heard the rumors of the King's men coming to root out the heresy of the temples, but we thought the Goddess would protect us. The night they came, I… I fled. They knocked down the doors, setting everything ablaze to force us out. I hurriedly grabbed a few items in my room and stole through the secret exits before they reached the interior. I didn't stay to help my sisters. I didn't look back. I ran like a coward as they murdered them."

She pauses, taking another steadying breath before continuing, "One of the elder priestesses was in the alley by the apothecary today. I was trying to help her when the soldier spoke to me. I was so afraid he would take me. That's why I ran. I was so consumed by my fear that I couldn't think straight. I did it again. I just ran."

A sob escapes her, and sorrow is written in every line of

her face. Grief from years past falls on the pillow and feather bed below. My heart breaks for her as I pull her against my chest, wrapping her in comfort. She tenses briefly before melting against me, and I press my cheek against her soft sable hair.

I had followed her to the apothecary's shop so I could make sure she was safe, but slipped across the street to Madame Serena's to remain unseen. Apparently, I wasn't as stealthy as I had planned based on her earlier words about the brothel. When she left the shop, I trailed her again. I had seen the soldier and the beggar woman, but hadn't connected them to her flight.

I understand her guilt — her regret. I carry the same burdens.

How many nights had I reviewed it in my head? If I had fought harder, or been stronger on those docks, I could have escaped. I could have saved my mother and brother-in-law. But I know I am only one man; I would have likely ended up dead alongside them.

"You couldn't have stopped them any more than I could have, Andromeda."

"Nerissa," she breathes against my chest.

"What?" I pull back to study her face.

"My name isn't Andromeda. That's who I became at the House of Starlight," she whispers. "My real name is Nerissa." A secret truth.

"Nerissa," I repeat it like a prayer and run my thumb over her full lower lip. She has given me this; I can offer a truth in return.

"Then please, when we are in private, call me Billy."

No one, except those who know me intimately, refers to

me by the nickname my mother and sister knew me as, and I can see her eyes crinkle with amusement at the boyhood name. It holds none of the notoriety I possess as *Captain Lennox*.

"Well, Billy," she tests the name, "any other deep secrets you'd like to share?"

"Oh, I have many secrets," I lean forward and quickly press a kiss on her rosy lips. "None of which I will be sharing today."

If she only knew all the secrets that swirl behind the eyes staring back at her, she would run from these quarters. I smile at her, squeezing her in my arms briefly, then gently release her. Standing from the bed to retrieve my shed clothing, the scars on my back are fully visible to her now. I wait for her to gasp or recoil, but when I glance over my shoulder, her full lips are taut as she inspects them. Anger flashes over her pretty face, but she blinks it away as quickly as it came. It's obvious to anyone familiar with the lash that I was beaten often. Often enough to shred my skin and leave thick scars. I spent most of the time I learned to sail in pain or fevered, biding my time.

"I think it's time we get underway," I announce, drawing her eyes up to my face.

Her gaze lingers for a moment as I fasten my pants, then quickly brushes over my chest and stomach as I pull my shirt on. She is quick with her looks, but I watch her inspect the tattoos across my chest and arms before they're fully covered again. I pull on my boots and coat, and catch her still watching me from the corner of her eye, earning a smirk at her admiration.

I am aware that most women find me physically attractive, even if they fear the stories that precede me. I've never had trouble finding a partner, but none of them have ever been who I truly want.

I only want her.

She stands gracefully, gathering her underskirt and dress. It pleases me that the flush on her pale skin is my doing. If I watch her for too much longer, though, I might strip her back out of her garments, and we will never leave the docks. As she pulls her dress over her pink skin, she starts, "Your hair…"

I freeze.

"Yes?" I raise my brows in question as I approach her, motioning for her to turn around so I can help with her buttons, and to keep her from looking at me too closely.

"It seems… lighter?" she casually observes, glancing over her shoulder. "I don't know why I thought it was black when I saw you in the House of Starlight, but it isn't at all."

The look she gives me would normally make me run my lips over the sensitive side of her neck that's bared to me, but as it stands I need to get out of the room and away from her curious glances.

"Ah, well, a trick of the light I'm sure." I clear my throat and answer quickly as I fasten the last button at the top of her dress. Grabbing a hat from a peg, I cover my hair with the tricorn and head toward the door.

"You can let yourself out whenever you wish," I bow to her and exit.

Fuck.

My footsteps pound on the wood as I descend to the hold, leaving her in my cabin without a backward glance. Pike and Erik share a smug, knowing look as I pass where they stand to oversee the cargo that's carried down into the hold. I probably should have made sure there wasn't anything of interest lying about on my desk, but I needed to get away from her questioning. She is proving to be far more inquisitive than I expected. Talking about my mother and my time in the navy is already a raw wound; I am not ready to divulge any other secrets yet.

Instead, I need to see Lyra.

CHAPTER 14

The door swings shut behind Lennox, but, I linger in his cabin, reflecting on the intimacy forming between the Captain and myself. The items from the apothecary are somehow still in the pocket of my dress, even after being tipped upside down and carried up the gangplank. Pulling them from my pocket, I separate the items specifically for him and place them on his desk.

Lying on top of several maps is the book I noticed beside him after my ordeal with Crewes. I turn the cover towards me, running my fingers across the title of an old play about star-crossed lovers. I can't fight the smile that immediately comes to my lips – *the dear Captain: vicious pirate or heartsick lover*? The discovery lightens my heart after the treachery of the city, and I nearly float to my surgery to organize my new herbs.

The next few hours pass quickly while I busy myself in the surgery. I'm unsure if my good mood is the result of a proper bedding or the new connection I feel to Lennox. It still feels unnatural to think of him as Billy, as if he is some village boy I've taken up with, even if I find the nickname endearing.

Once I've organized my new supplies, I retreat to my shared cabin to visit and dine with Lyra. The door swings open, and I open my mouth to greet her, but she is not there. We have already weighed anchor, so I know she isn't on shore, but I've been so preoccupied that I haven't kept track of her today. Panic forms a tight ball that grows in my chest the longer I search.

There is no sign of her, or Charlie, anywhere in the darkened hold, so I mount the stairs to ascend to the deck to find her. A quick glance around the main deck also reveals nothing — crewmembers at their tasks, but no cheerful youths. Finally, after wandering forward to the bow and turning back to walk toward the stern, I spot Charlie fluttering in the space leading to the Captain's cabin. When she sees me, her face grows uneasy, her steps hurried as she moves to intercept me.

"Good evening, Missus. Do you need something?" Charlie fumbles with her hat as she looks at her feet.

"Hello, Charlie. I'm looking for Lyra. Have you seen her?" My panic fully takes root with each nervous movement Charlie makes, warring with jealousy, as I scan the deck.

"Oh, uh, well, she's in with the Cap'n, Missus. He requested her a little while ago, and told me to make sure no one… interrupts." Charlie refuses to meet my eyes, but I can see that she shares my sense of unease at the order.

"Is that so?" I ask rhetorically, continuing my march as Charlie grasps at my hand. She grips my forearm as I move past, fingers slipping to circle my wrist, the same one wrapped by Lennox's bangle. "Please, Missus... I'm sure she's all right."

"Remove your hand from me right now, Charlie," I order, using a tone I haven't sought out since my days as a priestess. The girl drops my wrist as if it is made from molten lead, but scurries behind me nonetheless. I don't know if she is more afraid of the Captain, me, or what is happening to her lover behind the closed door that looms in front of us.

"Stay here," I command, hand on the knob. As the cool metal turns in my hand, dread settles in my stomach. I push the door open, anger coursing through my veins both for my own foolish mistakes and at the repulsive behavior of this man I was beginning to trust.

"What do you think you are doing to — " I stop short.

The Captain sits in one of the chairs from his dining table, stripped to the waist with a towel draped over his shoulders. Standing behind him is Lyra, wearing her shift, the sleeves rolled up to her elbows. She has a small dish in one hand and a comb in the other. Both wear shocked expressions as I plow through the door, slamming it behind me.

My eyes dart around the room, trying to make sense of this scene.

"*What* is happening here?" I look between the two of them and, if I wasn't so taken aback, I might even laugh at their sheepish expressions. The worries that plagued me as I marched up to the cabin have vanished, replaced with sheer curiosity and confusion.

"Hello, Andromeda!" Lyra greets me brightly, an uneasy smile breaking across her pretty face. "The Captain, well, he asked me to assist him. I only undressed because I didn't want my dress to be stained if the water became rougher."

She has nothing to explain — if the Captain had ordered her to lay naked on his dining table, she would be expected to do so. No matter how kind and polite he is to her at breakfast, or how convincing he is with his affections and shared secrets with me, we are still his property until the end of this voyage.

"Are you..." I tilt my head questioningly at Lennox, "coloring your hair?" I gasp as understanding settles in. "The black walnut hulls! You *are* dying it!"

It *was* black at the House of Starlight and has faded the more time we've been away from shore.

"But, why?"

"Lyra, please help me wash this off," Lennox orders, exasperation tinting his deep voice. Lyra muffles a derisive snort and grabs a bucket of water to sluice the paste off his hair.

"One moment and I will try to explain," he directs to me.

I watch in silence as Lyra helps scrub the color off Lennox's hair while he leans forward over another bucket. After the rinse, he rubs it with a towel, the ends standing up wildly from the motion. Lyra scrubs her hands with lye soap and rinses them clean before slipping into her dress. As she heads toward the door, Lennox stops her.

"Lyra, wait. I think it's time to share some things with...," he pauses before saying my assumed name, and I give the smallest shake of my head in response. I am not ready to share my true name with anyone else yet. "Andromeda."

Lyra turns, returning to sit beside the Captain. He gestures for me to join them at the table. As I sit, he seems to reconsider the nature of our impending conversation and rises to retrieve the decanter of brandy from his desk, grabbing three glasses for us to share a drink.

"So…," I prod, taking a small sip of the burning liquid.

"So," he sighs, "it seems several more secrets will be revealed today. First, yes, I dye my hair to darken it. I have an image to uphold, and an identity to protect. The dark hair helps on those fronts, plus it keeps me looking a bit different at each port as it fades, so no one has a true portrait of me. Keeps up the mystery." He pauses to take a sip, then thinks better of it, and drains his glass before continuing.

"Secondly, you do not have to keep rushing through doors worrying about Lyra. At least worrying about *me* harming her. She is… "

I lean forward involuntarily at the confession, waiting for his explanation.

"She is my niece. None of the men will harm her; they all know she is my family, and that their punishment would be death. I have no idea what to do with poor Charlie. She's clearly in love."

At this deduction Lyra blushes up to her eyebrows; it seems the feelings are mutual. I sit frozen in my seat.

"Your… *niece*?" My eyes shift between the two of them while my mind hurries to catch up to this new information.

Lyra only smiles, her smooth skin dewy and tan with youthful, feminine beauty, a mass of tight, dark brown curls framing her lovely face. In contrast, Lennox is serious, angular, and all masculinity, minus the dripping darkened strands of hair hanging across his forehead at the moment. They look nothing alike.

"I don't understand, you *bought* her. I heard you talking to Celeste."

"Ah, yes. Well, if Lyra is my niece, you must then realize that Celeste is my sister. Apparently, unnatural hair color preferences are hereditary," he explains.

Lyra stifles a giggle at the statement, the memory of her mother's bright red hair assuredly popping into her mind, but I begin to feel unwell.

"I had to be sure the image of buying young women was upheld. I couldn't very well announce her true relationship to me, not without putting Celeste in danger, or undermining authority the next time I'm in Artemisia."

"So, you're saying, you only bought *me*?" I rise from my seat, anger replacing my earlier confusion. "To be a companion and nursemaid to your niece, and somewhere warm for your cock when you seek *entertainment*."

After so many years, shame fills me to have allowed myself to think I was anything more than a chase for him; a vixen escaping a hound until she tired and relented to capture. I curse my imprudent heart for softening for the first man who touched me with kindness and finish my glass of brandy in one deep drink.

Lennox holds his hand up to stop my flight, but I turn my back to the two, embarrassed at being deceived by them both. I stomp to the door without a backward glance, ignoring any protests they may have prepared.

Charlie still waits outside the great cabin, but I pass her by without a word and continue to my room. Once secure inside, I bolt the door and let my angry tears fall.

My back still rests against the rough wood of the door, my tears having run dry long ago, when I hear the softest knock. Lyra's gentle voice reaches my ears through the wood. "Andromeda, I'm so sorry. May I please come in?"

I relent, unbolting the door to let her enter. This isn't her fault. I'm sure, between her mother and uncle, she has been warned to not trust me with their secrets — I'm just a whore, after all — but the lies still sting. She cautiously enters our cabin and takes a seat next to me on my bed, gently taking my hand in between both of hers before speaking.

"Mother and Uncle told me to wait until they were sure you were trustworthy." Her words confirm my earlier thoughts. "They thought you would be, but one can never be too cautious. Please don't be mad. You've been such a lovely friend and I feel so terrible," she says softly, keeping her eyes cast downward.

She is so young and trusting that it breaks my heart. I remember when I still felt like there was good in the world, and that people were trustworthy. I lost that faith long ago.

"Uncle sent this note to you. Please don't hate him either."

I take the folded note from her hand and open it, despite wanting to tear it into pieces out of spite.

N-
Now that our secrets have been spilled, it's time to be our true selves. The moon is full tomorrow, please join us on deck for a ceremony. I think you have the proper attire. You and Lyra can join the crew and me for celebrations afterward. –B

M_Y BREATH CATCHES AS I READ HIS WORDS, THE ANGER AT HIS deception softening as I review the note a second time. We have been at sea long enough that the moon is already full again, but I have been so preoccupied with the Captain and my surgery that I haven't paid attention. My hands tremble with nervous anticipation at the thought of donning my robe for the first time in so many years. I fold the note and bite the inside of my cheek in thought.

I don't know how many moments pass before I stand from the bed and go to my trunk, kneeling to carefully remove the silver robe and gold jewelry from the case. I pull the gold dust from the smaller compartment, placing it on the table. Lyra watches, a look of awe on her face as I lay out my garb and run my hands over the silky fabric.

At her age, I doubt if she has ever seen a priestess in her ceremonial attire before; not many younger people have. Those who grew up near the temples or worshipped in the villages perished when Blackwell sent his men to clear out heretics. Tomorrow will be a special night for all of us, it seems.

CHAPTER 15

The next day I stay in my cabin, while Lyra and Charlie agree to bring me food or items I might need from my surgery. I sip tea and bathe, making sure my hair and body are as clean as I can get them on a ship with limited fresh water. Alone, I am free to sit in prayer and contemplation at my leisure now, no longer worried about prying eyes who might turn me into the King's men, or customers to satisfy. The fear that has weighed me down for so many years lifts momentarily today, replaced with the pleasant tingle of anticipation for the sight of the full moon over the open sea.

I am still vexed with the Captain, even though he truly owes me no explanations or honesty, but that irritation is tempered with gratitude and curiosity at the invitation to hold ceremony tonight. Pushing my tumultuous emotions aside for this evening, I gather my jewelry and robe. My eyes close on a deep inhale, holding it for only a moment, savoring this feeling that I have missed for so long, and begin my preparations.

The sun has set fully by the time I step from our cabin. Lyra walks ahead of me up the stairs, and I focus on climbing the slick steps without stumbling. My hands still tremble, but I cannot let my nervousness be seen. Tonight, I will be the priestess I once was, whether these men believe in me and the Goddess or not.

My robe is cut low and fitted in the front, revealing my collar bone and sternum, then gathers at the waist before falling to my feet. A deep slash up one thigh allows space to move and dance freely, or, in the case of fertility and other rites, to make love without removing the garment. The gold choker lays against my skin, visible on my exposed neck and breastbone. A chain connecting it from the front of my throat to my navel drapes between my breasts before attaching to another thin chain that brackets my waist. My hair is braided in a crown with the back flowing loosely down to my waist, and the gold circlet floats across my brow.

As my bare foot touches the main deck, I'm greeted by a collective intake of breath. The crew stands pressed against the rails, while Captain Lennox and Erik stand on the quarter deck overseeing the entire group. I look up at Lennox once, and the romantic fool in me thinks his breath catches when our eyes meet. I quickly direct my gaze to my destination in the middle of the deck; I cannot allow myself to be distracted by him now.

The moon is full over the calm sea, her reflection illuminating the crew and slick boards of the deck. Brilliant pinpricks of light sparkle across the sky as the stars join in a show of twinkling light. For the first time in many years, my heart lightens and joy spreads over me.

I'm free, even if just for tonight. I'm finally beneath the stars again.

I take a deep breath and begin.

Before King Dargan outlawed the Old Ways, full moon celebrations were used to thank the Goddess for blessings, to harness the height of the moon's energy, and to manifest desires. Although each moon phase has its own uses, emotions and desires of all types are heightened during the full moon time. Nervous energy radiating from the men on deck surrounds me, and even though the King has outlawed their practice, the power of the Old Ways is felt strongly amongst these men.

My breasts peak in the cool ocean breeze, and my mind wanders to nights at the temple when I performed other, more pleasurable, rituals under the white glow of the full moon. I stoop, lighting a candle and filling a small cup with wine as an offering to honor the Goddess. Rising to my feet again, I raise my arms and begin an ancient chant of thanks to Her.

My voice stumbles once as warmth spreads in my chest, a sensation that was once commonplace, but has been absent for almost a decade — since I lost the companion-ship of my sister priestesses. The heat blossomed when other voices joined me in my prayer. I continue speaking the words, but as the chant ends and a song begins, more voices lift. Higher-pitched feminine voices.

The heat in my breast radiates through my limbs, and I don't know if I am more shocked at the return of this feel-ing, or at the fact that there are far more women on this ship than I knew. My gaze snaps from the moon to the faces that surround me, and understanding dawns on me as to how many secrets have truly been kept right in front of me all along.

The fresh-faced boys that work alongside these hardened sailors… they're all *women*.

I turn quickly to face Lennox and Erik; both are moving their mouths with the lyrics even though they are too far away for me to hear. The Captain's eyes burn into mine, a wry smile forming as he moves his lips to the words of the song.

How many more secrets lay in wait for me to uncover on this voyage?

My curiosity dims when I inspect my hands and find that, although they feel warm and tingly with power, they appear outwardly unchanged; only long, pale fingers greet me in the white moonlight. I blink several times, willing the heat in my chest to strengthen, to outwardly show what has been kept hidden so long, but even as the song crescendos, my hands remain the same, with no hint of the *glow* I once possessed.

———

AFTER THE CEREMONY, I RETURN TO MY CABIN TO CHANGE OUT of my robe, laying it lovingly across my bed to allow the hem to dry from the sea spray on the deck. Glancing at the dresses I have laid out, I decide that if we are venturing into the men's — well, crew's — mess area, perhaps I should look the part.

Setting the dresses aside, I pull out one of the plain shirts and grey trousers that were provided in the collection from my trunk. I have never worn men's clothing before, so the idea of my body being exposed without being nude is novel to me. A smile spreads across my face as I slip into the outfit, carefully tucking my shirt in, before walking down the hold toward the bow where the crew awaits.

From the open doorway, my eyes immediately find Lyra in her cobalt dress. She sits next to Lennox in one of only a few chairs at the head of the noisy room, like a princess and a king on their dais. The rest of the crew crowds together on benches gathered around tables that pull down from the walls. They clutch the side of their plates with one arm and shovel food into their mouths with the other as they laugh and talk. Lanterns swing from beams on the ceiling and hang from sporadically placed hooks along the walls to cast the room in an amber glow.

When the first table notices me walk through the entryway, silence descends on the room. Several crew members, some of the ones I mistook for boys before, stand and approach me. They each gently take my hand, kissing my fingers in respect, and I squeeze their fingers in acknowledgment. Each time, they quickly return to their places and allow me to continue my walk to where the Captain sits. Lennox stands to pull out the chair to his right for me when I approach. Once I take my seat, he raises his glass of wine. The crew mimics his motion, raising their ration of the fine wine that was distributed on this celebratory evening.

"To our priestess and healer, Andromeda." He cuts his eyes to me when he says my name, our little secret passing between us. "May she bring us blessings and comfort in the days ahead, remind us of the good times we've had in the past, and the vengeance we seek in the future."

The crew cheers and I join in the toast, clinking my glass

with Lyra's and Lennox's before drinking, the red wine smooth on my tongue. Everyone seems to settle back into their meals, the volume rising again as the crewmembers joke and shout to each other. I quietly observe them all, noting the ones that are obviously female now that I know the truth, inspecting the men with curiosity.

Surely they all knew the truth?

"You were brilliant tonight," the Captain whispers in my ear. "Like the Moon herself."

Shivers scuttle down my spine, and gooseflesh springs on my arms, as my stomach tumbles at his nearness. His warm breath reminds me of our time together yesterday, and I blush, wondering if the men really could hear me cry out from his cabin.

"Oh, they heard you." He smiles against my ear as if reading my mind. "And if they didn't, we should make sure they do next time."

"Who says there will be a next time, Captain?" I retort, glancing at him with my brows raised in feigned innocence.

"The way your body responds to me says so," he murmurs. His smile is wicked, fitting for the arrogant pirate that he is, and I can't help but narrow my eyes, offering a lopsided smile in return as he runs his thumb across my lower lip.

"Or are you still mad at me for earlier, my pretty priestess?" His voice turns husky and sends tingles over my skin.

"Thank you. For tonight." I change the subject, sitting back in my seat. Otherwise, I might not be able to stop myself from climbing into his lap and straddling him in front of the entire crew.

That would be some fine entertainment indeed.

"What do you have to thank me for?" he replies. "You did everything."

"No. For the robe, the jewelry. The opportunity to be something other than...," I trail off, the word bitter on my tongue. I don't fool myself into thinking that I am anything other than a whore anymore, but I cannot say it. Not tonight.

"You are everything, Andromeda." His tone is serious as he looks deeply into my eyes. "Never think you are anything less than a priestess who commands respect and honor."

For a moment, I no longer hear the din of the crew or the scrape of silverware on wooden plates. I only feel his gaze, and hear the command in his voice. I exhale and the moment is gone. The world comes back into focus, and I shake myself to remind myself where I am.

"Now, how about some entertainment?" Lennox announces loudly turning away from me. The crew cheers in response.

My mouth goes dry at his choice of words, fear creeping over me and paralyzing my muscles. Is this the moment I have been dreading, where I must perform for them as I am bid? But, all panic subsides when he claps his hands with a broad grin. A few of the crew members quickly retrieve something from the corner of the room — instruments — and begin to play.

One man saws on a fiddle, while a woman blows a happy tune on a pennywhistle. Yet another man holds a concertina at the ready, waiting for his cue to join in. The others stomp their feet or clap to keep time with the raucous tunes, and many sing along to the bawdy songs. I can't resist joining them with my own clapping and stomping. Lyra glows with joy at the celebratory atmosphere. Even the usually stoic Erik smiles and drinks heartily as music fills the room.

After a few songs, the tune turns mournful. Pike, the older man who gave me the list for the apothecary, stands and sings in a rich baritone. The ballad tells the tale of parted lovers — the man searches for his beloved, but he perishes at sea before being reunited. Gooseflesh rises over my skin as a clear soprano soars through the air to join Pike's deeper tones for the heartrending chorus. When I trace the sound, surprise fills me to discover that the mournful words pour from Lyra's lips. Tears trail down my cheeks from the emotion in the song, and I am astonished when I glance at the Captain; he, too, has tearstains on his sun-kissed cheeks.

After the tragic song, the music resumes an upbeat tempo with the entire room joining to sing the bright lyrics. I can't resist grabbing Lyra's hand, twirling with her to the beat, weaving through the midst of the crew. Laughter bubbles from my lips when I realize she knows the words to all of the songs, both the lewd and the romantic. I can't believe I've never heard her sing before at the House.

Several others join us in our dance, and it feels like a grand party rather than a group of unwashed pirates in close quarters. I haven't danced joyfully since my young and carefree days at the temple, and I cannot disguise the joy that is surely shining on my face.

Each time I spy Lennox, seated next to Erik on one of the benches, he wears a grin. His eyes never stray from my form. Eventually, the flow of drink slows, and men begin to stumble to their berths. I walk alongside Lyra to return to our cabin, but Lennox clasps my hand in his when I turn to bid him goodnight.

"Don't go," he whispers. "Let her go to her bed with Charlie tonight. Come with me."

I wet my lips in indecision. This isn't a command, even though he hasn't asked a question. It's a request. A request I accept with a smile.

The Captain holds my hand the entire way to his cabin, stroking his thumb across the back of it tenderly, almost as if he is a suitor paying court to his intended. My chest tightens with emotion at the thought, much to my surprise. How have I allowed myself to forget that I am only here because of a business agreement?

I try to remind myself to be careful, to rein in my feelings, but my mind starts to lose its battle with my long-stifled heart. Lennox holds the door for me to enter, and I step into the dim cabin illuminated with a few oil lamps, casting the faintest glow in the darkness. The white of the moon pours through the back windows and reflects off the surface of the dark sea beyond.

I turn to the Captain, glancing up at him through my lashes. "So, Captain, what shall we do tonight?"

"Billy, remember?" He beams at the reminder, brushing my wild hair away from my eyes. "And we can do anything you like, Nerissa." He pulls me closer to him as he breathes my name.

I smile devilishly and push away from him, dancing to the table. My backside leans against the wood, standing casually like a man waiting for a drink at a bar.

"Well, Billy," I test the name. "I think you will have to

work for *me* tonight. Come here."

I beckon to him with a crook of my finger and smirk. He curls his lips to match, stalking across the rich carpets, placing his hands on either side of my hips when he reaches me.

As he leans down to kiss me, I place my hand on his chest to stop him.

"Ah, not so fast. On your knees," I command. His brows lift, but he slowly kneels at my feet, looking up at me as he rests his hands on my hips. "Remove my boots and pants."

Slowly, Lennox pulls the leather boots from my feet, tossing them across the room before unbuttoning the front of my pants. His eyes stay on my face while he slides each button from their place so painfully slow that I almost give in and push him to the floor, but I enjoy this game too much. I bite my lip, watching him, allowing a ghost of a smile to show, as my breath hitches. Once the buttons are each freed and he begins to slip the pants down from my hips, I catch him chuckle under his breath.

"Is something funny... *Billy*?" I ask imperiously.

"I believe this is the first time I've ever had to remove someone's *pants* before fucking them." His grin is wild, the same brightness of the stars above shining in his gaze.

"There's a first time for everything, isn't there?" I can't mask my own huff of laughter at his revelation while he pulls the pants to my ankles and removes them, leaving me in only my long shirt. My breath is ragged at the touch of his calloused hands on my skin, fingers roaming my bare thighs. He rucks up my shirt to bare me to him and begins kissing my inner thighs as I part my legs in encouragement, leaning against the table.

"Is this what you want?" His breath tickles against my thigh, and my belly tightens at the anticipation of his mouth higher up.

"Yes," I whisper, running my fingers through his soft hair. It's dark brown now, but I briefly wonder what the true color is under the black walnut paste Lyra applied.

All thoughts of hair color evaporate when his hot mouth reaches the apex between my thighs, and his tongue caresses between them. I moan, letting my head tip back, and pull at his hair, grinding against his mouth. He grabs my hips, pulling me toward him, increasing the friction as I move. Gripping the edge of the table with one hand, I feel myself nearing my release, and press him closer.

"Please, don't stop." The words come out as a plea.

He obliges, alternating between sucking the bundle of nerves and running his tongue against me.

"Oh, Goddess!" I moan, arching my back as I come against his mouth, still gripping his hair in one hand while I shudder against him.

When I release my hold, his dark hair is in disarray and he wears a smug masculine look when he glances up at me. He still kneels in front of me, as if waiting for further instructions. The sight unleashes me — I run my fingers through his hair and pull him up. Our mouths meet, and I feel his lips part to welcome my tongue against his, the heat between us making me melt against his hard body. My taste lingers on his mouth and it makes me smile, it's as if I have marked him as mine in some way. With a wicked grin, I pull away to run my hands down his chest and stomach over the fabric of his shirt, inching closer to his erection pressed between us.

"Your turn," I whisper against his neck before rising from the table, then slowly dropping to my knees.

I deftly unbutton him and release his cock from his pants. He groans as I kiss him low on his belly and grip him in my hand. Glancing up through my lashes, I slide my mouth over him as I keep working him with my hand. He firmly guides my motions with his fingers twined in my hair, and I match his request, sliding him all the way to the back of my throat; his moans of pleasure and breathy curses reward my actions. I increase the speed, slipping him in and out of my wet mouth until his hands grip my shoulders roughly and pull me to my feet.

"Not yet," he says breathily, sweeping my feet out from under me and carrying me to the bed. He swiftly removes his shirt, and kicks out of his boots and pants, while I pull my shirt over my head. Arching my back, I recline against the plush pillows on his bed, exposed fully to him with my loose hair spread around me. For the first time in a long time, I feel pride in my nakedness and an ache of longing for the man I am bared to.

"You're beautiful," he states, sharp green eyes taking in every inch of me.

"You are well-versed in what women love to hear." I arch my back more, running my hands over myself seductively. I wish I had it in me to accept the compliment outright, but I can't fully let go of the armor I have worn for so long.

"No. *You* are beautiful, Nerissa." He strides to the bed and presses me into the soft mattress and coverlet with a kiss.

Tired of fighting against what my body and heart want,

I relent, throwing caution to the wind as I wrap my arms around his neck and return his kiss with everything I have. At the end of this voyage, I know I will likely be lost and alone again, but, for tonight, I can pretend that he's truly mine, and I am his. Not just because he bought me for the novelty of laying with a priestess, but because he wants *me*.

He deepens the embrace, tongue meeting mine, and settles between my thighs. I raise my hips in response and he pushes himself up on his forearms to look me in the eyes before entering me. Even though it has only been a day since our last joining, the sensation of him filling me pulls a gasp from my lips. I haul him back to my mouth for another hungry kiss as we begin to move together.

This time, we aren't hurried. There is no punishing pace. Our bodies move in tune, and the friction coils in my core with each deep kiss and deeper thrust. Lennox kisses down my neck, sucking at the place where it meets my shoulder, wringing a moan of pleasure from me at the sensation. I grip his shoulders as I near my release a second time, and when I come, I call out his true name. He finishes close behind me, crying out against my mouth, kissing me deeply.

He rolls off of me, and we lay side by side for a few moments, catching our breath. As our panting evens out, he inches his hand close to mine over the coverlet, our finger-tips delicately brushing one another almost shyly despite what we have just shared. As he lifts my hand into his own, little shocks tingle where our skin meets. When I look over at him, he is studying my face with a furrowed brow until our eyes meet and he gifts me a small, bashful smile.

CHAPTER 16

Over the next days, as we leave Selennia further in the distance, my life falls into a comfortable routine. My days are still spent in the surgery, tending to injuries and illnesses; the crew seems to be more at ease around me now that their secrets are in the open. In turn, I relax in their presence, feeling safe with the men I now know willingly work alongside women.

While some meals are spent dining with Lyra and Charlie, I often slip into the Captain's cabin, sharing dinner, heated glances, and easy conversations about books or the many places he has visited. As for my nights – I take advantage of Lennox's passionate kisses and skills in bed, readily sleeping curled in his comforting arms after.

We rarely mention our agreement or the end of the voyage, and never discuss emotions, but being in his presence no longer makes me anxious, except when I think of what comes next. Logically, I know I'm becoming more attached to him than I should allow myself, but after feeling alone for so long I can't seem to make my heart understand that.

One morning, I wake to find that I'm alone in the large feather bed, the protective warmth I've quickly become accustomed to is missing from my side. Daylight streams through the windows along the stern, and my eyes squint at the bright sunlight. Once they adjust, I pull my discarded shirt over my head and stretch before looking out at the sea. Since I'm alone, I also take the time to wander about the cabin, openly admiring the collection of books on the desk, piled alongside rolled maps of places I've never seen.

It still amuses me that I caught him reading a romantic text the first time I woke by his side, but I have since learned that he has a wide variety of books, so I've yet to ask him about that particular title. He has never said how he came by so many of these, but I assume they are stolen goods from prior pirate raids as so much of his cabin's finery is.

My hands run across the leather-bound tomes, eyeing the other contents of his desk. Amongst the books and maps is a crystal inkwell, quill, and a journal with notes about the voyage. Before I can sate my curiosity by peeking at the contents of the ledger, the door swings wide. Lennox bursts into the room startling me so badly that I jerk my hand away from the desk.

"Get dressed, quickly!" he commands.

Gone is the gentle lover from previous nights. This morning, he is the consummate pirate lord, no longer dressed in elegant wool and clean linen that could be mistaken for gentlemen's attire. He now stands before me in a long weathered leather coat and pants, and a faded black shirt with a gleam of violence in his eyes. My mind races through possibilities of what could be happening on deck for him to speak so brusquely. His mouth is a hard line and there is a nervous, angry tension surrounding him like I've never seen. As I dash to grab the trousers I wore the previous evening, he rapidly loads a second pistol, grabs his cutlass, and sheathes a shorter knife in his boot.

"What's happening?" I ask as I tuck my shirt in and braid my loose hair back, wrapping the thick plait into a messy knot at my neck.

"There's a ship on the horizon. We're going to raise the flag and send a warning shot soon, then prepare to board," he answers matter-of-factly.

When his eyes drift back to my face, I know I can't hide the way the blood has surely leached from my face at the mention of another ship. If we are captured, Lyra and I will no longer have any protection from a strange crew. His brow draws down as he paces toward me, sensing my fear, and his demeanor softens as he approaches me.

"Don't worry," he assures me, touching my cheek, "they'll know who hails them, and they almost always surrender. It isn't worth a battle with me or my crew."

Almost always. I swallow hard and nod, trying to be brave. I will need to stay with Lyra just in case, but I don't know if I am more worried for our safety, or for the Captain's. He pushes the extra pistol into my hand – a twin to the one he wears in his belt. He quickly strides to the desk and pulls out another knife from a drawer, placing its handle in my palm when he returns to me.

"For Lyra," he states, glancing at the short blade. "Have you shot a pistol before?"

I nod in the affirmative, even though my brain is foggy, and I hope I remember what to do.

"Good. It only has one shot. I don't have time to teach you how to reload, so only use it if you're desperate. I trust you with your dagger if you need it."

Lacing one arm behind my back, he pulls me tight to him and kisses me hard on the top of my head before leading me out into the brilliant sunlight. I squint, glancing around at the men scurrying on the deck.

"Be fierce today, my she-wolf," he says, squeezing my hand once before leaving me and heading up to the quarter deck where Erik waits for his commands.

"Raise the colors!" One of the men shouts.

My eyes are drawn upward to the mast where a black flag is being raised. The neutral flag that has flown since our departure is missing, and the true flag of the *Bartered Soul* ascends. As the flag travels higher, the wind catches it, unfurling the canvas, and a shiver runs up my spine both from the cold air and the fear the sigil instills. It's emblazoned with an animal's skull, and a cutlass and pistol are crossed under its gaping maw. With a crack, it opens fully in the breeze, and recognition sweeps through me as I stare up at the skull — a wolf.

Heart pounding, I retreat below deck to my shared cabin to find Lyra. Charlie is here, comforting her, and I'm relieved she has this companion. As soon as I brush through the door, the sprightly young woman is on her feet, leans over and kisses Lyra hard on the mouth, and runs out the door to join her crewmates in preparation.

My hands slightly tremble as I pour myself a glass of water from the pitcher on the table and sit by Lyra on the bed. With a heavy breath, I realize that I am the last person who can offer comfort to the girl; I am just as worried about the fate of the crew as she is. No placating words come to me as I stare into my glass of water, and the silence is heavy between us. Wordlessly, I pull the knife Lennox gave me from my boot and press it, handle first, into her hand.

"This is from your uncle. Let's hope you don't have to use it." I pull the pistol from the back of my waistband and place it on the table beside the bed, then I retrieve my dagger from under my mattress to wait, returning to her side.

"Have you ever killed a man, Andromeda?" Lyra asks as we sit together, our anxiety filling the small room. We aren't touching — I'm not the kind to offer gentle, reassuring gestures, but I hope my steady presence eases some of her fear. We are together, for whatever may come next.

"Yes, Lyra. I have," I reply. I shudder, shoving the memory of the act back into the place I've kept it buried for all these years. This voyage continues to make me revisit my past, but I don't need the distraction right now. "And I won't hesitate to do it again if someone threatens us."

After what feels like an eternity, but is not much time at all if our little clock is to be trusted, shouting and a single cannon shot breaks the heavy silence of our cabin. My breath catches, anxiety washing over me while expecting the side of the ship to blow out at any moment. Noise — footsteps and shouting mostly — surrounds us from above and just outside in the hold where the guns are, and my eyes dart around the cabin following the sound. The hair on the back of my neck stands on end when howling begins on deck, like a pack of wolves surrounding their prey.

Locked in this cabin, not able to see what is happening, is worse than being in the thick of it on deck and my breaths come raggedly. Clearly, Lyra's imagination is running as wild as my own as she twists her skirts between her fingers. I close my eyes in silent prayer, begging the Goddess for her protection from whatever comes next. She didn't answer us so many years ago, but I have not lost faith.

A lengthy silence has my eyes flying open, staring through the wooden door as the ship creaks and loud banging sounds above us, followed by more shouts and footsteps pounding. The anticipation gnaws at me, and I can sit still no longer, pacing in circles, trapped in our tiny cabin.

Finally, I can take no more. Grabbing the pistol from the table, I return it to my waistband and tuck my dagger in my boot before approaching the door.

"Stay here," I command Lyra, but the girl has steel in her hazel eyes as she rises as well.

"No. If you're going up, I'm coming with you. I don't want us to be separated and I need to see what's happening."

I'm taken aback by the forcefulness in her tone, but I can see in her eyes that she is terrified, both for our safety and the crew. I relent, and she follows me out the door.

One gun crew still stands poised at a single cannon below deck, but the remainder of the crew must be overhead. Lyra and I creep up the stairs to the deck. As my head rises above the deck, I swivel it, taking in the scene around me. We are tied off to another ship, and my blood runs cold at the sight of the King's flag flying from its mast.

If King Dargan's men catch me, my life is as good as forfeit; I cannot hide the sigil at my brow to ensure my safety outside the walls of the brothel.

I don't understand the finer points of piracy, but I can't fathom why we hailed a vessel of the King. I thought the goal was to steal from merchant ships and to avoid the crown altogether.

Scanning the deck of the smaller ship, a few men hold weapons, but the remainder of the crew is out of my sight-line, and the worst of the battle seems to be over. I cannot stop my feet from propelling me farther onto the deck, to look across the rail and ropes for a better view. Erik's hulking frame holds a battle axe in one hand, while another smaller one is tucked at his lower back. He looks more menacing than I've ever seen him — his dark hair glints with gold tied into the thick braid down his back, and leather vambraces cover his forearms.

While I am glad to see the quartermaster safe, he is not the desired target of my searching gaze. My eyes are instinctually drawn to Captain Lennox's broad shoulders in his faded leather coat as he stands shouting to the captured men. I can't hear his words from here, but there is no sign of the man who gently caressed me last night. Billy has vanished, replaced by Captain Lennox who offers no quarter, and his glare is hard as he stares down the men awaiting their sentence. At this moment, he is every bit the fearsome captain I avoided so deftly at the House of Starlight.

Several of the crewmembers from the *Bartered Soul* guard a man I assume is the captain of the King's ship. Unlike the rest of his crew kneeling in the plain uniforms of the King's Navy, his military coat, epaulets, and fearless demeanor set him apart from the rest of the sailors. This man doesn't cast his eyes downward when Lennox approaches him, meeting his stare boldly and spitting on the deck just short of Lennox's boots when Lennox chucks him under the chin with his cutlass. Lennox makes a comment to the man before laughing at him on his knees, twisting the cutlass slightly to make the man flinch. A cruel smile turns his lips upward at the prisoner's reaction before he turns his back to give additional orders.

From a distance, I continue to watch, and suddenly realize I am not the only one focused on the rival captain. Several of the men on his crew seem to be focused on him as well, and dread stirs in my chest. There is nothing I can do, no warning that will carry to our men.

When did I begin to think of them as mine?

My heart stops, and things seem to move in slow motion with the slight nod of the King's captain's head. That small dip of his chin unleashes his crew with unbridled fury. They quickly rise to their feet, attacking the pirates without hesitation, pulling hidden weapons from their boots or other hiding places, not yet searched, along the deck.

A shout rises in my throat, but I can only watch and pray to the Goddess that the tough men and women of our crew can stand against them. In my distress, I've nearly forgotten Lyra, standing at my back in silence, until she grabs my hand with a sudden sob. I grip her hand tightly, but cannot pull my eyes away from the chaos unfolding.

Erik towers above the other men brutally swinging his axe, while Lennox slashes with his cutlass, saving his pistol for an opportune moment. Sound fades, the heavy whooshing of my blood in my ears is the only thing I hear as I watch the other crewmembers hold their own against the King's sailors, and it isn't long before the opposing Captain falls under one of Erik's blows.

Even the women from the *Bartered Soul* fight like demons. A sweeping sense of pride swells in my chest as I watch them. Everywhere I look, chaos unfolds, but still, my eyes scan each member of the crew until I find Charlie's slight frame battling with a large sailor from the other ship. A sob rises in my throat, but I hold it back, hoping she can gain the upper hand.

Charlie's eyes glance my way, and I realize, too late, that she has seen Lyra's bright form hiding behind me. The moment of distraction is all her opponent needs. Lyra screams at the same time that his blade comes down on Charlie's shoulder. Within moments, Pike cuts the sailor down, then turns to rejoin the fray. But Charlie remains motionless on the deck — a pool of crimson spreading around her limp form.

I'm in motion before I can consider the danger, running toward the boarding bridge between the ships. By the time I reach the rail, Erik has retrieved Charlie's limp body and bellows commands to the crew. My eyes light on Lennox as he delivers a few final blows, blind fury clouding his face. I can only hope none of the blood that covers him is his own.

This close to the railing, I can see the full picture of the carnage of this attack. Fighting slows — our crew has taken the victory, and the King's Navy has given in to the inevitable, but we are not without casualties. The remaining King's sailors are on their knees once more, weapons at their feet.

My fingers dig into the wood of the rail as Lennox walks behind each prisoner, drawing his sharp blade across their throats as easily as if he is slaughtering a lamb. Only the sound of the seawater crashes in my ears as I watch them collapse forward.

This is the brutal pirate I feared when he lurked in the shadows at the House of Starlight.

This is the savage beast who offers no quarter to his foes.

And yet, the sight of the men in the King's colors dying on the deck of their ship doesn't make me recoil in fear.

Instead, this feels like justice. Justice for the pain Lennox endured under the lash when he was pressed into service and lost his family. For the pain the priestesses felt when our temples were ransacked, and they were staked and set ablaze. For the nights I sought refuge in memories of being touched by the gentle boy from the rites instead of the greedy hands of men in the House of Starlight. For the losses we have all suffered for this new King's reign.

At the end of the line, when the last limp body hits the deck, Lennox raises his fierce eyes to meet mine. His chest rises with deep breaths, and his smile is a bright gash of white across his crimson-splashed face. The moment lingers, pride swelling in my chest where fear should be, but for this Captain, my fear is gone.

THE REMAINDER OF THE BLOOD-COVERED CREW RETURNING across the boarding bridge snaps me back to the present. My heart lurches as Lyra pushes past me with a sob, running to Erik's side as he cradles Charlie. I glance back once at Lennox as he mounts the bridge, then turn to see if there is anything to be done for Charlie. Lyra is kneeling on the deck, her fine gown soaked with sea spray and Charlie's blood, as Erik lowers the limp form of the young woman to be cradled in her lover's arms. Before I can even reach them, I know there is nothing I can do.

Charlie is already gone.

Lyra's keening surrounds us, and my chest aches. Even the hardened crewmembers watch the beautiful girl with sorrow in their eyes, tears streaming freely down her tan cheeks as she curls herself over Charlie's still form. I crouch next to her, running my hand over her back in an attempt at comfort, but I am not foolish enough to think I can soothe the pain she is feeling.

After a while, her shaking subsides, and I stand, glancing to see if I can be of aid to any of the other crewmembers, leaving Lyra to mourn. As I take in the battered crew, heat spreads across my skin in a tingle, and I know *he's* behind me. Spinning, I catch green eyes shining fiercely in his blood-coated face.

Before I can think twice, I run into his arms, our mouths slanted together. I don't care whose blood I am tasting, or if the crew sees us. All I can focus on is his strong body pressed against mine, his scent mixed with the salty sea air and the coppery tang of bloodshed. Relief washes over me.

He survived.

He's safe.

The kiss can't last long enough; I never want to let him go. After several moments, he releases me, and I pull back with heavy breaths. There is work to do. Lennox cradles my cheek in his palm briefly, his eyes never leaving mine as he gives commands to raid the hold of the captured ship for weapons and supplies.

"See if there is anything you can do to help the wounded. If they're beyond help, offer them some of the strong rum or whisky to ease their pain until it's their time," he whispers to me before returning to the other ship with his men. I exhale a sigh of relief at his steady command before I return to the wounded.

CHAPTER 17

After the battle, I mentally categorize the crew into two categories: those with minor flesh wounds that I can clean and bandage, and those who are near death — far beyond my capability to help. As I told Lennox at the beginning of this trip, I'm not a physician or barber-surgeon; there is only so much that my herbs and prayers can do. Their crewmates and I both know it is only a matter of time until the latter group joins Charlie in the afterlife.

As Lennox mentioned, a strong drink is the only comfort I can offer to ease their pain, so I set my face into the calm, expressionless veil I am used to wearing, all emotion buried deep inside. I cannot allow my sadness and worry to seep into the injured.

We remain tied to the crown's ship for several hours while I work. Lennox and Erik stand in deep discussion for a while before the Captain retreats to his cabin. When he returns to the deck, he is free of bloodstains and dressed in fresh clothing, appearing as though he hasn't been in a battle at all.

The sun sinks lower in the sky, and I rise from the last of the crew I'd been tending, ready to seek out Lyra. Worry for her has been a constant in my mind this afternoon, knowing she has likely witnessed more brutality today than she has ever endured. Following the sounds of soft murmurs, I find the young woman tucked away behind a crate still cradling Charlie's cold body, stroking her mousy brown hair softly.

Lyra's tears have long since dried, and she simply rocks and hums a song to herself as she comforts a lover that can no longer feel pain. Leaving her be, I rush to my surgery and quickly prepare a tisane with valerian in it to help her nerves, hoping it will allow her to relax and sleep peacefully tonight. When I return to the deck, I lower myself next to her, leaning against the side of the ship with my knees tucked up to my chest, and offer her the warm mug. Instead of accepting my offering, she simply meets my eyes with her sad hazel ones.

"What happens now?" she asks in a ragged whisper, her voice rough from her wails.

"I'm not sure," I reply honestly. "I believe sailors are buried at sea."

As a priestess, I have been present at births as well as deathbeds — welcoming souls into the world and easing them back out — but I've never attended a ceremony at sea. The cycle of life isn't new to me, but Lyra was sheltered in Artemisia, even under the roof of a brothel, and I wonder if she has truly seen death before.

Before my thoughts can wander further down that trail, I realize my ignorance — she is more than old enough to remember the chaos and bloodshed when the Usurper King moved through the countryside, violently claiming his new kingdom after defeating the Queen. I don't have the heart to ask the girl if she remembers the invasion, but I am sure she must to some degree. Hopefully, Celeste had made it to the safety of the House of Starlight before they witnessed much of the carnage.

"Well, she must be prepared then." Lyra interrupts my thoughts, and my head jerks to study her again. Her beautiful face is stony, and understanding settles in — she wishes to do the honor of preparing Charlie herself.

"I can help you if you need me to, Lyra," I tell her gently. "You don't have to be alone." I would be happy to use some of my herbs to create the ceremonial wash water for Charlie's body if Lyra has intentions to honor her in the Old Way.

"Thank you, but I want to say goodbye alone," she nods solemnly, acknowledging my offer. "Can you bring me what I need? I'll use our room if that's all right."

"Of course. Whatever you need." I touch her hand as it rests on Charlie's still chest, then rise to my feet to retreat to my surgery to gather the supplies.

There aren't enough herbs to make a large batch of the scented water, but I should have plenty to anoint each of the deceased before their burial. Fresh water is precious aboard the ship and I don't want to waste it, but for this day, for this cause, we can spare it. An hour passes quickly as I blend the sweet herbs and steep them in the bucket of freshly heated water. Before returning to the deck to clean and anoint the other dead, I knock gently at the door of my shared room, leaving a mug of the mixture outside the door for Lyra.

Many of the able-bodied crew are still aboard the commandeered vessel adjacent to us, sorting through supplies and moving crates and weaponry, but none are bringing those items across to the *Bartered Soul* as I would expect. The dead from the King's crew are no longer visible on deck, so I assume they have been given a swift burial at sea. In the end, we have lost six of our crew, including Charlie. Not a large number, but the loss makes the crew somber as they go about their duties.

Stars rise above me before my preparations are complete, the moon shining down on the deck around me as the deceased are sewn into shrouds of canvas for their watery grave. When I finish sewing the last stitches, I rise to my feet, stretching as I gaze around the deck. Lyra stands at the top of the stairs leading from the hold, still wearing her stained cobalt gown, but has straightened her hair into a tidy chignon and cleaned her face and hands, all traces of blood and tears mere memories. Erik walks to her side and speaks softly with her, gently placing a large hand on her shoulder. He then nods before walking below, returning a few moments later cradling another shroud to place next to the other five I have prepared.

The crew gathers around me, their faces expectant in the lantern light.

They're awaiting the ritual.

It's been over a decade since I participated in death rites. My gifts leaned toward the arts of love and the flesh, along with healing once I completed my initiation, so I was removed from comfort and death duties shortly after becoming a fully-fledged priestess.

For a moment, my nerves threaten to pull me under; my

palms grow slick and my body prickles with anxiety as I meet their friends' eyes. I cannot possibly honor these men and women properly.

But I raise my chin, and my gaze settles on the only eyes that matter – the assuring dark green of Captain Lennox's. Sweat shines on his brow, even with the cool evening breeze, but we all look haggard after the battle and its aftermath.

Lennox stands tall and gives me a small nod of encouragement, fortifying my nerves. What speech I can offer is better than none at all, especially for those who have not been able to openly worship for so long. With this reassurance, I dip my hands in the herbal water to cleanse them and stand tall to begin.

Words find me of their own volition, and I beseech the Goddess to watch over the departed souls who prepare to take their last dip into the sea, asking Her to ensure they reach the underworld. The name of each fallen crewmember is called, and their friends and crewmates step forward to remark on their life, virtues, or talents. Charlie's name is called last — Erik, Lennox, and Lyra all step forward to speak.

"Charlie was a brave and fierce crewmember. She fought valiantly at the end, and died a death that one should be proud of, man or woman," Erik states, his light accent lyrical in the twilight.

"Charlie was always bright, always quick, and always a steady friend. She will be missed," Lennox adds, silver lining his eyes as he looks at his heartbroken niece with deep despair.

Lastly, Lyra steps forward, far more composed than I would expect — back straight, shoulders squared.

"I met Charlie the last time she was ashore while I was in town with my mother," she pauses, taking a deep breath, before continuing, "I had never met someone, man or woman, who made me feel beautiful and strong like she did. I regret we will not have more time together, but I don't regret the moments we did share. I know I will see her again in the afterlife."

On a shaky breath, she steps back out of the lantern light before her body is wracked with sobs. Lennox carefully places his arm around her shoulder for comfort, and Erik looks at the boards of the deck in sadness. Surprisingly, Pike steps forward to wrap an arm around the girl as well, materializing from the rest of the crew. Lennox leaves her hugging the older man, stepping back to Erik's side.

My eyes burn as a tear rolls down my cheek; I cannot hold them back any longer.

After goodbyes are dispensed, each shrouded figure is hoisted over the rail to their watery grave, each one enclosed with a prized possession chosen by a friend on board to carry with them to the beyond. I stand at the rail long after the last body — Charlie's — is dropped over the edge and sinks beneath the waves.

As I stare at the stars, listening to the lapping of waves on the side of the ship, familiar footsteps sound behind me. Without a glance, I know the Captain stands at my back. Warm arms bracket my waist, and I turn to look up into Lennox's eyes. His skin is damp, but sea-mist sprays freely over the deck often, and I lean against his chest to allow him to hold me.

"I'm so glad you're all right," I murmur into his chest as he surrounds me with warmth.

"You're not terrified that I am truly a sea monster after you witnessed what happened on the other ship?" He asks against my hair, cheek pressed to the top of my head.

I pull away slightly to study his face. "You're not the monster. The man — the *King* —," I say his title on a growl, "who made us what we are with his cruelty is the monster."

He nods, reassured by my words, and I bring my hands up to cup his jaw, studying this man in the moonlight. A sheen of sweat coats his face, and his usually golden skin is pale. I push away further, examining him more closely.

"*Are* you all right?" I ask.

"Yes…" he hesitates. "Nothing to worry about. Just, just a little scratch," he says swaying on his feet. I clutch at his coat as he begins to fall.

"Erik! Pike! Help me!"

The two men are talking near the mast when they hear my shouts. They immediately start toward us, but they're too slow. Lennox's eyes roll back, and I am not strong enough to stop his body as he buckles to the damp deck at my feet. I stumble, gripping at his coat and falling with him, as I try to keep him from hitting his head. When Erik and Pike reach us, I kneel next to him on the deck.

"Get him to his cabin. Now!" I order them as they work together to carry his tall frame between them to the great cabin. Other crew members look on with concern as we pass, but I am more concerned with Lennox than their gazes.

"Get his clothes off. I need to figure out what caused

this!" I shout once the door shuts behind us in the great cabin.

Erik obeys as Pike stands guard at the door, keeping the prying eyes of any curious crew members from seeing the Captain in distress; no matter the crew, a pirate captain with any weakness is not good for anyone. Once Lennox's shirt is off, I notice a bloodied bandage around his middle. Grabbing my dagger, I cut it off and inspect the deep gash across the side of his ribs. He has to have been bleeding for hours.

I was so distracted by Charlie's fatal wounds, the burial preparations, and my worry for Lyra that I hadn't noticed anything off about the Captain. When he escaped to his cabin to clean up earlier, he must have bandaged it himself, donning his black coat to hide the sight of any seeping blood. My eyes dart around the cabin until they land on his, now damaged, leather coat, discarded in a heap alongside a bloodied shirt. He deliberately hid the wound from me.

"Damn you, Billy," I murmur under my breath. "Erik, I need clean water and boiled wine. And grab honey and comfrey from my surgery. Now!" I demand. Erik nods once and immediately departs the cabin.

"I will stand outside the door, Mistress," Pike states in his rich baritone. "I am at your service for anything you may need." The cabin door closes silently behind him, leaving me alone with my panic.

My fingers roam his skin gently; the wound is red and warm to the touch, and much deeper than I expected. Herbs and tonics I can handle, but a wound this deep may very well be beyond me. My hands shake as I check for any other injuries and wait impatiently for Erik to return.

Nausea threatens as I fret over the worst-case scenario, fighting to hold back tears.

"Please, please, stay with me," I whisper shakily, placing my cool hands on his face. He leans into the sensation in his restless sleep, and my heart clenches in fear. Lyra returns with Erik and the supplies I requested. She has changed into a pair of trousers and a shirt, and her face is schooled in a neutral expression as she views her uncle unconscious and wounded.

"I will help Andromeda, you two can go about your duties," she tells Erik and Pike, who still stand in the doorway, before coming to my side. "How can I help?" she asks me quietly as the men depart the room.

"Tear the linen into bandages while I clean his wound, then we can make the poultice," I guide her.

Having her present allows me to focus and pull myself together, forcing the panic back down to keep her calm as well. I sponge the wound with clean water and then rinse it with boiled wine. Debating whether I should suture it, I chew my lip in contemplation, trying to remember everything I have ever learned. However, the idea of sticking a needle through someone's flesh makes me feel faint. Plus, if it is inflamed and I seal the wound, I'm afraid I will be sentencing him to death. I have no way of knowing if he collapsed due to the injury itself, or from the loss of blood throughout the day.

Anger rises in me, easily overpowering my fear — a tactic I have relied on to keep myself going this long without falling into despair. I need more training to be able to handle this fully; training that ended when my temple was destroyed, and my lessons were cut short because of King Dargan's bigotry.

With a visible shake of my head, I force myself to refocus, channeling the excess energy into my work instead. The only thing that betrays my true emotions are my hands, which still tremble as I sponge boiled wine on the wound.

Lyra has completed her task and holds a handful of bandages, ready for me to guide her. I show her how to mix the honey and herbs to make a poultice that will hopefully help the wound stay clean, and keep the inflammation from spreading. Once I've spread the sticky mixture over the wound, Lyra and I work together, passing the bandages across his body to wrap them around him. I secure the fabric with a tight knot, then cover him with the coverlet and rise to sit at the table with Lyra. Shadows have taken root under her eyes, and she droops in her seat.

"Lyra, go to bed. I will let you know if I need assistance. We will be fine."

"You still haven't changed yet," she observes, looking over my stained clothing. "May I at least bring you clothes? A fresh shift? Tea?"

Genuine concern for me coats each of her words, and I realize how much I have come to adore this sweet young woman. Even after a day of so much loss, she still cares for the living.

"Actually, yes. Please bring me one of my simple dresses and a shift. I think I have enough water to rinse off a bit," I answer, offering her a small smile. She departs quickly and returns within fifteen minutes, the articles I requested in hand and a female crew member in tow with a warm bucket of fresh water for me, despite my protests against it.

"The other ship has clean water stores, too — don't worry about wasting it," the woman says, dipping her head in respect, then leaves the room with Lyra.

Once the door closes behind them and I am alone, aside from the unconscious Captain, I allow my emotions to bubble to the surface. I curl inward as I sit at the table, my hands covering my face.

Tears fall quickly and silently as sadness and fear leak from my eyes. When my lamentation is exhausted, I strip my clothing off, rinse the blood and honey from my hands, and slip into my clean shift. Before joining Lennox on the bed, I retrieve a novel from his desk and quietly place the lantern on the table next to the bed. Propped against the headboard, the book in my lap to read, I am determined to distract my mind while he rests.

CHAPTER 18

D*eep in the forest grove, strong hands caress my hips and thighs as I ride the handsome young man beneath me. My hair, dark as a crow's wing, is free over my breasts and hangs down to my waist, softly tickling my flesh as I near release. He raises up, holding me against his smooth chest as I rock against him. Our lips meet in a passionate kiss, masks brushing against each other, as we reach our oblivion together.*

MY EYES BLINK OPEN AS I JERK AWAKE IN THE DARK ROOM. Longing aches in my belly from my dream before it's extinguished by the heat of the body at my back. Sometime in the night, I dozed off, drifting down on the bed next to Lennox. When I roll over to check on my bedmate, the book I was reading slides from my hip to lay between us.

Lennox's brow is flushed with fever and burns against my palm. The sun peeks over the horizon, but the light is still dim even with the wall of windows, so I scramble out of the bed to light the lantern. The bucket of water from last night is now cool, and I grab it along with a clean cloth, pulling one of the chairs with me to the bedside. As I sponge his flesh, the cool water rouses him, and his eyes blink open.

"You damn fool," I scold as he wakes. "Why didn't you tell me you were wounded?"

"Nerissa?" his voice is rough with sleep. He brings his hand up to touch mine as I wring the cloth out. "I thought it was a dream, but you're here."

"Of course, I'm here! You passed out on the deck, and are burning up with a fever from this fucking wound. Where else would I be?" I chide gently.

"I'm sorry," he says as he tries to sit up, grimacing at the pain the motion causes. "I didn't think it was urgent. I'll be fine,"

"Lay back, you stubborn thing." My irritation hides the fear creeping over me at his high temperature and flushed skin. "I'll make you a tea of willow bark to ease the pain. We need to get this fever under control." Standing, I fetch the water, pouring it into a glass for him before pulling on the simple navy dress Lyra brought me. Once dressed, I reach for the door, letting in the dawn light as I go to gather supplies.

Lennox's eyes track my movement across the cabin, and I glance back at him before leaving. "I'll be right back."

Erik is awake, despite the early hour, and meets my eye as I exit the cabin. I wave in acknowledgment before heading down to my surgery to gather any herbs that might be of use at the Captain's side.

The sight of Lennox sitting in bed when I return has the

worry in my chest releasing its grip slightly. His head is tipped down as he toys with the pages of the novel that still lays on the coverlet.

"I hadn't guessed you were a hopeless romantic, but then I saw you were reading that, so I had to find out more," I smile, walking past him to place the supplies on the table. Mixing some of the willow bark into hot water, I leave it to steep and then return to his side.

"It's one of my favorites. A remnant of my youth, I suppose. I blame unrequited love," he responds, glancing down at his hands, running his fingers over the scarred knuckles.

I chuckle softly, watching his hands fidget, twisting one of the rings on his finger. "A lonely pirate searching for lost love, hmm? Sounds like a novel in and of itself."

My smile slips from my face when I take in his countenance. His color is high from the fever, and his full lips are chapped from the wind and sea and dehydration. But his eyes... they are ablaze as he meets my stare, and tightens his jaw.

"I asked if you participated in the rites," he says solemnly, gaze never leaving my face. I nod silently in response and swallow nervously, unable to speak or look away.

"You gave yourself in honor of the Goddess eleven years ago this past summer. In a grove outside the temple we saw in ruins at the Port of Athene."

I blink at his statement, taken aback that he would know this — I had never provided those details to him. Realization dawns on me, and my body begins to shake as the truth finally washes over me.

The masked figurehead on his ship.

The green eyes haunting my dreams.

His false hair color.

"It was you," I breathe, heart galloping wildly in my chest.

"It was me," he whispers in response. "I loved you the moment I saw you step into the firelight that evening. You were the most beautiful thing I'd ever seen." He takes my hand carefully, as if he fears I may bolt.

"I was tormented every day knowing what happened at that temple while I was trapped at sea. I feared you were lost with the rest of your sisters. When you came to Celeste's, she told me about you, but I couldn't be sure until I set eyes on you again. As soon as I saw you, I knew it had to be you."

"I don't understand." The words leave my mouth as I shake my head, trying to make sense of this. "Why didn't you tell me sooner? What about all the girls you took and never brought back? Why are you telling me this now?" The questions tumble from my mouth. One hand is still cocooned in his warm grip, but my free one toys with the seam of my skirt.

"I had to keep up my reputation — a pirate lord with a weakness? I couldn't allow it to be known. Couldn't risk your security. Once I knew I was taking Lyra across the sea, I knew I could bring you to safety, too. As for the girls… " His eyes roam over my face, trying to read my response, "have you not noticed the gender of many of my crew?"

I open and close my mouth several times, but no words come. I don't know if I feel betrayed or exalted. In response to my silence, he continues.

"I give the girls an option once they are aboard; they can learn the trade and go on the account, or they can leave at another harbor with a pouch of gold and make their own life. Outside of a brothel. Outside of the King's law. They know they will be safe here, and many choose to stay. Any who wish to return, and there aren't many, don't dare speak the truth to anyone to protect the others."

I continue to sit beside him in stunned silence, his hand hot in mine. Remembering his tea steeping, I shakily rise to retrieve it.

"I just needed you to know, in case..." He swallows. "In case this wound takes me. I needed you to understand. I don't expect anything from you," he says quietly to my back.

His gaze is locked on his fingers when I return to his side, nervously twisting one of the gold rings he wears around the long digit again. Gone is the vicious creature I watched on the deck of a conquered ship, and, in his stead, sits a gentle boy fearing rejection. I place the mug in his hands and sit on the mattress next to him.

"I— " I begin, but falter, needing to gather my thoughts. "I have dreamt of that night. It's surfaced here and there over the years, but it's come to me several times since boarding this ship. I think... I think I knew it was you, Billy," I say, taking his hand again.

At the gesture, he looks up at me in surprise.

"You will *not* succumb to this wound. I forbid it." My eyes burn fiercely into his, and our lips meet in a desperate kiss, his rough and hot with fever, mine cool with the chill of the early morning.

I break the kiss with force, leaning back. "Now, drink

that, and rest. We still have a long journey ahead of us, and the ship needs a captain."

"Yes, my she-wolf. I wouldn't want to disappoint you," he says weakly, cupping my cheek in his rough palm before taking a sip of the bitter liquid. Once the cup is drained, I sponge cool water on his brow as he falls into a fitful sleep.

CHAPTER 19

Almost a full week passes while the Captain burns through his fever. I rarely see the light of day as I fretfully sit at his side, his confession replaying in my mind often, mingled with memories of the rites and our youthful innocence. My courses arrive, dampening my mood and fraying my emotions further.

The few times I leave his side, it is to carry updates to Erik, who, as quartermaster, is in charge by default while Lennox is abed, or to make offerings to the Goddess, pouring wine or whiskey in the sea as I beseech her to heal him. Lyra visits often, aiding me in caring for her uncle, the little cat that is supposed to rid the ship of vermin trailing her. Other than helping me with my tasks, she sits at his side reading aloud, cat curled in a ball on her lap. The ship we breached is still tied to us as we drift, but I haven't had the energy to question why.

Fear is a constant, and unwelcome, companion as I spend hours trying to force broth, fresh water, or willow bark tea into Lennox, avoiding the thought that he might not wake. When I do sleep, which isn't often since he is restless as the fever burns through him, I dream of the past — waking uneasily to memories of pleasure and pain, moonlight and flames.

As I sit staring at a book on the table one afternoon, eyes not focused enough to read, the mattress creaks behind me. I whip in the direction of the sound to find Lennox sitting on the side of the bed, feet touching the floor for the first time in days.

"You're awake!" I gasp and spring to my feet, nearly knocking the chair over in my excitement. His fever broke earlier in the day, but he remained asleep for hours after. "Are you well enough to be getting up?" I ask as I approach his side.

"I'd better be," he says, running his fingers through his hair in frustration. "We can't afford for me to be down any longer over this nonsense."

"You could have died; it isn't nonsense," I remind him gently as I brush his overly long hair from his forehead. The black walnut coloring has faded significantly to a dark blond; I can see the true golden hue peeking through at the roots and in the thick stubble covering his jaw.

My hands slip beneath his forearms as I try to help him stand, but he brushes me away, stubbornly insisting he do it himself. His bandage is no longer seeping, and the last time I changed it, all signs of inflammation had abated. Still, a week in bed is sure to have his body weakened.

"Would you like something to eat?" I ask.

"Yes, I think that would be fine. And I need some water to clean up with," he replies, running his hand over the rough beard he has grown.

My steps are hurried as I rush from the cabin to fetch the items, happiness surging through me that he has recovered. I return with the water, and food will be brought when it's ready. He is already dressed in a clean shirt and pants and is in the company of Erik as the door shuts behind me. They quickly end their hushed conversation, and Erik sweeps past me with purpose.

"Getting underway, I assume?" I ask, placing the water on the table. Lennox has already pulled out his razor and block of shave soap to remove his beard.

"We are," he perfunctorily replies, seating himself before a small mirror to shave, barely glancing in my direction.

I'm confused by his behavior. No longer is he the gentle man I nursed back to health. Here sits the brash Captain I met my first night aboard the ship. Irritated at his demeanor, I gather my remaining supplies and walk silently from the cabin.

When I reach my quarters, Lyra sits at the table reading a book. She has grown thinner in the past week, and her skin is pale from staying under the deck. I change out of my soiled dress and shift, replacing it with a pair of trousers and a linen shirt before laying down on my small bed.

Exhaustion from worrying over Lennox weighs me down, and my thanks is a surly, stubborn man. I'm surprised at his behavior after what was nearly an outright declaration of love while he burned with his wound. But, I'm more embarrassed by my own response. Shame stings my cheeks – *how could I be so foolish to be wrapped into these tender feelings?*

"Your uncle is awake and seems well," I tell her curtly.

Then, to avoid examining my bruised heart too closely, I curl into a ball and will myself to nap.

THE HAND IN MY HAIR GRIPS HARDER AND PULLS ME BACKWARD in the darkness of the tunnel. I thrash as strands are ripped from my scalp, but the grip doesn't relent. He has me in his grasp now, dragging me backward with an arm around my waist as I kick and struggle.

Tears burn my eyes, and my ragged feet scrape on the ground as I try to free myself. I don't know what awaits me when we are back in the temple, but I have to get away. Suddenly, the darkness is gone, and a blaze lights my vision as stacks of texts on fire in the center of the temple come into view. Men wearing the red and black of Dargan Blackwell, the new King, build pyres and stakes. I shake with terror at the thought of burning alive.

I know what Blackwell and his clergy say about us: that we are wives of demons, that we are whores for the Devil himself, that we are damned, and feel no pain since our souls are forfeit. I know this isn't true; the pain in my feet and scalp is proof enough.

We know no Devil or demons. We simply worship the Goddess, utilizing the energy that fuels all nature and life around us. Our sacred sexuality sends energy back into the world as much as it drifts between two lovers in their embrace. Women have known the power of this energy since time began; why are these men so fearful?

As I twist and turn in my captor's arms, other younger priestesses are herded toward the camp while our older leaders are beaten and bound, awaiting the pyre. My mentor, our High Priestess, lies still on the marble floor. A dark stain surrounds her broken body, covering the sigils inlaid on the floor that should have protected her, and I can't control the wail that escapes me. I know my fate as the man holding me laughs and drags me toward the tents being erected outside the temple grounds.

My mind clouds and I drift between reality and insensibility as my robe is torn from my body. Rough hands grope my skin, bruising the pale flesh. A sob echoes in my ears as I am crushed beneath his weight, it takes me a moment to realize the sound comes from my lips. When I try to scream for help that I know won't come, he covers my mouth with a hand crusted in blood, and I struggle to breathe through my fear and the barrier of his skin. His hot breath makes me shudder, but I cannot escape any part of him.

I have never been touched so savagely, the pain of his violation makes me retreat further inward. Surely this will be over soon? *But then new fear bubbles to the surface when I comprehend what will happen when he is done with me. That I might then meet the pyre myself, or be tossed into another tent for more of this misery, causing me to choke on my tears.*

When he is finished, I am pushed unceremoniously to the side as he puts himself back together. He doesn't notice his sword belt lying behind him, dagger and sword still attached. He never sees the dagger, even when it juts from the front of his throat, and he chokes on his blood.

I FEEL HANDS ON ME AS I SCREAM AND THRASH TO ESCAPE THE man dragging me.

"Andromeda. Andromeda!" A voice shouts my name as I kick. "Andromeda, wake up!"

Lyra.

My eyes fly open as I relax back onto the bed, the fear of only moments before leaving me gasping for breath. Lyra grips my shoulders with a frightened look on her face, her thin fingers digging into my shoulders. My hands claw across the bed, reaching for the dagger I almost always keep nearby — the one that saved me that night — for reassurance. The memories of that night have always haunted me; each time I ventured into the streets in Artemisia alone, each time a red and black uniform caught my eye, each time a man gave me the wrong kind of look, but the stress of our journey seems to be pulling my old life to the surface in many ways.

My body trembles as she wraps her arms around me delicately, stroking my hair as if I am a child waking from a bad dream instead of the older woman in the room.

"Andromeda, are you all right?"

"Yes," I gasp. "I survived. I'm all right," I reply quietly.

The salt of tears settles on my lips as they fall of their own volition, and my body shakes as I try to hold them in.

"Were you dreaming of Crewes' attack?" she asks gently.

"No," I whisper.

"Ah, before, then?" I pull back in shock, searching her face. "I was eight when they came. Mother and I had already left for the city, but they killed my granny and my father. Just because of what they believed – because they wouldn't give in. They loved the Queen, and they loved the Goddess. They gave everything for them." Her face is somber, but her eyes are angry, and I find myself continually surprised by the young woman I always dismissed as just a pretty face.

"You said before that you killed a man," she trails off.

I hesitate for a moment before replying. "Yes."

"You're brave. I wish I could have killed the man who hurt Charlie," she says fiercely. "The men who hurt my family."

"I hope you never have to do such things," I tell her, holding her hand as she sits with me, "but I understand the desire."

"I loved her," she whispers sadly.

"I know, Lyra. I know. I'm so sorry."

We sit together quietly in our sorrows, holding hands with our shoulders pressed together. The sun sinks outside our little porthole – the creak of the hull and the crash of the sea beyond a requiem for our losses.

CHAPTER 20

L ate that evening, Lyra and I make our way to the mess area, ready to join the crew for our evening meal. The sound of laughter and merriment only heightens the melancholy feeling clinging to me, and I am ready for my share of alcohol tonight — wine, rum, whiskey, I don't care. I haven't seen Lennox since I left his cabin earlier in the day, and am unsure whether he will be present for dinner or if he will dine in his private chamber.

A hush falls on the area as we enter, and the eyes of many of the crew fall on us, appraising our masculine ensembles. We almost blend in with the other female crew, except our hair is longer, and we haven't spent as much time in the sun.

I feel the Captain's gaze upon me before my eyes find him sitting at the table in the front of the group, where he has joined his crew for the evening. Lyra and I walk to take our places where we ate before, but the Captain is frosty at best.

My hand drifts to the pitcher to my right, and I quickly

pour a glass of whatever is in it into my glass, drinking it down quickly, then gagging after I swallow. *Grog*, as the crew calls it — a blend of several different alcohols, guaranteed to get one drunk quickly. Swiping my sleeve across my mouth, I pour another glass, ignoring the hard stare the Captain passes my way.

"Feeling better, Uncle?" Lyra whispers to him from my left.

"I am, thank you, Lyra. Andromeda is well-skilled," he replies, pointedly ignoring me.

A laugh escapes into my glass as I continue to drink, pouring one glass and then another into my cup, choking down the burning liquor. I secretly long for the fine wine or brandy in the Captain's cabin, but I will be damned if I speak the words to him to say so.

The liquor sloshes in my stomach, reminding me to dig into the ration of salted beef and beans that was placed before me. In the weeks we have been at sea, the variety of food has diminished and become repetitive. I had hoped the captured ship might have more supplies, but based on tonight's meal, it seems that it's more of the same.

I can't quite explain the anger simmering under my skin, but anger has been a familiar companion over the past eight years, and tonight I am restless with it. Since departing Athene, I thought the Captain and I had become close. The nights we've spent together, plus the confession of his true identity — the memory of our night together at the rites all those years ago — made me assume that the feelings I have tried to stave off were mutual. But based on his current actions, it seems like those words were the final regretful statements of a dying man, and now he wants to dismiss me, returning to my lowly status: a bartered soul.

Scraping the last of my meal from my plate, I pour another full cup before standing, swaying slightly from the movement of the ship and the alcohol coursing through me. Without a word, I walk out of the room and back into the hold.

If he wants me to know my place, I will make sure he sees that I understand completely.

I continue to drink as I stumble to my cabin, pulling the door open with far more force than is needed. Clumsily, I kick out of my boots and pants and rifle through my trunk, tossing the fine clothing aside until I see the few pieces I brought from my time at the House of Starlight.

My hands slide across a gauzy dress the color of smoke that barely reaches below the curve of my backside, and I separate it out, stripping my shirt from my body. I wear the chain Lennox gave me to wear with my priestess robe, clasping it around my neck and waist, and then slip the dress on over it. The front is cut deep, almost to my navel, so the chain connecting my neck and waist is visible on my exposed skin.

I leave my feet bare, as I would have at the House, and smear kohl thick around my eyes — my own form of war paint. My lips are stained as red as ripe berries, and I remove all adornment from my tresses, allowing them to flow wildly down my back. With a glance in my mottled mirror, I look every bit the part of the feral women the King's religion fears so deeply. Laying the mirror back down on the table, I gulp down the last of my drink for courage, then storm out the door.

Time stops when I step back into the mess area. The scraping of cutlery against wooden plates ceases, and the only sound is the creak of the ship, and a few cups set down in astonishment. My gaze is locked on Lennox though, and I prowl toward him.

If he wants a she-wolf, I will be a predator tonight.

Air ruffles against my bare skin, raising goosebumps at the chill and reminding me of how much of me is exposed to the room. When I look into the Captain's eyes, it pleases me to see both lust and anger warring in them. I smirk at him, almost baring my teeth, and continue my approach. My anger at his earlier dismissal is a fire in my blood, and the alcohol I consumed adds fuel to the flame.

My voice is a snarl when I say, "Good evening, *Captain Lennox*."

I lean forward slightly over the table, a glimpse of my bare behind surely on display for the crew. Chair legs scoot across the wooden floor planks, and in my peripheral vision, I can see men's eyes averted from the sight.

They know who I belong to.

"What the *fuck* are you doing?" Lennox growls at me. His hands are clenched in fists on the table, and a tremble runs through them as he grits his teeth.

"Isn't this what I'm for… *Captain*? Your *entertainment?* You said it yourself, I am *well-skilled*. Would you like me to put on a show of my *skills* for your crew?" My mask is back, and armor of cloying sarcasm drips from cherry-red lips.

"You need to go back to your cabin and change. *Now,*" Lennox hisses.

"Perhaps I need you to take me to your cabin and get your money's worth, Captain. After all, you did purchase me for quite a lot of coin. Surely it wasn't just for me to act as a healer and occasional bed warmer," I croon, batting my lashes in mock seduction.

His eyes are ablaze; I just can't tell if desire or anger is winning. Truthfully, I don't care. Lyra bites her lip where she sits next to him, a nervous expression on her face as she glances between me and her uncle.

"Enough," his rough voice cuts through the silence of the mess area as he stands suddenly and walks around the table.

I turn to challenge him as he approaches, but before I can protest, he pulls me into his arms and flips me over his shoulder. Then, he strides out of the room, holding my dress over my bare bits as if the whole room hasn't already seen all of me. As if it matters at all.

As soon as we have cleared the room, he releases his hand from the hem of my dress and slaps me on my partially bare behind. The sting sends a shock of desire through me, and I can feel heat surging low in my belly. He grips the same cheek firmly as he continues to forge ahead to his cabin.

"Is this what you want?" he growls at me. "To be manhandled and mistreated? To be punished?"

"Whatever brings you pleasure, Captain," I reply cheek-ily, my chest bouncing against his back as he takes the stairs. "I am *yours* after all."

The huff of a laugh rolls across his skin and mine before the hand that isn't wrapped tightly across my knees slides up the back of my thigh. It is all I can do to keep from trying to spread my legs as he carries me, but we are soon in his cabin, and he plops me down unceremoniously on his bed. Retreating across the room, he stops by his desk, next to the pretty decanter of fine liquor I was thinking of earlier. His eyes never leave me, staring daggers with his arms crossed over his chest.

"What was *that*?" His voice is far more calm than I would expect.

"What you want, isn't it? My *skills*?" I rise to my hands and knees on the bed, arching my back so my dress sides forward off my rump. Gathering my lip between my teeth, I meet his gaze. "Let me show them to you."

He turns his back to me and pours a glass, drinking it in one gulp. Slipping lightly off the bed, I approach his back, slowly sliding my hand down his firm stomach to cup his erection through his pants.

"See, it *is* what you want," I whisper to his back and press my breasts against him. I can't disguise the anger and hurt I feel as they bubble up as ugly words on my tongue. I want him to be just as angry. "You bought a whore for a voyage. Use me, you fucking coward."

That does it.

He spins toward me and grabs my wrists, hissing at me through gritted teeth. "Watch your mouth."

His grip is firm but doesn't hurt, and I rub against him like a cat in heat.

"Why don't you put it to better use?" I breathe against his lips.

Lennox's resolve cracks and his mouth crashes into mine, our teeth clashing as our tongues meet. I rub against him again, and, before I know what is happening, he gathers the front of my dress in his hands and rips it open down the front, a feral snarl escaping from his gritted teeth.

The fabric falls to the floor, leaving me bare except for the chain I wear and his bangle at my wrist. The intensity of the action has me gasping in surprise, but he grabs my chin roughly before kissing me again to quiet any words I might speak.

Just as abruptly, he ends the kiss, spinning me in front of him to run his hands over my back. The wood of the desk bites into my skin as his fingers lace through my hair, roughly tugging on my loose strands as he pushes me down onto the surface. I arch my back, pressing against his arousal as he runs a hand up my thigh and moans at the wetness between my legs; one finger, then two, slide inside me, and I push back onto him, riding his hand, knowing he's watching every move.

"*Fuck*, Andromeda." His voice is rough. "You're so fucking wet."

"Fuck me, Captain," I moan against the desk. "Take me now, *please*," I plead, anything to get more of him inside me.

When he removes his hand to unbutton his breeches, I arch my back again to give him a full view. A sharp gasp escapes my lips when he plunges into me in one motion. My gasp quickly turns to moans with his thrusts — furious and rough, matching my mood. Just when I think he's about to come, he stops and pulls out of me, turning me around and lifting me onto the desk. He pulls his shirt over his head as I part my thighs, begging for him to rejoin me. He doesn't disappoint, driving into me as I move with him.

"Oh Goddess, Lennox," I moan.

"This is what you wanted," he snarls as I begin to lay back on the desk, grabbing my hair and forcing me to watch as he slides in and out of me. "Now watch me fuck you, Andromeda. You're *mine*." I moan at the sight, and rub my hand over the apex between my thighs, greedy to come.

"Uh-uh-uh," he grabs my hand, forcing it away. "I'll let you come when I want you to. I'm not done with you yet."

A whimper leaves me in frustration at the denial.

Lifting me off the desk, he carries me to the bed, laying me on my back before kicking out of his boots and pants. I squeeze my thighs together, seeking any friction to relieve the ache between my legs. Once he is naked, except for the bandage around his midsection, he kisses my stomach, alternating between trailing his tongue over my heated skin and nipping my flesh. I arch as he dips below my navel, and my knees fall to the side, all but begging him to lick me between my legs. But he smiles up at me, denying me again. The bed dips as he lays down next to me, then reaches over and pulls me onto him.

"Ride me, Andromeda. Ride me until you come all over me," he commands, finally permitting me to seek my release.

I almost scramble in my urgency to straddle his length and slide slowly down on him, enjoying the look on his face as I take my time. When he is seated deeply within me, I rock my hips in earnest, his large hands grip my waist as I rub my own over my breasts. I can't get enough friction all over my body.

This isn't gentle and loving like when we made love under the trees at the rites — that innocence is gone. I lean forward and slide up and down his length, causing him to throw his head back in pleasure as I near my climax. My muscles coil and the waves of pleasure overwhelm me once I get into a rhythm. I grip his inked forearms, digging my nails into his flesh as I cry out when I come. He smiles and pushes me off of him, pulling me on my hands and knees before taking me from behind again.

He slaps the same place as when he carried me up to his quarters, grabbing it in his hand to soothe the sting, and I know I will bear his mark on my behind in the morning. The thought inflames my senses and causes me to push back harder, meeting him with each thrust. His grip is firm on my hips, squeezing the flesh beneath him, and after a few more deep thrusts, he growls when he finds his own satisfaction. After, we lay side by side on his bed panting, my makeup smeared and my dress destroyed, staring at the ceiling of his cabin.

"Is that what you wanted?" he finally asks quietly.

"Is it what *you* wanted?" I return.

I will not be the one to say how I truly feel. I am used to wearing a mask; I can continue to do so until I leave this ship.

"I certainly didn't want you bending over so my entire crew can imagine your pretty pink pussy when they abuse themselves," he looks over at me with a slight frown.

"Well, after the frosty reception you gave me after you woke today, you didn't seem like you'd mind what I did. Or with whom," I say, trying to keep emotion from my voice. "You seem to be healing nicely, no issues in manhandling me."

I stand abruptly and find one of his shirts to pull over myself, then head toward the door.

"Where are you going?" He sits up quickly when he realizes I aim for the exit, grimacing slightly at the sudden movement.

"To bed. Most of my customers don't want me to stick around."

"Nerissa, wait —"

"Oh, I'm Nerissa again, now? Andromeda the whore, Nerissa the saint? Let me tell you something — the girl you *think* you fell in love with that midsummer night died the night her temple and the life she knew were taken from her. The things that have happened to me —" I pause, swallowing bitter tears that threaten to escape. "The things I have had to do to survive killed her. Just like the things you've done killed Billy. If we are being honest, we are exactly who we present to the world – Andromeda and Captain William Lennox. Nerissa and Billy are a dream that died. Another victim of the King."

I turn to the door. I cannot allow him to see me cry; if he does, he will know how badly the words hurt me to say. If I can just get on the deck before he sees, it will be fine; I can choke down my feelings again.

Before my fingers graze the doorknob, his hand lands gently on my shoulder. He spins me to him, tucking me in tight against his warm chest. "I'm sorry," he says to the top of my head. "I'm sorry for what you've endured. I'm sorry for how I treated you. I'm sorry."

I let him hold me as I cry, releasing the anger and hurt from his earlier dismissal along with the losses I have experienced over the past eight years.

"A Captain on a pirate vessel is by vote. I hold this rank at their pleasure. I had been abed for a long time and had no idea what was happening while I was out. For all I knew, Erik had taken over, and we were halfway across the ocean. I trust him, but I just... I needed to get my affairs in order. To make sure the plan was still in place. I also... I'm ashamed to say... well, I was embarrassed at having told you the truth. I didn't know how you felt about it," he confides into my hair.

Enveloped in his warmth, I take my time to process his statement as my tears dry. "I see. I understand. Like I said before you fell into a weeklong fever dream, I think I knew it was you. I started having dreams about the rites once I boarded the ship. I was never one with a talent for divination, but things have been coming to me — memories resurfacing — and I think it was my subconscious pointing to the truth."

I don't tell him what's truly in my heart; I'm not ready to be completely bared to him yet — to admit my feelings.

"I'm sorry if... if I hurt you. Tonight." He stumbles over his words, examining my face. I can't imagine what I look like to him right now with my heavy makeup smeared and the flush from the strong drink coloring my skin.

"Oh, Captain — I can handle much worse," I smirk at him with a twinkle in my eye. "How many weeks do we have left on this voyage?"

"At least two, I'd say." He looks at me with uncertainty, a furrow between his brows like he is sizing up a wild animal.

"Plenty of time for me to show you, then," I reply, raising my eyebrows.

At that, he laughs — a real, deep laugh for the first time since I've been around him — and sweeps me into his arms and back to the bed.

CHAPTER 21

The next morning, I scurry to my cabin and use a damp cloth to scrub the residual kohl and stain from my face before donning a more demure dress. The pleasant ache between my legs reminds me of my night with Lennox, and I can't hide my smile as I ready for the day. Lyra rolls towards me as I sit braiding my hair, and she gives me a knowing grin. If she hadn't been raised in a brothel, I would be mildly embarrassed at her viewing my performance in the crew mess last night, but she has been exposed to far more provocative scenes in her sixteen years.

"He's not a bad man, Andromeda." Her voice is rough and drowsy as she stretches and rubs the sleep from her eyes. Her eyes, puffy with dark circles beneath them, still bear the evidence of her tears, but I, of all people, know grief takes its time.

"I know he isn't," I reply with a hesitant smile.

He's far more like me than I care to admit, the thought crosses my mind, but I don't confide it, not wanting to inspect it too closely myself.

Today the crew will be split between the *Bartered Soul* and the recently captured sloop. The *Archangel* is a smaller ship, faster and more maneuverable, and Lennox has ordered Erik to take command of it with a smaller crew to sail alongside us to our destination. When Lennox informed me of the plan this morning, I simply nodded, then took my leave so he could meet with Erik and Pike to discuss the details.

The sun beats down on Lyra and me where we stand on the deck, watching as crewmembers move between the ships, distributing supplies, and readying the vessels to sail. Despite knowing our destination is the islands to the west, I can't truly comprehend what that means. I've heard stories of the exotic islands and have seen drawings of tropical plants and wild beasts that supposedly live there, but I know nothing of value about the island Delosia, other than the small outline representing it on a map. My mind drifts to what life on a tropical island might be like while the crews continue to work, and the ropes connecting us are pulled in. With a loud crack, the sails flap open and catch the wind, sending us on our way, swiftly moving away from the rising sun.

———

"ANDROMEDA, WILL YOU TEACH ME?" LYRA ASKS ONE morning while we push some sort of pale gruel around our wooden bowls to break our fast. I study her face for a moment before answering, trying to determine what *exactly* she wishes to learn.

"Do you mean...?" I start, quirking a brow in question.

"Herblore. Healing. About the Goddess. I want to have skills and knowledge when we arrive at our new home. I want to be useful for more than my pretty face, or what's between my legs," she replies, her lips tight and her expression more serious than I have ever seen.

"Of course," I answer, offering a smile to her. "You can join me in my surgery after we are finished eating, and I can share the basics and the most helpful things to know."

Pride swells in my breast at her request. Lyra has grown into a woman on this voyage, between her loss of Charlie and assisting me with healing her uncle. It honors me for her to seek my instruction, even if I've never thought of myself as much of a teacher. That she sees me as someone worthy of her respect and emulation pleases me, and I find that I'm even a bit excited to take on the role. If my life had been different, if I were still at the temple, this is what I would be doing — preparing young initiates for the rites and aiding them on their path to become a priestess.

We spend hours in the surgery reviewing different herbs and their uses — chamomile for nerves, peppermint for upset stomach, willow bark for pain relief, and raspberry leaves to prepare a woman for birth. I don't touch on the stronger herbs that she might find useful should she end up helping women in a House like the one we left, or on how to create blends or tinctures yet, but she is curious and eager to learn.

Hopefully, I can teach her more before we arrive, and I decide to ask Lennox for parchment or a journal so Lyra can create her own notebook to keep. Then, she will have the knowledge at hand, whether she is with me or not.

The thought of being parted from the young woman

opens a pit in my stomach. The last time I had someone I called a friend was at the temple, the need to protect myself always winning out over the desire to allow anyone to truly know me since the day I fled. But Lyra, I find, I've come to adore.

Perhaps we won't have to part. We could each find work at a public house or tavern at our destination, share lodging, and keep each other safe. A protective instinct flares to life in me at the thought, even if the fact that she has come to feel more like a little sister or a daughter in these weeks brings an unbidden smile to my lips.

The sun is high in the sky, glistening over the water as I walk the deck that afternoon. I nibble on a hard biscuit, ignoring the holes made by the unavoidable tiny bugs that have stowed away in the hardtack, and allow myself to ponder a possible future. In the past week, since opening our sails and moving alongside the sloop, the temperatures have climbed and the time on deck is invigorating — hot sunlight on my skin and cool sea mist tickling my face.

The water has changed from treacherously dark, mysterious depths to crystalline blue and turquoise the farther west we travel. The clever creatures the sailors call dolphins are a delight as they frolic alongside the ships, jumping from the waves with joy. Sweat drips down my back in the hot sun, and I'm thankful that the Captain provided Lyra and me the lightweight pieces made of cotton and linen. It hasn't escaped my notice that he has taken to only wearing a linen shirt on deck instead of his grand overcoat, when he dons a shirt at all.

As if summoned by my thoughts, Lennox steps from his cabin, tattooed chest and arms glistening in the sun's rays.

He claps one of the crewmembers on the shoulder as he passes them with a smile. It's only been a night since I last shared his bed, and yet, I find myself mesmerized by his easy confidence. His hair has faded to its true golden hue, and it hangs a bit longer than it did when I first stepped aboard. Days-old stubble along his jaw glints in the bright sun, shimmering against his tan cheeks. The menacing sea monster I feared in the House of Starlight is nowhere to be found in this man. Instead, he is as bright as Helios himself, almost outshining the sun.

When his eyes meet mine as they linger on his frame, he gives me a wry smile, one brow raised in question. I avert my gaze and fail to contain my own smile as he approaches, stopping to stand at my side.

"Good afternoon, my pretty priestess. The warmer weather seems to suit you. Or is that flush on your cheeks my doing?" he flirts.

"I'm quite certain it is a sunburn, thank you, Captain," I reply smartly, although I can feel my cheeks darken with a blush at his rakish comment and the memories of where his stubble has grazed them, and other places, recently.

Warmth blooms in my chest when I glance over at him standing at my side at the rail. My heart aches knowing our final port grows closer with every day, and that I will have to part with this man. The man I hated for coercing me to agree on this journey in the first place. The man I gave myself to in honor of the Goddess years ago. The man who is causing the emotions I have kept bound tightly in my chest to finally loosen.

The man I might even — dare I say — *love*.

I can't bear to admit it, even if only to myself, though

what I feel for him goes beyond the physical. I gave up the hope of finding love years ago — first when I committed to becoming a priestess, then again when I lost everything and found myself on the steps of the House of Starlight. But the tightness in my chest and flutter in my stomach when I look at Lennox is unlike anything I've felt before, no matter how much I try to ignore it.

It's ironic that initially, I worried that the Captain would use me and discard me, that he would leave me so broken that I wouldn't be able to return to my life in Selennia. Now, I am more afraid of being separated from him and the freedom I have felt these past weeks, than I ever was of stepping onto this ship. But, the thought of being cold and alone again is too much for me to consider when the sun is warm on my skin. He owes me nothing more than what he agreed to at the outset of this voyage, and I have no right to expect more. There is no room for me to explore these wistful thoughts now, I am determined to make the most of the last few weeks we have together.

"Lyra tells me you agreed to teach her your knowledge of herbs. That's kind of you," he says, gazing out at the horizon. The sun sinks lower in the sky, and I look forward to another beautiful sunset with pinks and oranges fading into the blues of the sea.

"She's clever, I am happy to share my knowledge." His hand rests near mine on the rail, and the nearness makes me feel like a young girl being courted when his little finger brushes against mine softly. The small motion sends chills skipping up my arm and desire coursing through my belly.

"I hope you aren't sharing *all* of your knowledge." My eyes shift to him, and he purses his lips as he grazes the edge of my hand again. "I would rather that be kept for my *private* instruction."

The rogue knows exactly what he's doing to me, teasing me on the deck in front of everyone. Turning to stare at him, I casually lean my hip against the railing and close the small space between us. My fingers trail slowly across the tattoos of his bare chest before dragging down to the waist-band of his trousers. He clenches his jaw slightly and inhales sharply. Glancing up through my lashes, I bite my lip and watch him swallow as my touch lingers on the fabric.

"Well, Captain, I am happy to begin your lesson at your leisure." My smile is languid as I pull my fingers across his stomach, dropping down to my side as I move to walk away. Only a heartbeat later, he catches my wrist in his warm grasp and stops me. I quirk my lips in a secret smirk as I still face away from him, more than satisfied with his reaction.

"Oh, I think now will work just fine. I am an eager student," he whispers in my ear before turning me to march in front of him to his cabin, lightly gripping my shoulders as we go.

LYRA CONTINUES TO JOIN ME IN THE SURGERY EACH DAY, assisting when one of the crewmembers needs my aid, and listening to my lessons when we are alone. The monotony of hours at sea is broken up by joining the Captain in his bed. One afternoon, as I lay in the crook of his arm, shouts reach us from on deck. The boom of cannon fire sounds in the distance and

Lennox's body tenses beneath me. Dread sinks into my gut at the thought of another battle. He's on his feet, pulling his pants up before I can allow that thought to materialize further.

"Get dressed. I'll be right back," he says, striding from the cabin as he pulls his shirt over his head.

I hurry to fasten my underskirts and pull on my dress and boots. Anxiety courses through me at the thought of waiting for him to return, so as soon as I am clothed, I step out onto the deck. Lennox surveys the other ship, looking through a spyglass, and my eyes naturally follow the direction it points. As I feared, another vessel floats on the horizon, and my fists clench with panic. Heart racing, I spin to go warn Lyra when I catch sight of the Captain's broad grin, and my worries disintegrate.

"Hail them, Pike," he tells the man standing in for Erik as Quartermaster. "It's Jackson."

The older man nods, his gold earrings flashing in the bright sun, and yells instructions to the crew who spring into action at his directions. Lennox hands the spyglass off to Pike before striding to where I stand.

"Friend of yours?" I ask when he reaches me, raising my brows in question.

"Of a sort. It looks like he may be heading to the same destination we are, and it never hurts to travel together. Captain Jackson is an interesting character, but we have been on the same side numerous times." He runs a soothing touch along my arm, reassuring me. "You don't need to worry."

When did my mind become so easily read? In the past six weeks, I have allowed my mask, my carefully forged armor, to fall, revealing my emotions and thoughts to those around me. I'm not sure if I'm happy to be free of the self-imposed restraint, or if I am worried about how I will protect myself when this trip ends.

Quickly, the new vessel, a smaller ship than the *Bartered Soul*, comes close enough for me to see its crew. The man who leads them, Captain Jackson, is a brilliant figure near the helmsman as he hails Lennox. Where Lennox is muted in fine fabrics, this man wears multiple bold colors and patterns, varying between calicos and silks, florals and linens – a tropical bird compared to the falcon at my side. His long, dark hair is neatly clubbed at his neck, but I can't make out his features well enough to tell much more about him.

Jackson's crew appears rowdy like the hardened sailors I saw come through Celeste's door, toiling in the sea spray and chanting a song together. Through whatever methods pirates use, Lennox confirms that the new ship — the *Selkie's Tears* — is indeed traveling in the same direction as we are, and our group becomes like a pod of dolphins continuing west.

"Do pirates often travel together?" I ask that evening over a plain dinner of salted meat, beans, and hardtack in his cabin. "I didn't think you would be friends."

"I wouldn't say *friends* so much as useful allies. We don't usually sail together unless we have a specific cause, but in this case, I don't think we will have any other raids along the way. We should arrive in a day or so with good wind. This close to Delosia, it's easier to hail one another in open waters and move together rather than surprise each other closer to shore. Plus, Erik, Jackson, and I have a shared history; I don't fear treachery from him."

Another day or so.

The statement is all I truly hear him say. I knew we would arrive soon, but it feels as though my world is collapsing. For the first time in a long time, I have felt valued and respected here on this ship. What will Delosia hold for me in the next few days? What will I do without him at my side?

I end up pushing my food around my plate for the remainder of our meal, lost in contemplation. I've become accustomed to having him close, what it will be like to say goodbye? With a breath, I shove the emotions deep down to the place I have stored them many times before, and nibble at my small ration.

At least the food will be better soon.

After dinner, once other physical hungers are sated, I lie awake in the dim candlelight. Lennox sleeps peacefully, his features soft in slumber without worry or strain. I long to stroke his cheek, to memorize his face like this, but don't wish to wake him. Instead, I slip from the bed and onto the deck. The night air is cool, but no longer holds the crispness it had when we departed Selennia. Standing at the bow of the ship, I gaze out into the pitch blackness of the sea. The figurehead, so like me, is my only company as I allow the tears I've been holding to quietly fall.

The Captain hasn't mentioned his feelings for me since the night he confessed his true identity under the duress of fever and possible death. We have studiously avoided it, in fact. It is plain to see that he enjoys my company and my body, but I can't be sure of his other emotions.

Despite what my heart tells me, I can't bring myself to tell him that I broke the most important rule girls in the Houses know — don't give your heart to your customer. I can't risk that he will scorn me, or tell me he will pay to keep me as his courtesan, holed away in a room while he is off at sea, forever waiting for him to return.

No matter how much my heart aches, this is my chance to finally start over. This is why I accepted his offer in the first place, isn't it? I wrap my arms around myself, trying to ease the ache in my chest, and turn away from the Captain's cabin, walking slowly toward the stern, heading down to my shared room with Lyra.

"LAND HO!"

The words ring through the ship to where Lyra and I work in the surgery, and my head whips up. I knew we would arrive soon, but the call is like a shard of ice to my heart. Granting a small smile to Lyra, who has lit up at the announcement, we climb to the deck to stand at the railing and view our destination.

The water we float in is crystalline, so clear I can easily see the brightly colored fish that swim below its surface. The land we approach is lush with palm trees and a beach that glows white against the turquoise sea. Rough camps are set up in clusters on the sand, and buildings that make up what appears to be a town rest far behind, nestled in the trees.

My skin prickles and I know when I turn I will see green eyes following me. Lennox stands outside his cabin, smiling when our eyes meet, but it doesn't reach his eyes. I return the look, my lips barely turning up, before turning to watch our destination grow larger as we approach. The *Archangel* is still at our side, while the *Selkie's Tears* moves in behind us, all preparing to drop anchor and go ashore.

PART TWO
DELOSIA

CHAPTER 22

Rope creaks as the rowboat I sit in is lowered down to the water joined by Lyra, Lennox, and several other crew members. The *Bartered Soul* has anchored in a small bay rather than at the main port for reasons unbeknownst to me, so there is no simple walk down a gangplank. Lyra grins at the pretty fish swimming beneath the waves, but I stare ahead at the beach. Sailors drift between tents and stacks of supplies on the white sands. I shiver despite the heat, imagining their eyes on Lyra's fresh face as we approach.

Lennox's arms slip around me, lifting me from the boat once we reach the shore and carrying me to the dry sand to keep my skirts and boots from getting wet in the salty tide. He returns to do the same for Lyra, leaving me to look around while he retrieves his niece. The men on the beach glance at me, but no one approaches. Several gather around a spit with a whole pig roasting, and I catch myself before I actually drool at the sight of the fresh food. It smells almost good enough to risk joining the men for a piece of the fatty meat.

A sigh of relief escapes me when Lyra and Lennox are back at my side, hating that I still feel so uneasy around strange men even this far from Selennia's shores. My dagger is secreted away in my pocket, but drawing blood as soon as my feet hit the sands isn't how I want to introduce myself to the island of Delosia.

Our footsteps sink into the sand as we start walking toward the town when Lyra's breath catches, then she breaks into a run. Before I can lunge to stop her, squeals of delight erupt from her lips, and Lennox chuckles softly at my side. I shoot him a quick sideways glance, but my eyes continue to follow Lyra's form along the sand until she throws her arms around an older woman walking toward us.

The woman's silver hair is braided in small rows tight to her scalp, pulled together at her nape and twisted into a thick bun. Her rich, ebony skin is smooth, contrasting against the brightly colored linen dress that flows loosely around her slim frame — ideal for the tropical heat.

When Lennox and I are closer, laughter lines etched lightly at the corners of her eyes and lips are evident, but she seems to shine with youthful joy despite her age. Raking my eyes between her and Lyra, my mouth pops open at the shock. They have the same full, smiling lips, the same eye shape, and the same inner glow.

"Andromeda! This is my Grandmama," Lyra announces, beaming and hugging the older woman again. I stand gaping — the stories of Celeste's departed sailor, the murdered husband, the flight from Blackwell's men, it all runs together. Truths and lies, covers and secrets.

"You must be the priestess Celeste sent to protect my darling Lyra!" The woman smiles and takes my hand, laying a gentle kiss on my knuckles. I start at the gesture.

"I am hardly—" I begin to deny her statement, but Lennox interrupts.

"She is, Mistress Marie. And a fine job she did. Our Andromeda is a wonder." He smiles at me as he compliments me to the woman. A blush sweeps across my skin at his words.

"She's been teaching me herblore, too, Grandmama," Lyra gushes. "So I can help in town!" Her grin is broad as she clasps her grandmother's hand happily.

"Oh, that *is* helpful. Let's all head to town to catch up. I would like to hear more about you, Andromeda." Marie speaks with authority as she smiles at me, then shoots a knowing look at Lennox.

The reunited pair walk arm in arm as we trod together through the warm sand toward the distant town. The trees here are lush and green with bursts of bright tropical flowers and fruits hanging from them, reminding me of things I saw in a hothouse when I was young. My senses are filled with the beautiful colors and textures; even the smell of the place is decadent and rich.

The heart of the town greets us with buildings in a mixture of warm colors that seem like they're growing out of the jungle itself. Laundry hangs from lines across the alleys, presumably from living spaces located above small shops that line the street. I note public houses, taverns, and what are likely a few brothels, sprinkled in the mix.

Rough men and women of all types mingle in the streets, but all of them step from our path as Lyra and her grandmother lead the way. Some nod their heads in greeting to the older woman or Lennox as we pass, and Marie greets her friends and neighbors warmly as we stroll along.

We soon stop at a cozy pub on a side street. Lennox holds the heavy front door for all of us to pass through, and the laughter and merriment inside quiets at our entry. After a moment, my eyes adjust to the dimness of the room. Tightly packed tables fill the space, and the open shutters allow a pleasant breeze to cool the overcrowded room full of men and women drinking from tankards and goblets. A bar runs across the back of the building with a curvaceous blonde serving the customers seated along its edge. Her face is pleasant, and by all accounts, she seems to enjoy her job, smiling and joking with each customer she greets. Her grin grows wider when her eyes light on Lennox, and she steps quickly around the bar.

As she nears us, it's evident she is at least a decade older than me, and her smile is missing a few teeth, but it doesn't dim the warmth radiating from her. She walks up to our party and slaps Lennox in a tight hug before I register what is happening.

"You scoundrel! You left the last time without saying goodbye and here you show up with not one beautiful maid, but two! Explain yourself you blackguard," the woman laughs, releasing him from her embrace.

"Hell, Maryanne, you were sleeping off a bender! There wouldn't have been a way to wake you had I tried. And you know I always come back," Lennox teases back with a bold smile on his face.

"And what have you done to your hair this time? You look far less handsome and mysterious this way," the woman called Maryanne scoffs, rubbing the top of his head and rumpling the golden hair that has been growing out since the voyage began.

"Well, unfortunately, this is the true me — far less handsome, but far *more* mysterious. Blame this one here for my aesthetic changes." He winks, gesturing to me.

"Mistress Marie, who are these two beauties? Surely you aren't going to let them work at the bar — they'll take all my good tips!" I glance between the two older women, not certain if Maryanne is serious, but she grins broadly at me indicating it is only a jest.

"Maryanne, my dear — this is my granddaughter, Lyra. Finally come home to me," Marie beams as she presents Lyra to the barkeep. "And this is," Marie steps aside to present me as well, pausing briefly, "Andromeda, a surviving Selennian priestess."

I'm sure she assumes that Andromeda is not my true name, but I do not wish to divulge my secrets just yet. Nevertheless, I study the woman — somehow, I get the distinct impression that Marie knows far more than she lets on. The fact that she uses my priestess title is a shocking reminder of how far I've traveled from home.

Maryanne practically glows with joy as she hugs Lyra, holding her at arm's length to examine her beauty, but as she approaches me her smile slips. Shock stills me as she takes my hand and bows her head to me in an honor I no longer deserve.

"Priestess. Welcome," she breathes over my hand.

Her eyes are lined in silver when she rises. I'm over-whelmed with emotion, but I quickly shove it back down before it can bubble up out of my own eyes. The reverence she shows me tells me right away that Maryann comes from our country as well, perhaps has experienced the same things my sisters and I have. I clasp her hand gently in thanks and she steps back, rearranging her face to be cheery and bright again.

"How 'bout a drink to welcome you and celebrate?" she offers to us, surreptitiously wiping her eyes as she walks back to the bar.

She pours five glasses of something from an earthen-ware pitcher and expertly carries all of them between her two hands to a table in an alcove near the bar. As I move through the space, I allow a ghost of a smile to grace my face; comparing it to the House of Starlight is like differenti-ating between night and day.

The people here are happy and full of life. The women join the men in their drinking and gambling because they want to, not because of the coin that they might scrape from them with favors. Everyone is sunkissed and smiling, drunk of course, but not angry or hateful when I walk past. Maybe it's the warm weather and sunshine, or perhaps because we are out from under the King's thumb and constant scrutiny, but the atmosphere altogether is lighter than I have experienced in many years.

Freedom washes over me anew, and I take a deep breath before following the group to have a seat. The drink is some sort of punch made with rum and spices, and it burns pleasantly in my chest as I taste it with the rest of the group.

Sipping along with us, Maryanne flits between our table, and the bar, where she doles out more of the punch or harder liquor from casks to the clientele.

"Is this her place?" I ask, gesturing toward Maryanne with my cup.

"No, my dear. It's mine," Marie replies with a small smile. "Most of the establishments on this street are, in fact."

I sputter a little, surprised that the older woman has so much property. Across the sea, women no longer have the luxury of owning properties or businesses unless they are inherited or owned by their husbands.

"Have you been here long then?" I wonder out loud. "That's quite the accomplishment."

"Yes, for the past ten years. I owned several places across the sea. I believe you might know one, I passed it to my daughter-in-law when I departed for warmer shores," *when she escaped Dargan Blackwell's approach, she means, "* — the House of Starlight."

So *she* is how Celeste acquired the House. Loose ends begin to knot, and I start to get a more complete picture of Lyra's family tree and history.

"Yes. I am quite familiar with that establishment," I reply softly, taking a long pull of my drink.

"Lennox tells me you hail from the Western Temple at Athene, near the village where he grew up. Are you originally from that area as well?" Marie prods gently.

Hesitating, I swallow another sip of the strong punch, hoping Lennox can feel the daggers in my eyes when I look at him. I'm not ready to revisit a past that I have spent almost a decade trying to escape, especially at a table with a stranger.

"Um…" I stumble, trying to find a polite way to tell our hostess to mind her business. "I'm so sorry, I think the heat and this punch have gone to my head," I redirect, "Is there a room where I might lay down and cool off a bit?"

"Of course." Marie graciously allows the subject of my past to drop, even though the look she gives me from the side of her eye makes it clear she knows more than she is telling. This topic will be revisited. "I forget you and Lyra aren't used to this climate. Lennox, take her across the way. I had the suite prepared adjacent to your usual accommodations."

She turns to me before continuing, "If you need anything, my dear, ring for one of the servants to assist you. I believe the crew has already brought your things from the ship."

I give a weak smile in response, trying to look the part of someone overcome with the heat, and allow the Captain to take my arm as we walk out of the tavern.

Across the sandy street is a beautiful boarding house with an open courtyard in the center and another bar in the back. Stairs lead to rooms above with doors that open to overlook the shared space. Vibrant colors of corals, blues, and yellows dazzle my eyes after living in the dark House and then the unembellished hold of a ship for so long. Trees grow in the courtyard, and tropical plants are scattered in large pots arranged around the open room to add more pops of color and beauty to the space.

"Are you all right?" Lennox asks when I stop in the center of the courtyard to look around.

"Yes. Yes, of course. I just needed some air. I would rather my past... stay there," I try to explain. I swear there is a flicker of hurt in his eyes, but it's gone as soon as I blink.

"Of course," he replies, leading the way up the stairs to one of the rooms and handing me a skeleton key. "This space was set aside for you the last time I was here. When Marie heard I was bringing you with Lyra. If it isn't to your taste, please tell a servant and they will do whatever you need. I am right here," he points at a door next to mine. "There is a door that connects our room inside as well, but I understand you may not wish to leave it open."

I clench my jaw at the insinuation that what happened between us on the ship was purely for pay, but hold my tongue.

"How long will you be staying this time?" I question, hoping it sounds like curiosity, not because I can't quite fathom being in this strange place without his now-familiar presence. "You mentioned you were here before you returned to pick up Lyra; do you come here often?"

"I'm usually here for a week or so, depending on the cargo and the crew." His hand reaches up to his neck, rubbing across the skin exposed above his shirt. "I need to go check on the crew and take care of some things. Just ring for a servant if you need anything."

He moves as if to touch my hand, but checks himself, then dips his chin once before taking his leave without so much as a kiss on the cheek. My breath catches in my throat as I watch him descend the stairs, his broad shoulders passing through the door of the courtyard before disappearing into the streets. With a sigh, I turn to open the door to my new quarters.

The suite is nothing like the plain, dim room I shared with Lyra the past several weeks, nor does it compare to the dark velvet- and satin-lined quarters I haunted at the House of Starlight. Louvered shutters cover the large windows on the back wall, giving the space a fresh and airy feel. I walk to one and push it open to a view of the lush jungle beyond, sunlight streaming across the brightly tiled floors.

Trailing my fingers across the light-colored wood furniture and the soft off-white linens, I can't help but appreciate how the yellow walls make the room feel like the sand and sun of the island. A vase of fresh flowers sits on the table in the center of the room — orchids and blooms I don't know the name of, but recognize from our walk from the beach — add a sweet and fresh fragrance to the space. A new silver-backed hand mirror and comb as well as a pitcher of fresh water to freshen up with wait for me on a nearby vanity as well.

My trunk sits between the vanity and an armoire, but I can't bring myself to unpack it. Even though the space is beautiful and light, a part of me misses hiding in the shadows of the House.

From the line of questioning that began this afternoon, I feel as though my carefully crafted façade may start to crack on this island, like the plaster on some of the buildings near the shore, battered by the salty air and Marie's knowing stare. I'm not sure I am ready to face what that means.

I won't even think of my traitorous heart, which nearly

stopped when Lennox said he might be leaving as soon as a week from now. Can I say goodbye and start over here?

Breathing in the sweet-scented ocean breeze, I sigh deeply. For the first time in quite some time, I have the freedom to relax and think about what *I* want — free of the yoke of servitude of the House and the terror of King Dargan Blackwell. No matter, there is part of me that can't let go of the past, and that sliver of fear stays wedged deeply in my soul as I ring the bell for a servant to help me with a proper bath.

CHAPTER 23

After what may have been the most refreshing bath of my life, I stand wrapped in a soft linen cloth staring out the window. The sun sinks in a deep pink and red sky, and the golden-hour light colors everything it touches in flame. I smile thinking of the old saying: *Red skies at night, sailors delight*. The sailors on the island, and aboard the vessels anchored offshore, are sure to be in a good mood tonight.

My long hair drips onto the floorboards behind me as I step away from the window, using the soft towel I clutch to dry my clean tresses. Rummaging through my trunk, I remove one of the last clean shifts, thankful that I thought ahead to save one for our adventure on land. Shrugging it on, I pull out the other various articles of clothing and lay them in a pile.

Many pieces need to be laundered, so I make a note to hand them over the next time a servant appears. One of the lightweight pieces calls to me; a cotton dress with a simple floral pattern, but still in my usual darker palette. I will never be bright and cheerful like the other women I see on the island, but the purple tones and flowers will suit just fine, and the fabric is light and breathable for the warmer climate.

Slipping into the dress, I notice this one has added boning for structure built in. Somehow, Lennox knew I would continue to fight against wearing stays, even here. This way I am still able to dress without assistance, even though assistance is readily available, and I cling to that sliver of independence. The other women I have seen so far on the island dress simply, nothing like what fashionable ladies across the sea wear. The heat and lack of the King's judgment make everything more relaxed, it seems. My fingers run across the soft fabric, thinking of the day it was given to me so many weeks ago, and the thought of the Captain brings my mood back down. I must speak with him plainly at some point soon.

As I stand at the vanity, pinning my hair back, a light tapping echoes at my door. "Come in," I respond, my back turned to the sound.

The door opens and Lyra's reflection shines brightly in the mirror as she stands by the door. She glows radiantly in a bold turquoise dress I have never seen before; perhaps her grandmother had it waiting for her. Her unruly tight curls aren't pinned back neatly like she usually styles them, so they create a dark halo around her pretty face.

"Hello, Lyra. Are you well?" I ask as I finish my hair and turn to her.

"Oh yes, Andromeda. I've been so excited to see Grand-mama again and to see Delosia. Isn't it beautiful?" she asks, excitement making her bounce in her dainty shoes.

"It is beautiful. What brings you to me tonight?" I am not unhappy to see the girl, but I assumed I would be on my own for the evening.

"Grandmama wanted to invite you to dinner at her home. Will you come?" she asks hesitantly. "Uncle Billy will be there, too!" she adds, like bait on a line. My ruse of feeling faint earlier must not have been as convincing as I had hoped.

"Of course. I would be honored to join you."

Slipping my feet into the boots that I have grown accustomed to wearing, we head toward the door. I forego any slippers or other delicate footwear like Lyra favors; the ability to run quickly without thought as to whether I'm going to stumble or roll an ankle remains a priority for me.

I follow Lyra out of the boarding house, winding down several different streets until we end up in a residential area. Small houses neatly line the sandy street, and locals sit on open porches or sing through open shutters as the refreshing briny breeze flows through the wooden slats. At the end of the street sits a much larger house, not ornate like the aristocracy has back in Selennia, but understated and elegant.

Lyra's turquoise dress swishes with each step as she leads me up the steps and onto the verandah before opening the front door. I was expecting this to be a small dinner with Lyra and her family, but several other men I don't recognize also wait inside, and my footsteps falter. Even though I was raised around nobility, and have dined in mixed company in the past, my most recent history has taught me to be wary of strange men.

Several moments pass while I lurk in the open doorway,

Lyra oblivious to my hesitation as she is halfway down the hall, before Lennox's eyes land on me. His smile calms my nerves, and I curse my body at the reaction he draws from me. The sight of him breaking free of the group he stands in to approach me nearly undoes my careful restraint. Without pause, he gently lifts my hand like a gentleman and leads me into the group for introductions.

While I try to focus on each of the other captains as they are introduced, my eyes are drawn to the man at my side and my heart flutters from his hand resting on my lower back. Lennox wears yet another finely constructed coat for tonight's dinner, this time in dark blue linen instead of emerald wool, with his cutlass still at his side. His golden hair is a tousled mess as if the wind has run her fingers through it just to spite me, and light stubble covers his jawline.

He's beautiful, I think to myself, studying the way he moves among the group. They are cordial, but somewhat wary of him, and give me a wide, respectful berth. *And dangerous,* I add silently at their reactions.

A boisterous man wearing a flashy patchwork coat laughs with Lyra's grandmother, and I recognize him as Captain Jackson from our voyage into the bay. Erik is also present, a looming comfort in my periphery, along with five other men I do not know. Both the varied colors of their skin, ranging from ice pale to deep ebony, and their different wardrobe choices lead me to assume that they hail from different places around the globe. I swallow my nerves as I plaster a smile on my face, hoping it looks as if I'm excited to be there, not like I'm going to be sick.

"Ah, our guest of honor, Mistress Andromeda." Marie

smiles broadly at me, her straight white teeth all still present despite her age. "Savior and avenging goddess of the *Bartered Soul*."

"I don't understand," I insist to her as she approaches. "I didn't save anyone."

"You nursed this one back to life." She nods toward Lennox with a smile. "And you helped anyone you could while you were at sea. *And* you served justice better than I've ever heard anyone do before, man or woman," Marie replies, eliciting grimaces from the men present.

She takes my arm and leads me toward the large table. The seat she indicates for me is at her right hand, with Lennox across from me, and Lyra to my right. I happily accept a glass of wine from the servant, sipping it as I try to determine why exactly I am here. Sweat pools at my back as I sit perfectly straight in the cane chair, staring across at Lennox while the other men file into the dining room and take their seats. A low murmur of male voices washes over me as the men settle into their places, the din of old friends becoming reacquainted after their respective journeys.

"Gentlemen. And ladies," Marie begins once we are all seated and served drinks. "I welcome you all to my home for this meal, to mingle and to discuss life, loyalty, and, dare I say, politics?" Marie smirks toward the men and they chuckle, sipping their drinks. Lyra smiles as well, and I feel like I am the only one not in on the joke.

A rich-smelling seafood stew is brought to the table and ladled into our bowls while Marie talks. I can only focus on the smell of the spices and the soothing taste of the broth while I take in snippets of conversations. No part of me wishes to discuss politics, or anything else, with these people; I took this voyage for my freedom, not to be trapped at a table of strangers to talk idly.

Despite my best attempt to tune everyone out, my hearing focuses on Marie's words. "We all loved Queen Adelaide, may the Goddess bless her. The King's defeat over her is still a bitter pill, but there may be hope."

My head snaps up at that, and her eyes find mine. The sweat that has been dripping at my back turns cold.

I glance back at my empty bowl, searching for something to be distracted by, but there is nothing; I must heed her speech or appear dreadfully rude.

"We have hope that an heir to Adelaide's throne may be found," Marie continues to no one in particular. "Although she had no consort or children of her own, it was rumored that she had a sister. And through that sister, a niece."

With a raise of my brow, I feign shock at this information, hoping the shaking of my hand isn't visible to the room as I take a dainty sip of wine. The men are listening attentively, and I glance up to see Lennox's stare meet mine.

"What do we know of the heir?" a man at the end of the table asks, but I cannot recall his name. His dark hair is tied back in a knot at the nape of his neck, and his olive complexion compliments his dark eyes. The light from the candelabra catches on one of his front teeth, as gold as the rings he wears on each of his fingers. He's handsome enough, and hasn't seemed unpleasant, but these men are all pirate captains — I know the violence required for that title and don't think I would like to meet any of them alone.

"We only know she was training to become a high priestess when Blackwell defeated Adelaide. The temples were all destroyed and the priestesses..." Marie trails off. I suck in a breath as Marie continues, "Well, as many of you know, met horrible fates. No one knows if Adelaide's niece perished or escaped; there has been no word of her for the past eight years."

Again, Marie's eyes drift to me and I refuse to meet her gaze, to rise to her bait.

"How did *you* survive, Priestess?" the black-eyed man asks, inspecting me closely.

"I stabbed a soldier through the throat with his own dagger." My words come out as a hiss, but it cannot be helped. "It was a kinder end than he deserved."

Familiar restlessness rushes through my limbs, urging me to flee the table if this continues; I will not be questioned and prodded by these strangers. As I move to push back from the table, I meet Lennox's steady gaze. Mild shock registers on his face at my admission, and my gaze swings wide around the room; expressions ranging from surprise to respect fill the faces of everyone in the room.

"I'm sorry to have caused you distress, Mistress. My curiosity often gets me in trouble," the man with the gold tooth smiles at me and inclines his head in respect. "I am Captain Mario di Micios. Of the *Hellcat*."

"Mario of Cats?" I question the meaning of his surname.

"Ah... Mario the Tomcat, Mistress." He gives a winning grin and winks at Lyra and me. "A fitting nickname."

"Indeed," Lennox mutters under his breath, lips thinning. I can't help but smirk at his terse response; it's clear to me that the Tomcat isn't a close friend. My emotions have muted slightly at the change of topic until Marie's gaze settles on me again.

"What do you know of the Queen's heir, Priestess?" Marie's head tilts with the question, casually sipping her wine as the servants clear the table for the main course. "I was told she may have resided at the temple near Athene where you hail from."

"If she did, I knew nothing about it. I doubt her identity would have been made known to us though," I confide.

"I see," Marie replies as roasted meats and vegetables are presented to us.

Dinner being served seems to have shuttered her line of questioning, but I still feel her keen eyes on me, and my cheeks pink involuntarily as I cut into my meat.

CHAPTER 24

Despite the questioning, I can't help but savor the food after our long journey and repetitive meals. Courses are presented, one after the next, and the rest of the meal passes with casual conversations and pleasantries. The captains discuss storms, raids, and ships, while Lyra and I speak with her grandmother about Delosia and its inhabitants.

Occasionally, Marie leans into my side, whispering commentary about the other guests as they speak to one another. The names all begin to run together, but a few stand out — Morel, Trevino, Gunnarson, and di Micios, are all seated around the table with Lennox, Jackson, and Varangr.

Although pirates hold to their own superstitions and rituals, Marie informs me that many of the captains share the old religion. This knowledge is a boon for my nerves, knowing that before Dargan Blackwell allowed the new priests to run rampant through Selennia, women were held in high regard. The Great Goddess was worshipped throughout the different islands, each culture infusing Her myth with their own flavors, but all revering Her. The way these men exhibit respectful behavior to the three women in the room does seem to be in line with the Old Ways, and tension leaves my shoulders as fear for my safety eases.

"How is it you are all able to move about so freely here?" I ask Lennox quietly across the table. "Are there not laws against piracy here as there are at other ports? Or is that why we anchored in the bay?"

From my limited knowledge, I know heavy bribes are often required to pull into port at most harbors if you sail on a vessel well known for piracy, otherwise, you risk hanging or other harsh sentencing. The more I think on it, I vaguely remember witnessing Erik hand a pouch to one of the harbormasters in Athene when I was disembarking, and now assume he was paying the man off.

"Delosia is a bit of a wild card on that front. We have an agreement with the locals, and one another, when we are on these sands," he replies. "Everyone is on their best behavior, for the most part, to avoid upsetting the leadership." His eyes sparkle in the candlelight as he cuts them to Marie.

"Most of the inhabitants of the island are running from the same things you are," Marie adds smartly. "They're willing to be friendly with the captains in exchange for the goods and commerce they bring as long as they behave and charge a fair price. Those who stay here year-round are almost all refugees of some sort, but we have sailors of all kinds who visit us frequently. The rules are a bit different than you're probably used to."

The conversation turns to other topics before the dessert

course is served — a delightful sponge cake with light icing and fresh fruit. The taste is so sweet and delectable I can barely stifle an almost sexual moan at the taste. I catch Lennox watching me as I eat, and can't resist licking the icing from my lips in a far more suggestive manner than is truly proper, ignoring the lust in some of the other captains' gazes. Heat pools in my belly, and hope fills me that he will breach the shared door to our quarters tonight.

Once dessert is cleared and digestifs are consumed, I plan my exit. As I prepare to depart, a smooth hand lightly touches my arm to gain my attention, and I turn to Marie, glancing down to where she holds me.

"May I speak with you privately, my dear?" she asks, as if she is *my* grandmother and just wants to have a chat with a loved one. Reluctantly, I agree and follow her down a tiled hallway to a tidy study.

Dark wooden shelves line the walls, laden with books with thick leather bindings. Other artwork and sculptures are interspersed with seashells and various other trinkets from the island among the books and on the walls. I can't imagine how she was able to acquire some of these pieces all the way across the sea, so I briefly admire the titles and paintings before refocusing on the older woman. She sits at the large gilded desk in the center of the space and indicates I should sit at one of the chairs facing it. For a moment, I feel like I am back in the House of Starlight bargaining with Celeste; she learned much from her mother-in-law.

"You were very quiet at dinner, Andromeda," Marie again pauses at my name. I swallow and sit straighter.

"I don't know what you mean, Mistress. I spoke as expected when I had knowledge of the topic or could contribute something interesting to the discussion. I'm not sure what Celeste or Captain Lennox may have told you, but I have never been a verbose woman. I don't see a point in speaking without something valuable to say."

"I see. And what do you know of this?" Marie asks as she pulls something from her desk drawer.

She steps around the desk and gently lays a painted miniature in my hand. My heart speeds to a gallop in my chest, and my dinner threatens to make a reappearance when I look down. The painting is of the former queen — Adelaide — as a younger woman, likely my age or a few years younger. Her sable waves frame milky skin and deep-set sapphire eyes. It's like looking in a mirror, not a painting of my aunt.

A shallow, shaky breath leaves me and I can't hide the tears on the edge of my lashes as I stare at the painting. I wish I could hold on to it to keep her close, but I hand it back to Marie.

"I don't know anything about it at all," I reply as I rise from my seat. With a small curtsy, I turn and walk steadily from the study.

As I breeze past the captains who are gathered drinking whiskey and brandy in Marie's parlor, they all turn to watch me, surprised at my brisk pace. Lyra calls my name as I stride through the door, but I cannot stop. I will not look back.

I have not looked back in eight years until this damn voyage, and I am *done* remembering the past. The girl Marie is looking for died at that temple, and I refuse to stay for further questioning.

The quick step of boots on the verandah follows me before clomping down the stairs as I continue stomping down the sandy street. Pleasant songs and laughter drift from the houses surrounding me on both sides, but neither of those exist in my future if I don't keep moving. It only takes a moment before Lennox is at my side, matching my pace, barely out of breath.

"Why do I always seem to be chasing you through the streets?" he asks, a smile evident in his deep voice. The smile fades when he looks at my face, his arm shooting out to still my hurried steps.

"What's wrong? What did Marie say to you?"

"Why did you bring me here?" I demand, trembling slightly with frustration. "Did you know?"

He shakes his head in confusion at my words, glancing over my face. His hands drift to my shoulders, but I shrug out of his grip. "I knew it was you when I saw you at Celeste's, knew you were the girl I shared the rites with that summer. I've never cared about anything else. What are you upset about?"

"Why is Marie asking questions about Adelaide's niece? What is it to her? What is her standing on this island?" I can't stop the questions from falling from my lips. "Did you tell her my name?"

"Your name? You mean— "

"Don't. Don't say it." I start walking again.

"Stop. What are you saying?" Lennox tries to grab at me again, but I pull my arm from his grasp. The armor I rebuilt around myself when we entered the bay cracks as I edge toward panic.

"Nothing, *she* is dead. Queen Adelaide's niece died at the temple. Never use that name again. Do you understand?" My eyes burn with tears as I stare into his. "Please, please just take me back to my room." I hate the plea in my voice, but cannot mask my distress.

Instead, he pulls me into his arms, holding me in the middle of the sandy street as the moon shines down on us.

"I understand. None of that matters to me," he says, a quiet growl in the night. His hand runs gently down my back as he holds me, comforting the ache in my chest, but he doesn't take me back to my room.

We walk through the moonlit street until we reach the tavern from earlier. Laughter and music pour through the open shutters, and the flicker of lanterns and candles illuminate the small, cozy space. Maryanne leans against the bar, this time accompanied by another younger woman who seems to be doing all the work at this hour.

"Lennox! Andromeda! Come have a drink!" Maryanne cries when we approach.

She is deep in her cups, but I can tell she is a happy drunk, not a vicious one. I accept another rum punch from her, and Lennox does the same. Maryanne is oblivious to the tension between us while she continues to laugh with the men that line the bar, more carefree than I have ever been. Lennox pulls me into the alcove from earlier and allows me to sit in silence, sipping the strong drink as I drown my thoughts.

"Can I ask you something?" I finally break my silence halfway through my second cup.

"Of course," he replies. I am not sure if he is on his second or third glass, but his cheeks are ruddy in the candlelight. The heat in my cheeks surely means I am similarly colored.

"Why a wolf?" I ask. He quirks a brow at me as if he doesn't understand, so I continue, "You have called me a she-wolf several times, even if you don't think I heard you." When I cut my eyes to him he looks abashed at the observation, but I go on. "Your black flag has a wolf's skull on it, does it not? Why?"

"You're far more astute than anyone realizes, aren't you?" He smiles from behind his cup.

"I was taught that symbols mean things. What does the wolf mean to you?"

"Well, the wolf can be a symbol to strike fear into men's hearts. They're vicious, wild, and free. But... they're also loyal. They work together and they protect the pack. The females are fierce, sometimes more fierce than the males, but they're nurturing." He cuts his eyes to me as he explains, "In some cultures, the Goddess of Battle can shapeshift into a wolf."

I huff into my cup. "I assure you I cannot shapeshift into anything, let alone a wolf. Don't hold your breath, Captain."

"Can you not? Have you not worn multiple masks these weeks? Priestess, healer, hand of justice, friend?" He leaves out a few glaring descriptions, but continues, "You inspire loyalty. You're the fiercest creature I've ever met. You care for Lyra as if she was your own blood, and cared for my entire crew and myself for the past weeks at sea."

His eyes are guileless as they take me in from across the

table. I finish my drink, and he tips his cup back to down the rest of his as well.

"Shall I don a different mask tonight, Captain? Or are you ready to retire on your own?" I smirk as I stand, the rum making my limbs feel loose and my tongue bold.

Lennox pushes up from the table to offer his arm as we walk to the doors. "I can think of many things I would like to do tonight, none of which are solitary deeds," he breathes to me as we walk arm in arm into the night air.

CHAPTER 25

The breeze from the ocean is refreshing, but my dress and shift cling to my flesh with sticky sweat as we walk to the boarding house — I can tell it is never truly cool on Delosia. Head muzzy, and body tingly and warm from the punch, I lean into the Captain like we are lovers out for a romantic stroll. If only our story was that simple.

No one pays us much attention when we enter the boarding house; trysts are happening in the darkened corners, and sailors gamble and drink around the evenly spaced tables in the open courtyard, but eyes don't linger on me like I am used to. It's a welcome change. My entire life has been observed in some manner, and the freedom of anonymity is as sweet as the smell of the flowers climbing the walls of the building.

I trip on the stairs as we ascend, and stifle a giggle as Lennox keeps me on my feet. My gaze meets his momentarily, and he is smiling like a fool, surely reflecting my own gleeful expression.

"Well, Captain. Thank you for escorting me to my

room," I tease, holding out my hand to him, looking up through my lashes once we reach my door.

"It was my honor, Mistress." He kisses my knuckles and his hot breath sends a shiver straight to my core.

"Goodnight, Captain." With a small curtsey, I enter my room, glancing over my shoulder once before I close the door behind me.

Before the tumbler on my door fully locks in place, the adjoining door swings wide, and his mouth descends on mine. The banter outside our rooms has only inflamed his senses, and he runs his hands down my back, pressing me closer to him as he claims my mouth. Body loose from the punch, and mind adrift after my earlier panic, I cling to him as if he is a lifeboat while I'm drowning in the open sea. I gasp as he kisses down my throat, his warm hand holding my hair back to bare my neck to him. If I only have him for a few more days, then I want to savor our time together.

"I want you, my pretty priestess," he breathes against my neck in between kisses.

"I'm yours," I reply breathlessly. "Take me."

Our kisses turn urgent, and I run my tongue along his lower lip before sucking it into my mouth. At my response, he lifts me and carries me to my bed of sunlight and sand, laying me amongst the fresh, creamy linens.

"So fucking beautiful," he murmurs, looking down at me where I recline against the pillows. He pulls off my boots one at a time, then kisses my calf gently. His own boots are kicked off, and he lays his cutlass on the table with a metallic clang. I giggle at the noise, evidence of his slight drunkenness.

The moment he returns to the bedside, he pushes my

skirts up and kneels between my legs. My fingers lace behind his neck, pulling him back to kiss me again, and he is happy to oblige. Our tongues dance while I grip his hair, holding him close to me. His weight presses against me on the bed as we kiss and caress, like lovers with all the time in the world together.

Slowly, mercilessly, he trails kisses down my neck and across the tops of my breasts where they rise above the neckline of my bodice. Unhooking the clasps down the front, he bares the sheer shift I wear beneath the floral dress, continuing his kissing through the thin fabric over my breasts, teasing each nipple before slowly moving down my stomach. I shrug out of the dress quickly, and he pulls it out from under my hips, tossing it to the floor so only my shift remains between us.

My nipples harden, and his grin is lascivious at their rosy peaks. Skin tingling under his touch, he runs his rough hands up my thighs and hips, pushing the fabric of my shift up to my waist, kissing my thighs, slowly alternating between hot breathy kisses and dragging his slick tongue on my fevered skin. I part my legs for him, and he kisses up to the apex of my thighs before sliding his hot tongue between them, tasting me and sucking at the bundle of nerves between my legs in turn. Without a thought, I bite my lip to keep from crying out at his touch while he glides his tongue inside of me before replacing it with his fingers. Rocking my hips against his mouth, I feel my climax approaching.

Before I can stop myself, I cry out at the pleasure when I come, "Oh, *fuck!*" Lennox pops his head up quickly, and I can't help but release a breathy laugh at his expression.

"Was I not supposed to come so loudly that all the men *here* know I'm yours, too?" I ask smartly, blushing at the thought of the men downstairs gambling.

He laughs deeply before sliding back up my body for a kiss, pressing his cock against me, and rubbing it against my sensitive mound.

"I'll never mind hearing you scream for me, my pretty priestess," he whispers.

I groan in response, meeting his hips with my own in my desire. Feeling greedy to have him inside me, I hastily pull his shirt from his pants and over his head, then reach for his waistband in desperation. He helps pull them down and settles back over me, teasing my entrance with his hardness, sliding in the wetness he finds there.

Raising up on his knees momentarily, Lennox looks at me with a mischievous smirk. "I hope you have an extra shift."

Before I have a moment to process his statement, he rips the cotton down the front, exposing my nakedness. I gasp at the vicious action, but find myself even more desirous of him and arch myself to glide him against me again. Lennox flashes me a grin as he leans down to run his teeth across one of my rosy nipples, and I moan with the pleasure it sends through my body. It feels like lightning is streaking through me directly to my core.

"Fucking take me, Billy," I snarl in his ear, reaching for him.

My hands never make it to his face though; he captures my wrists in one hand, pinning them over me. I buck half-heartedly, biting my lip and writhing my body under him as he holds me firmly. His cock slides against me until I can barely think straight, never releasing my arms, before plunging into me in one stroke. I arch to meet him, gasping at the feel of him, and our mouths are hot against one another, nipping and claiming each other as he thrusts deep into me. My legs wrap around his hips, trying to pull him deeper with each thrust.

Maybe it is the knowledge that we will part soon, or the rum punch releasing my inhibitions, or the sheer weight of the emotions he brings out in me, but I have never wanted to be closer to another human, and I come again hard as he increases the speed of his movements. Waves of pleasure wrack my body, and Lennox follows me over the edge shortly, releasing my wrists, caressing my face with his hands, and nuzzling at my neck.

My arms fold around his neck, holding him against me as we pant in the afterglow. Tonight, we are merely lovers enjoying one another; my other worries sink into the fading blur from the rum and orgasms, and I hold him without hesitation.

THIN STREAMS OF SUNLIGHT WASH OVER THE ROOM WHEN I wake, and I'm surprised to find Lennox's sleeping form next to me in my bed. The door between our rooms still stands wide open from last night, our clothing strewn across the floor including my ruined shift. *He stayed.* A little kernel of sunlight gleams within my heart, and for the first time in a very long time, I allow it to kindle as I lay on my side curled up, watching him.

Like on the ship, he lays on his back with a hand across

his broad tattooed chest, face peaceful in sleep, and I want to memorize him like this. When I reach out to touch his hand with my own, his lashes flutter, and his eyes open. My hesitation lasts for only a moment, gone when he smiles, stretches, and grabs my hand, pulling me to his chest.

"Good morning," he says into my wild, wavy hair, arms wrapped around me.

"Good morning," I smile against his skin. "I see you decided to make yourself at home."

"Sorry to have invaded your room. I can go." He makes to move, but I clutch at him, hoping my desperation for him to stay isn't evident in the movement.

"You can stay, it's nice to have a familiar face around in a strange place."

"Oh, well in that case," I can hear the smile in his voice, and my heart flutters as I rest my head on his chest. His heart beats steadily under my ear, but it is a regular rhythm, not the speeding flip-flop that my own seems to be performing. "Andromeda, I – "

Footsteps outside the door interrupt his statement and a sharp knock sounds, causing me to sit up.

"Yes?" I call toward the door.

"Andromeda, we need to talk!" Lyra's voice pulls me from my lovesick reverie, dread replacing it.

She knows.

CHAPTER 26

L ennox pushes up, but I shove him back down on the bed and motion for him to stay put. Wrapping myself in one of the discarded sheets from the bed, I pad to the door. With a deep breath, I square my shoulders, turn the lock, and open the door. Lyra stands smiling in the walkway holding a tea service like a servant, but her eyes widen and brows lift at my attire and disheveled hair as I stare at her with pursed lips.

"How may I help you so early, Lyra?" I ask dryly.

"Andromeda, we need to talk. I'm sorry if Grandmama offended or upset you. Please let me in." The young woman is guileless as she pleads, her sparkling hazel eyes illuminated by the sunlight and tears she holds back.

Her reaction gives me pause; perhaps she truly didn't know her grandmother's intentions and is afraid to lose a friend. I sigh and let my shoulders drop, moving aside so she can squeeze into my room with the tea tray. A squeak escapes from her when she makes it far enough into the room to view Lennox. The noise makes my lips quirk in amusement as I shut the door, and spin to face the room.

Captain Lennox sits on the edge of the bed wrapped in the coverlet from the waist down, bare-chested and blushing like a maiden, while Lyra opens and closes her mouth like a landed fish. Refusing to meet her uncle's gaze, her eyes flit over my torn and discarded shift, our clothing in wild disarray, and the door that stands open between our chambers.

"I... um... I'm sorry to have... uh... interrupted," Lyra stutters, as if she wasn't raised in a brothel and doesn't know her uncle and I have been in bed together numerous times since we boarded his ship. Knowing something and seeing something are two very different things, though.

"Good morning, Lyra. I was just... uh, going." Lennox smiles at us as he tightens his grip on the coverlet and stands to dash into his quarters. I smile indulgently at him as he scoots past Lyra, sketching a small bow to me before he shuts the adjoining door behind him.

"Now that you have interrupted my pleasant morning, what is it that you want, Lyra?" I ask, facing her with my arms clutched around the sheet covering me. While I don't blame Lyra for her grandmother's words, a drip of acid seeps into my voice at the memory of feeling cornered in her study last night. Curiosity eats at me to know what she's been told, ordered to do, or to find out, as I sit on the stool near my vanity and indicate she should sit as well.

She gently places the tea service on a table and gestures to it in question. I shake my head in response, so she pours a single cup for herself — the aroma of bergamot and black tea wafts toward me. The silence lingers heavily as she adds milk and sugar cubes before sitting and taking a sip.

Once fortified, she begins, "I could tell you were uncomfortable last night at dinner, but I don't know why. Is it because we kept so many secrets from you?" She takes another sip, eyes studying me as I sit in silence, waiting for her to continue. "When you swept from the study and out the door, I wanted to follow you. But Uncle took off after you, and I didn't want to interrupt. Judging by what I walked in on, maybe I was right in that inclination."

Her eyes dance with mirth as she smiles wickedly over her cup, and from her playful tone, I can tell she has no ulterior motive. She is genuinely concerned for her friend, and I have been rude. Unable to resist her charm, I allow my lip to quirk up at the corner in response.

"Your grandmother... surprised me... last night with the direction of her questioning when I entered her study. I'm not sure what she may have told you about me or my past, but I would prefer to leave yesterday far behind. That's why I agreed to this trip. That, and watching over you, which now I know was a ruse to encourage me to get on the ship in the first place." I sigh, relaxing a bit as I continue.

"This was supposed to be my chance to get away from everything I've run from for so long. To be safe. But it seems as if all this journey has done is serve to remind me that the past is never truly buried," I confide without divulging any important details.

Lyra gently sets her cup on its saucer and looks at me, chewing on the inside of her cheek in thought. "Andromeda, I know that you are frightened of something that happened to you before. Grandmama didn't tell me what happened, but I know that she has been working with my uncle for a long time now to help women escape just like they did for you and me... and Charlie," Lyra's voice hitches when she mentions her dead lover.

She takes a deep breath before continuing, "I have no right to ask you, but please speak with her again. Alone. Without a party of sea captains in the house. She has presided over this island for so long, and they're prosperous and happy here. She isn't a bad woman. I can't imagine she has ill intent for you."

"What do you mean *she has presided over this island*?" I question. My curiosity, a blessing, and a curse, is piqued. I know this is bait to get me to talk to Marie again, but I cannot resist the pull.

"Grandmama is the head of the republic here on the island; handling the governing and trade. The men in the room last night are all elected from their ships to represent the different crews who do business here. Grandmama represents the permanent residents of Delosia. They all vote on it, and she has held the position for a very long time," Lyra explains.

"So the island is run like a pirate ship?" I ask, still confused.

"Ha!" Lyra laughs, "I guess you're right — that *is* the same way they elect captains. I hadn't thought of it that way, but yes. I suppose it is." She sips her tea quietly as I think about her statement.

I cannot quite comprehend the information. An island ruling itself? Everyone having a say? If this wasn't enough to pique my interest in learning more about Marie and

Delosia, the reminder of a time before Blackwell's reign, when women held the power in Selennia would do the trick.

Maybe I *should* speak with Marie in private once more. Now that the initial shock of her knowing my identity has worn off, perhaps I can manage to gather my thoughts and ask the right questions. If this is to be my new home...

"Fine," I say, standing from my stool with my sheet still held tight around me. "I will speak with her. Will you see if tomorrow around lunchtime is convenient? I can meet her at her house, but would prefer no other audience be in attendance."

"Of course! I will go to her straight away!" Lyra finishes her tea and stands beaming, her mission completed.

"Also, will you please ask around and find out who the best seamstress on the island is? I have a few things I need made." I glance down at the ruined shift, frowning slightly. It was fun in the moment, but now I have nothing clean to wear. "And a laundress?"

"Yes! I will ask and let you know," Lyra wraps me in a hug, despite my lack of proper attire or free arms to return her embrace, and practically bounces out the door.

Once she has departed, I tap gently on the adjoining door to the Captain's room, wondering if he might wish to share the remainder of the tea, but receive no answer. When I ease the door open, the room is empty and immaculate, with no sign of Lennox to be found aside from a small trunk of his things.

THE ISLAND SUN GREETS ME BRIGHTLY AS I STEP OUT OF THE seamstress' shop on one of the sandy side streets. It's sinking in the sky so that the rays streak perfectly down the alley and into my eyes, forcing me to blink rapidly to see again. The orange and pink sunset is beautiful, but the sun is powerful, even as it sets, so I am continually squinting just when I think I have grown used to it.

Lyra returned earlier to direct me to the favored tailor in town and I found the plump middle-aged woman at the shop to be a delight. The wide variety of fabrics she had available was a pleasant surprise — not just linen and cotton for the tropical heat, but fine wools and silks, too. I have never been able to shake off my love of luxurious fabrics and thus spent entirely too much time touching and cooing over the selection. Now that my request for assorted new clothing pieces is complete, I proceed down the street to the familiar tavern that we've frequented since our arrival. Lennox has been missing since he departed my bed this morning, and, although my main goal is to locate an evening meal, I also hope to find him lounging in the alcove when I arrive.

The raucous tavern is overflowing, but I am disappointed to find that there are no familiar faces to greet me except Maryanne behind the bar. "Andromeda, my dear!" she calls out warmly as I make my way through the crowded tables, a smile spreading across my lips in response.

"Hello, Maryanne! How has your day been?" The woman is so joyous, that it is hard not to match her tone.

"Oh, lovely! Just lovely! Can I get you more of the rum punch from last night? You and Lennox seemed to be quite fond of the flavor," she says with a wink, and I crinkle my nose in response.

"No, thank you. It went down entirely too easily and I fear my morning was a bit cloudy because of it," I chuckle. "But if you have something on the menu for dinner I would appreciate it, and perhaps a cup of ale or lager? Something that won't have me stumbling back to my room this time?"

"Of course, of course! Won't take a moment!" Maryanne replies happily and rushes to the back to the kitchen.

I settle in on one of the stools at the bar to await her return, keeping my eyes carefully downcast so I do not look like I'm seeking company. My lightweight linen dress is modest, and my long hair is tidy and pinned up; I look as pious as one of the women who follow the King's religion, but I don't know if that will matter to some of the sailors who frequent the tavern. Not a moment later, the stool next to me jostles, and a strange man plops down, grinning like a fool. I sigh and keep my eyes directed to my hands so as to not invite conversation. As soon as Maryanne returns with my food, I plan to escape to the safety of my alcove, alone.

"Hello, beauty — when did you arrive on this fine island?" the man asks, alcohol wafting from his lips as he watches me expectantly.

"Only a day ago, sir. If you please, I would prefer to have my meal alone," I reply curtly, barely cutting my eyes to register his scraggly dark hair and matching beard.

"Only a day! Then you must be in need of a friend, Miss. Let me join you and keep you company!" He is jolly and boisterous, and clearly drunk. Although he may not mean me harm, I do not want him to linger.

"I appreciate the kindness, but again, I prefer to dine alone. I am not in need of company." I sit straight and look him directly in the eye to accentuate my statement. When the man looks me full in the face, all glee falls from his expression, and his eyes display a hint of fear as they widen. His gaze flicks just above my eyes, and in the next breath, glances to my wrist where the bracelet Lennox placed on me that fateful night at the House still gleams.

"I meant no harm, Missus. Truly. Forgive me." He almost falls as he stumbles backward off the stool, backing away as if I have transformed into a venomous snake or rabid wolf.

"Of course, you didn't. Thank you," I reply coldly, masking my confusion and curiosity at the man's fear. My eyes track him across the room as he retreats to a table of men, whispering furiously. The table falls to a hush, and fearful glances turn my way briefly. Soon enough, though, they're all distracted again by drinking and cards, forgetting me. Maryanne approaches with a large cup of ale, almost choking on laughter.

"What did you do to that one, Andromeda dear?" she chuckles, carefully setting the mug in front of me.

"I merely asked to be left alone. At first, he seemed like he was going to be troublesome, but when he looked at me, he seemed afraid. Is Captain Lennox so feared on this island?" I jingle the bracelet against the bar slightly to direct her attention to it when she seems confused.

"Lennox? Well, he is certainly a force to be reckoned with here, most of the men respect him. He *is* known to be brutal when he needs to be. But it's *you* that struck fear into that one, love."

"*Me?*" I ask incredulously. It seems unlikely that a woman sitting alone at a bar would strike fear into a group of hardened seafarers.

"Oh yes. They've all heard of the resurrected priestess that sailed in on the *Bartered Soul*. The one that removed a lecherous man's cock for trying to touch her without permission. You are a sea witch that haunts their dreams. Men always love beautiful dangerous things, but not one of them would dare touch you without your consent after that." Pride is evident on her tanned face as she smiles at me with her gapped teeth.

"I see." I hadn't expected my actions to precede me, and it makes me nervous that I'm already known here after just over a day and a half.

The ale is refreshing as I drink deeply from the tankard, rotating on the stool to glance around the room one side at a time. Some eyes are on me, but they flicker back to their cards, dice, or companions when I meet their gaze. A few of the women catch my eye and give small smiles or nods. I need to talk to Marie soon and get away from here. I do not wish to be known.

After a few more minutes, a serving girl appears from the back of the tavern with a savory stew of fresh seafood, placing it in front of me along with a small loaf of crusty bread. My stomach growls and I dig into the meal at almost an indecent speed, forgetting all manners I may have learned between my childhood and the temple, burning my tongue in my haste. When the stew is gone, I finish by wiping the bowl with the crusts of the loaf and down the remainder of my beer before leaving coin for Maryanne. She is busy chatting with another customer at the bar, so I bid her a quick goodbye with a wave and swiftly sweep through the room and out into the twilight street.

The waxing gibbous moon illuminates the palms and other lush trees that line the back of the buildings, casting a pretty glow on the night. The full moon is not far away, and my heart swells at the thought of another ceremonial night. The thought makes me briefly wonder if anyone on the island celebrates in the old way now that I know many of the residents fled persecution from Selennia. Maybe there are even other priestesses that hold ceremony, or at least mark the passing phases. My heart warms at the possibility as I stand another few moments in the street gazing at the stars as they blink to life, then continue my trek to the boarding house.

When I step through the doors of the boarding house, I survey the courtyard, but again find no familiar faces to greet me. In need of liquid courage to sit with my thoughts tonight while I gather ideas for how to handle Marie and decide my next moves, I stop by the bar to request a bottle of wine and a fresh pitcher of water for my room. I have to fight the urge to ask the bartender if the Captain has returned, but restrain myself and ascend the stairs in silence. Reaching the door to my room, I pause, glancing longingly at Lennox's room next door.

Did he ever come back? Will he say goodbye before he departs for good again?

I shake my head at my foolishness and enter my chambers. The room has been tidied, and two notes wait for me: one from the servant girl letting me know that she has sent all of my soiled items to the laundress and that they will be returned tomorrow, which is good since I have no other options to wear besides what's on my back. The other note bears a deep purple wax seal and unfamiliar handwriting on the outside. I carefully open it, suspecting the heavy paper is Marie's before breaking the seal. I'm confident she won't be opposed to another meeting, but my heart still skips like a nervous child performing for an audience as I read:

ANDROMEDA,

I am sorry if I upset you at dinner last night. I won't make excuses — I was trying to test your mettle. I fear my approach has backfired, but I was so pleased when Lyra told me you wished to speak again. I would be honored to have you for lunch tomorrow. Please visit me around noontime. -Marie

WITH A SIGH, I PLACE THE NOTE ON MY VANITY AND OPEN THE bottle of wine — tonight I will drown my worries. Tomorrow, I will confront my past, and, hopefully, make a plan for whatever future I might have left.

CHAPTER 27

A nxiety rolls through me as I hurry through the streets towards Marie's home, but hopefully, it isn't written across my face. Luckily, the laundress was able to return my clothing with a short turnaround, but she was late enough that I was afraid I would be wearing a sweat-stained shift and a days-old dirty dress to my lunch with the head of the entire island.

As it is, I selected a navy dress of soft breathable linen for the occasion. My hair is braided into a coronet with the back free to my waist, the same as it was all those years in the temple and the House of Starlight. Old habits are hard to break, and the reminder of my identity brings comfort, even if my old memories do not.

I skip up the stairs to the verandah, tapping lightly with the knocker to announce my presence. The same butler who attended us at dinner opens the door quickly and escorts me inside. I catch my reflection in a mirror in the entry hall, noticing the color high in my cheeks, either from the heat or my nerves, and my eyes shine bright against my pale reflection. Forcing myself to breathe evenly, we approach the dining room.

At the head of the table sits Marie wearing bold purple and bright green, silver hair wrapped in a beautifully printed swath of fabric. The contrast between her and I is not lost on me — she is like a brilliant bird or hothouse orchid compared to my midnight skies and shadows. I dip into a small curtsey in greeting as she stands.

Once again, she seats me in the chair to her right, and the butler pulls it out for me to sit at her indication. He returns to my side momentarily, quickly filling my goblet with wine once I am settled in my place.

"Wine midday? Should I be worried already?" I give a smirk to my hostess as she raises her glass to me. I clink my goblet with hers, and we both take ladylike sips. She asks me idle questions about my room, what I think of the island, and how I'm faring with the temperatures while the servants bring in a light meal, but they leave it on the table for us to serve at our leisure instead of plating the meal for us — Marie must have told them this was to be a private meeting.

Once alone, Marie turns to me. "I would like to calm your nerves, even though I know that is unlikely to happen, my dear. You do not need to fear harm from me, truly. Don't you think if I had wished to hurt you, I could have already done so in the past years you've been employed in one of my establishments?" Marie asks, and although my blood chills, there is no malice in her words, only truth.

"What is it that you think of me, Marie?" I ask, toying with my food with the fine silver fork from my place setting. "What is it that you want?"

"The real question is: what do *you* want? You have been working as a prostitute for many years, but also healing the women you come across without recompense. Celeste writes that you haven't outwardly celebrated the Old Ways since she met you, but then I hear a rumor that you performed both a Full Moon and Death Ceremony on the *Bartered Soul* as if you've been doing it for centuries. And we won't discuss the justice you served in front of an entire crew that causes your name to be whispered like a nightmare in the streets. Who are you, girl? What do *you* want?" Marie is direct, which I appreciate. She doesn't allow passion to cloud her statements, even if I am having trouble controlling my own roiling emotions.

"I want what everyone wants — to be free. To not live in fear. To worship as I please. For actual justice to be served." I stop myself. *Have I ever been asked what I truly want before? Has it ever mattered?* "To find love, and to help people," I finish quietly.

"And?" Marie presses, staring at me with her head cocked slightly to the side, like a cat considering its prey.

"And?" I mimic, unsure what she expects. I have been honest and already offered her far more than I've ever admitted to myself.

"And what of your heritage? Your rightful title? The King?" she prods.

My expression flattens at her words. "I don't see what difference it makes at this point," I reply sternly. "I would love nothing more than to see Dargan Blackwell burning on one of his own pyres if I am truthful, but I don't know what that wish, or my title, has to do with it." I pause, taking a sip of my wine while I try to control the rage I feel at the words that tumble from my tongue. At her questions.

"It's not as if I can march to the castle steps and ask him to leave — he murdered my —," I catch myself, not quite able to fully admit the relation out loud. "The Queen... to steal her throne. I have no army. No siege weapons. I have no way to demand the justice that he deserves."

"Do you not?" Marie asks, raising a silver brow, before taking another sip of her wine.

"I am a displaced priestess of an outlawed religion, a former whore, and I'm at the mercy of a pirate lord to pay me the money he owes me in order to make my new life. How can you think I have any power or forces to wield? The only power that has gotten me anywhere the past eight years is the power between my legs and the stubborn will to survive."

Disgust fills me at my admission, but it's all true. I have used my beauty and my *talents* to eke out the existence I've lived, burying the hatred and rage I feel amongst my fear and sadness. I've sought numbness instead of wallowing in my true feelings out of necessity.

"Oh child, is that truly what you think?" Suddenly, Marie's eyes are full of pity, and I cannot understand why. Maybe my words were harsh, but they weren't untrue. My experience, however terrible, is still far less depressing than those of many of the women that still work in the Houses I escaped from, or who find themselves on the streets I left behind.

"Love, fear, and respect are the greatest powers in the universe, and you, my dear, command all of these. I thought when I met you that you knew that? But perhaps you are a better actress, or have been far better trained, than I ever imagined."

I study her face, trying to root out the cunning I'm certain is hiding there, but all that looks back is the gentle face of a grandmother, schooling a child in the ways of the world. For a moment I can't come up with the proper words to respond with, so I take another drink of the wine while I collect myself.

"Explain." I finally invite her to continue.

"Your aunt was beloved by the people, you know this surely?" she asks. I offer a quick nod, stuffing my emotion deep at the thought of my Aunt Adelaide. Marie continues, "When gossip started about the Usurper King threatening her rule, no one thought it would be troublesome; Selennia was strong and peaceful. But, of course, a group of foul men felt like it wasn't right for women to have so much power anymore. They paved the way for the treachery and defeat that began with Adelaide's death and the destruction of the temples, and ended with dismantling the way our society worked.

"I believe — and I am encouraged in this belief by the news that comes to me through the different pirate lords that pass through this island — that there are a host of people back home waiting for a uniting force to initiate a rebellion by the people. I think *you* may be that rallying force."

Fortunately, I had hesitated in my last sip of wine, and still only hold the goblet to my lips, otherwise, I would have spit the dark liquid across her fine tablecloth.

"*Me*? No. I am *not* looking to be a queen. I am not trying to rally a rebellion. I have given so much — my family, my beliefs, my body, everything I ever knew. I will not become the property of an entire country. I'm sorry. I can't." I push my chair away from the table to stand, but Marie holds up her hand to stop me.

"I understand, child. You have endured. You aren't ready to return to the source of your pain. I merely need you to understand that I am not a threat to you. Your secret is safe with me, but this is something you *must* entertain. If you truly want to help people — especially those women and girls still suffering — *and* be free, like you said you do, *this* may be your way."

"I appreciate your concern and your insight, but I can't… I just… I'm sorry, I can't." I stand and fold the napkin before placing it on the table next to my uneaten, much toyed with, meal. Remembering my manners, I turn to her before storming out. "Thank you for seeing me and for the lunch, Marie. I'm sorry, but I must excuse myself now."

"Don't hurt, Billy," Marie says as I reach the doorway, making me pause.

"Excuse me?" I snap, looking over my shoulder, a wave of annoyance cresting in my chest.

"Don't hurt him. Cut the ties now if you are going to run away. He has loved you since he bedded you at the rites, long before he had any idea who you truly were. I've known him since he was a young man — the thought of you possibly murdered in that temple helped drive him to become what he is now." She sighs deeply, as if the memory of a young Lennox is painful. "Don't fool him if you don't love him. I don't think he can handle coming back to find another woman he loves is gone," she confides.

Although my heart feels like it could burst at the idea that Lennox might actually have feelings for me, and at the sorrow for his losses, that feeling is overridden by boiling anger at her audacity.

"It's amusing that the way he decided to show his love was to terrify me at the House of Starlight. To *buy my company* to get me aboard his ship. And then to coerce me into agreeing to step foot onto that vessel by working with Celeste to use Lyra as bait. Do not presume to lecture me on his feelings, or my own," I snarl at her.

Marie recoils, her eyes wide at my words and tone, and doesn't say another word to me as I breeze past the startled butler, letting myself out of the house and into the blinding midday sun.

CHAPTER 28
LENNOX

"Billy... Billy!" Erik's hearty, accented voice jolts me from my thoughts as we sit in my cabin aboard the *Bartered Soul*. "What's the matter with you, man?"

I'm distracted. I've been distracted for weeks now.

I haven't seen Nerissa since Lyra interrupted our morning yesterday, her last sight of me being when I ran out of her room like a maiden caught in the hay with the stable boy.

What was I going to tell her before that interruption? Was I really going to lay it all out? That I love her — I've always loved her? That the idea of leaving her behind again makes me feel like I can't breathe?

My cabin here on the ship is one of the only places where I feel secure discussing important things with these two. While the other captains on the island aren't enemies, they aren't fully trustworthy, either, and I have no idea who might be spying for them. Whereas these two, I trust implicitly — it has been earned over the last seven years. We are supposed to be discussing the next route, whether we are going to New Aphros to spend the winter storm season or heading farther to sea first, but I haven't been able to focus on their opinions.

What feels like a lifetime ago, Erik was on the first crew I joined after the mutiny from the King's Navy, aboard the *Selkie's Tears*. He left Jackson's crew with me when I took my own ship.

Pike is an old friend of Lyra's father and Marie, having hailed from the same village they did. The older man is a steady force for the younger crew members during times of trouble. He knew my mother, too, from when he sailed with Lyra's father and visited us on leave. They're like family to me and know all my secrets. Including what's distracting me now.

Nerissa.

"You *know* what's the matter with him, Erik," Pike scoffs gruffly over the mug of ale he sips from, his dark brown cheeks wrinkling around his eyes as he teases.

"Could both of you kindly shut the fuck up?" I grumble back at their teasing, taking another drink of the whiskey I swirl in my glass aimlessly. The sun sinks lower, casting an orange and pink glow over the open sea beyond the windows of my cabin. The moon rises, and I can't help but think of Nerissa in her silver robe under its white glow. I make a mental note to ensure she knows there will be a ceremony for the full moon; watching her the last time was a thing of beauty, and holding one on the beach will be magical for her.

"You've been searching for the woman for years, Billy. You found her, you've won her. Why don't you just tell her what you want and be done with it?" Pike asks. Erik gives

268

him a sharp look but studies me closely. He, of all people, understands my predicament but has always let me process without the grief that Pike enjoys showering over me.

"I haven't won her, though, have I? I've given her the chance to get out of Celeste's place, but she hasn't said anything about wanting to stay with me. I don't know how to ask her without it seeming like I am trying to buy her or control her. Especially with Marie's dinner hanging over us." My gaze swings to the older man. "Did you know she was going to confront her about her past like that, Pike?" He has known Marie for decades and is always in close communication when we are on the island.

"I had no idea. And you say Andromeda wanted no part of it?" Pike asks.

"None. Told me to not even call her by her true name anymore, as if that will help conceal the truth."

"She was quite shaken, even though she thinks she hides her emotions," Erik observes. "Fear still clings to her skin."

My eyes shift to him — Erik's quiet way of watching and assessing people has always been an asset to me. Somehow, he manages to recede in a group and he catches more pieces of information and news than anyone I know, even as he towers over almost everyone in a room.

"I can't blame her," I answer, finishing my drink.

Her words of stabbing a soldier at the temple ring in my ears, and the memory makes me clench my jaw. I know exactly what they did to women there if they didn't burn them immediately, and I wish I could have done much worse to any bastard that ever hurt her. Self-loathing coats me at my inability to protect her, my mother, my sister, as it has for years. Even knowing she was safe under Celeste's protective watch, I raged while I was away from Artemisia, too far to offer assistance should they need it.

It took years of visits and conversations with my sister to determine when it was the right moment to send Lyra away, timing it so Nerissa would also be strong enough to consider the voyage. When she first arrived on the sidewalk outside the House of Starlight, Celeste had mentioned Nerissa was so broken that she would have risked cutting her hand off to ensure she wouldn't be trapped on a ship full of men rather than wear the bracelet I placed on her.

I swallow bitterness at the memory of seeing her there the first time. Her indigo eyes were empty, as she watched each patron like a wild animal with its leg in a trap.

It took nearly a year before she told Celeste she would be open to receiving customers, and somehow my sister passed it off as offering Nerissa control in their relationship, rather than showing favor to her over the other girls. A few weeks later it was agreed that she would only bed the men she chose, not anyone who wanted a taste of her — she was too volatile with her dagger, otherwise.

Having a strange pirate steal her away would have surely been met with that blade, either for me or herself, so I had waited. I watched her every time I was in town — observed her shape fill back out, stand straighter, walk more boldly, until the night I made the deal with Celeste and swept her and Lyra from that place. It's only fair that I let her make her choices now as to what she wishes for the future.

"I think New Aphros is the best choice," Pike interrupts my train of thought while Erik nods in agreement. They

270

both look at me expectantly as I sit behind my desk. Maps are strewn over the surface, but I haven't even glanced down at them.

"I agree. It has plenty of accommodation and is an easy port to sell the goods we still have onboard and those we will depart Delosia with. Plus, the crew enjoys it there during Winter Solstice," Erik speaks wisely as always, and it has been a while since we stopped for long in the port.

"It's also an opportunity for the lady to meet Madame Salome," Erik adds quietly, cutting his eyes at me.

The mention of Salome makes me smile, fond memories of my past rising up over the past decade of violence. I've known the priestess all my life — she was a close friend to my mother. She encouraged my parents' marriage, and then soothed our aching hearts when my father passed away. Nerissa would like her, I'm sure of it, and she could learn more about her heritage and the Old Ways of the priestesses from her.

"If she comes," I murmur.

"If you ask her, she will come," Pike says firmly, like an old uncle telling me I'm an idiot in not so many words.

"If I ask her," I breathe into my refilled glass. Topping off the men's cups, I sit back in my chair to discuss our course to New Aphros before we return to the shore.

"WHAT HAPPENED?" I ASK MARIE, SITTING ACROSS FROM HER at her dining table for dinner later that evening.

"Well, I thought she would be more receptive," the older woman grumbles, "but she was clearly still agitated about what I had to share." She pauses as her butler brings platters around the table to us.

"What. Happened?" I repeat firmly.

I love Marie — we have known one another for years, but she is not always the most delicate when it comes to sharing her opinions.

"I told her that I think she could be the rallying force to overthrow Blackwell," she states casually with a shrug.

"You, what? Marie –" I start, before she interrupts.

"And to not hurt you," she says.

"What!" I shoot to my feet in my anger.

"I told her if she is going to run away from her past, she should tell you outright to avoid breaking your heart. Billy, we have all watched you with her now. It's clear this is not some infatuation over a pretty woman and whatever talents she has in the bedroom. I didn't want her to run away and hurt you," Marie says sweetly with a smile that suits a grandmother – and a viper.

"Dammit, Marie!" the words burst from my mouth as I lean over the table towards her, "You are not my mother. You and Pike are worse at meddling in other people's affairs than anyone I know. *Fuck!*"

I retake my seat and run my hands through my hair, clutching the back of my neck with one as I stare down at my plate. *Just fucking great.*

"Well, what did she say?" I ask quietly, ducking my eyes to hide my desperation to know the answer. If Marie put it out there, I should at least find out what was said.

"She was furious," Marie chuckles. "If she wasn't so adept at restraint, I think she would have thrown her wine at me."

My head snaps up, blinking in surprise.

"She still wants nothing to do with a rebellion or being a queen. At least, she says she doesn't. I can see the rage in that woman. It practically ripples under her skin, even if she thinks she's a still pool — she could be terrifying if she decided to use her power. But it was obvious when I spoke about you that she is mad about you."

My eyes find her at her words. "I'll go to her tonight. Don't bring it up again, Marie. I mean it. Let her live her life, whatever that means for her. She's been through enough," I scold the woman seated across from me.

The knowledge that Nerissa may feel the same for me as I do for her has my heart racing, wanting to run to her room and take her in my arms right now, but I tame my emotions and continue our meal.

"Of course, Billy," she replies, that knowing smirk twitching at the corners of her mouth as she waves to her butler for more wine. "Whatever you wish."

My steps are hurried after dinner as I walk through the warm night air to the boarding house. Leaning over the bar, I snag a bottle of wine and confirm with the barkeep that Nerissa is in her room. She had food and drink delivered a few hours ago and no one has seen her come or go. The coin I drop rings on the counter as I push it towards him — a generous tip for keeping an eye out. Bottle in hand, I head up the stairs to her door.

Tap. Tap tap. No answer. I knock once more and listen closely at the wood. No answer.

For a moment, fear seizes me as my heartbeat stutters in my chest. What if she is sick? Injured? Has someone hurt her?

I listen again, almost resting my ear against the wood completely, and hear the creak of the bed as if someone has rolled over. My heart both sinks and lifts at once — at least she's all right, even if she is avoiding everyone since the lunch with Marie went as poorly as it seems. A sigh escapes me as I quietly go through my own door and silently check the door between our rooms. Locked. She needs time alone.

My body slumps into the chair at the small desk in the corner of my room as I glance at the paper laying there. I write a quick note, leaving it open for the ink to dry, while I undress and take a long pull of wine straight from the bottle. Half of a bottle later, I splay out on the soft feather bed and let the island breeze soothe me to sleep.

CHAPTER 29

A light tap draws my attention, but I do not stir from the bed where I lay. Hours ago I stripped to my shift, then had dinner and refreshments delivered to my room. I have no desire to speak with, or see, anyone. The tap comes again, and I turn my head to look at the offending noise, but still don't move except to roll over.

Let them think I am gone. Let them think I am drunk and sleeping it off. Whatever they think, I will not rise to entertain anyone tonight. I'm no longer at anyone's bidding.

I roll back towards the window, staring out into the night. The gauzy curtains blow gently in the sea breeze, and the air feels pleasant on my bare skin. Once the tapping stops, I close my eyes and take a cleansing breath.

The anger from earlier is safely secured in my chest, but Marie's warning about Lennox's true feelings still weighs heavy on me. *If he feels that strongly, why hasn't he told me?*

Waxing moonlight is just visible through my open windows, reminding me once again that the moon will be full in just another few nights. As I fall asleep, memories surround me, causing me to dream of silver robes, golden circlets, and dancing with my sisters in the moonlight at the temple that no longer stands on the hill in Athene.

THE ORCHIDS AND TROPICAL FLOWERS ARE AROMATIC — THEIR sweet vanilla and cinnamon scents cling to me as I follow my aunt through the humidity of the hothouse. Standing straight as an arrow, she is tall, her dark hair showing threads of silver at her temples when she turns her head to smile at me. The many exotic flowers with their bold hues and delicious scents easily distract me, but I try to remain attentive to her when she tells me about the different species and the medicinal qualities of new plants that have been brought back from faraway places.

At ten, I will be at court a few more years before I depart for the temple to learn from the priestesses, and each moment I spend with Aunt Adelaide is a treasure to me. She is dark, whereas my mother was fair, and her laughing eyes and quick smile are the opposite of my mother's stern and serious nature.

I want to be like my aunt, but I know that even though I look like her, I am as stoic and stubborn as my mother. It's been years since my mother passed, and in that time I've lived here with my aunt as her ward. Even after all this time guilt still surges in my chest when I think about how much I enjoy being here instead of back home.

"It's all right, Nerissa! You can get closer to look at them," my aunt indulges me, as if she isn't the ruler of our country with better things to do than teach a child about flowers. "Smell their fragrances. We have time."

I step closer to the beautiful orchids with their irresistible fragrance and inhale deeply. Giggles of delight burst from my lips over the bright little blooms and Aunt Adelaide chuckles along with me, giving me a tight hug around my shoulders.

———————

THE SWEET SMELL OF TROPICAL FLOWERS GREETS ME WHEN I wake, wafting through the open shutters overlooking the jungle. The memory of my aunt is yet another sting to my heart, but it doesn't take much for me to understand why, of all nights, this dream would return to me.

Even before Blackwell murdered her, I hadn't seen her for five years, not since I left for the temple. The discussions with Marie have opened a raw place in my chest that I locked away years ago, the ache sinking all the way into my bones.

Hot tears burn the back of my throat as I fight to keep them from falling on my pillow. I have already cried enough tears to fill the ocean over the loss of my aunt – shedding more will not change the past. With a deep breath, I sit up, wiping my cheeks roughly and sniffling lightly. A light tap at the door rouses me further, and I glance to the door at the sound — what pulled me from my memory-dream of the hothouse with my aunt.

"Yes?" I call out. My voice is rough this morning and my head throbs slightly, courtesy of the empty bottle of wine lying next to my bed.

"Tea and biscuits for you, Missus?" A woman's voice replies, accompanied by the light clink of silver on a tray through the door. I groan lightly, drop my feet to the ground, and pad to the door to open it for the servant.

"Good morning, Missus. I hope I didn't disturb you?" She looks at the tray instead of my face, dipping her blond head as if she is afraid she woke me.

"Good morning. No no, you're fine." I rub my temples with my hand as I sweep the other toward the table in the center of the room to usher her in. "Please bring the tray in. Thank you." She gently places the tray on the low table and quickly turns back to the door.

A folded note under the plate holding the sweet biscuit catches my eye, and cock my head. "Is that a message for me?" I gesture to the note before the servant can leave.

"Oh, um… yes, Missus — from the Captain. He left it this morning on his way out." She averts her eyes again, cheeks flaming at the mention of Lennox. I huff air out of my nose in amusement, but excuse the girl before grabbing the note. Was it him tapping at my door last night?

The note is indeed sealed with the dark green wax I associate with Lennox, and I shove part of the biscuit in my mouth before cracking the seal:

I ASSUME YOU HAD ANOTHER MEETING WITH MARIE — I hope you're all right. Tomorrow is the full moon, will you celebrate with me on the beach? The locals will be pleased. As would I.

I will be away today and tomorrow handling business, but I will meet you downstairs tomorrow evening at seven o'clock. —B

· · ·

SETTING THE PAPER DOWN ON THE TRAY, I LEAN BACK IN MY chair. I now have another day to amuse myself on the island with no plans. Pouring a cup of tea to clear my foggy mind, I nibble at the remaining biscuit, hoping it will be enough to prevent my headache from worsening.

After breakfast is finished, I take the time to sort through all of the belongings I have with me. My hands settle on the silver robe Lennox gifted me, luminous in the trunk. The only sign it's been worn at all is a faint stain of sea spray on the hem. The memory of the ceremony on the deck drifts through my mind like the warm breeze fluttering the curtains. Lifting the silky fabric, I gently lay it on the bed, placing the coordinating jewelry with it. The thought of wearing them tomorrow, here, on the beach with Lennox, has my eyes drifting shut, a smile ghosting across my lips.

Sometime later, I sort the rest of my clothing into piles based on climate. My three lightweight dresses — the floral cotton I wore the first night to Marie's, the midnight blue linen I wore yesterday, and the simple grey linen that I wore the day we arrived — I place where they are easily accessible. On a whim, I also set a pair of linen trousers and a few shirts that can be worn with them to the side. The other wool items and my fine fur-lined cloak I pack back into the bottom of the trunk, assuming I won't be needing them for a long while.

The flimsy costumes I included in my trunk from the House of Starlight lay in a gauzy pile. I chew the inside of my cheek as I mull over what to do with them, but in the end make no final decision, kicking them to the side and closing the top of the trunk.

The seamstress assured me that the items I requested from her should arrive within a few days, but for the time being, I have a choice between the three dresses. I gravitate to the dark purple floral for the day, carefully braiding back my hair and tucking it tightly in a knot at my neck to relieve the heat of the day. Once dressed, I make my way out of my room to descend into the sun-dappled courtyard below.

After a few inquiries with the servants who mill about with trays of breakfast, and a brisk walk down one of the side corridors, I find myself outside Lyra's door. After a light knock, I announce myself, and the door opens quickly with a smile. Lyra's hair is still in a disarray of tight curls, but she is clothed for the day.

"Good morning, Lyra. Would you like to explore today?" I ask, a small smile of my own tickling my lips as I raise my brows in a conspiratorial look.

"Andromeda! Of course, I'd love to! Come in while I finish getting ready." She steps away from the door to allow me entry, gesturing for me to sit down as she dashes to the vanity to finish her toilette.

I glance around at the grand room while I wait — Marie has taken great pains to keep her granddaughter in comfort here. Gowns lay scattered about the space and Lyra wears a dress similar to those her grandmother prefers — multiple patterns mixed with creatively clashing colors that look spectacular against her naturally tanned skin. She wraps her hair in a scarf like Marie did yesterday, pinning it in place, and turns to join me where I sit next to a pot of tea. Conveniently, the service has two cups provided, so we share a cup while the sun glows brighter through the shades.

"Where would you like to visit today?" Lyra asks as we prepare to leave her room.

"I'd love to see the town — I haven't seen anything more than here, the tavern, the tailor, and your grandmother's." I smile to disguise the slight shudder I feel at the memory of lunch yesterday. "Is there an apothecary or herbalist? I'm eager to learn more about my potential new home."

Truthfully, I want to get the measure of the inhabitants. Thus far, I have been respected as a guest of Marie and acquaintance of Captain Lennox, but what are the townspeople really like when I don't have two powerful leaders watching over me?

"Oh yes! Grandmama is very close with the apothecary. She hopes I might be able to help there depending on what you've taught me. Let's go there first, then we can explore the shops and maybe one of the beaches?" Lyra is practically jumping up and down at the chance to feel normal, so we link arms and head down the stairs and out into the warm sunshine.

CHAPTER 30

The apothecary shop is on the main street, not far from the tavern where we met Maryanne. The building itself is painted bright coral, nestled in between two similar structures that appear to be more boarding houses. As we push the spring green door open, a small bell overhead jingles and loud rustling sounds emanate from beyond the swinging door behind the counter.

"Just a moment!" A feminine voice calls from what I assume is a storage area, but my mind is distracted as I stand in awe of the bottles and vials lining the walls. The stock is shockingly varied for a small island, and the tinctures are multihued as the sun glints on their dark bottles. I resist the urge to stroke the glass with my fingertips, pulling back as a lovely woman steps from the back room.

Her rich copper hair is braided back from her brow in a style similar to mine – the color reflecting the sunlight coming through the wavy glass, surrounding her freckled, heart-shaped face with gilded flames. While she is stunning, her smooth creamy skin isn't what makes my eyes widen. A muted sigil sits above her brows, identical to my own. I gasp at the recognition — she is a priestess.

She pauses behind the counter, glancing up at us with a smile. When she catches my expression, her smile falters and turns into the same shock I wear. We stare at each other in silence, words lost to both of us, but Lyra, always effervescent, breaks the silence. "You must be Siobhan! My grandmama, Marie, spoke so highly of you!"

Siobhan drags her eyes from me as she turns to Lyra, her mouth snapping shut as she visibly shakes her head to clear her thoughts. "Of course! Lyra, correct? Mistress Marie has spoken of you many times, she even mentioned you might be coming by to talk. Is this your teacher then?"

At her question, Siobhan turns her light blue eyes to me, a small smile lifting the edges of her thin lips. Her voice has a light burr and I gather she must be from the Northern part of Selennia — another refugee running from the King.

"Yes, this is Andromeda." Lyra's hand drifts down to grip mine, and I allow it, knowing the touch comforts and encourages the young woman. "She began teaching me on the voyage here. I would love to keep learning and help you if you need assistance," Lyra explains.

"Andromeda?" Siobhan's brows raise as she repeats my name with curiosity. It isn't a common one.

"Priestess," I greet her, inclining my head, and a pleasant laugh bubbles from the apothecary's lips at my greeting. She toys with a heavy torc that rests on her delicate collarbones, the twisted gold the only adornment to her simple, grey linen dress.

"It's been an age since someone greeted me so; I am sure

you feel the same. How is it you come here, Sister?" she asks, her voice soothing to my ears.

"A long story, but I arrived with Lyra aboard the *Bartered Soul*," I reply, glancing at my bracelet.

"Ah, it might be a long story, but not an unusual one. I arrived here a few years back aboard the same ship. Seems as though we may have much to discuss. Are you also seeking work?" Siobhan inquires, looking hopeful.

I turn to hide my surprise at finding out she was also carried away on Lennox's ship, looking at the selection of remedies, teas, tonics, and cosmetics on the shelves with true wonder.

"Perhaps. My plans aren't settled as of yet," I confess.

"Come, have a seat with me in the back, ladies," Siobhan welcomes us back behind the counter with a broad smile. "I can brew some tea and we can discuss opportunities."

We wend our way through the swinging doors to a small kitchen space. Siobhan places a kettle on a little black stove with a fire happily crackling in its belly, preparing the teapot with a blend of dried leaves, while Lyra and I settle at the rough-topped table with seating for four. Herbs and flowers hang drying overhead and a host of potted plants line the back windows.

A large clear crystal rests in the center of her table, and I take it to mean she may have been trained in divination at her temple. Glancing around the space, I breathe deeply, feeling a sense of calm I haven't felt in years as the pungent aroma of different medicinals mix to wrap me in a redolent hug – this is an existence I could get used to. Lyra sits close, both of us silent, until Siobhan joins us with the steaming herbal tea.

"So, let's start with the difficult topic first. Which temple are you from, Andromeda?" Siobhan asks, pouring tea more carefully than strictly necessary, to avoid meeting my eyes.

The question is a stab to the heart, but my hands are steady as I take a sip of the tea. "The Western coast. And you?"

"Northern point," Siobhan replies. Her temple was one of the first hit by Blackwell's men.

"How did you escape?" I ask quietly.

"I'm sure in a similar fashion to you." A flicker in the muscle of her jaw and tightening of her lips are the only indication of discomfort at the topic. Lyra stares into the red-hued tea silently.

"And you were brought here by Lennox?" I continue, the pang of jealousy I feel carefully tucked away so neither of my companions notice. *Was the surgery space on the ship hers before it was mine?*

"I was. Lennox found me in an alley on the Western coast a few years back and swept me up to bring me here," she explains while sipping her tea. "I was in… unfortunate… condition at the time, but I was lucky enough to have Marie offer me the chance to help the elderly man who ran the apothecary.

"I aided him in the shop and through the end of his life. When he passed, I was able to purchase it. My training at the temple meant I already knew the remedies, so I only had to learn the business side of things. Having an assistant — or co-owner — would be very helpful," she looks at me now with hope in her eyes. Perhaps I am not the only one who misses the sisterhood of my fellow priestesses.

Quickly, she shifts the subject, and I am glad for it. "So, Lyra, tell me what Andromeda has taught you."

The afternoon passes pleasantly while the three of us discuss remedies, island gossip, and other blissfully inconsequential things. As we prepare to leave, I turn to Siobhan and take her freckled hand in my own.

"Will you be celebrating the full moon tomorrow night?" I ask.

"I usually celebrate quietly on my own to mark the phases, but... do you mean...?" She trails off before asking her question, brow lightly furrowed in question.

"On the beach, for a ceremony. Please come," I implore, lightly squeezing her fingers. It would be lovely to have another sister on the beach.

After a moment of thought, Siobhan's grip tightens in return. "Yes, I would love to. I'll be there." Her bright smile reaches her eyes as she bids us goodbye. When we step into the afternoon sunlight, my mood has brightened to match its rays.

Lyra and I spend the remainder of the daylight soaking in the warmth of the sun as we stroll along the white sandy beach. We kick off our shoes and hold up our skirts to allow the cool clear waves to wash up over our feet and ankles. For these few hours, the worries that continuously turn over in my mind are forgotten, tossed into the breeze with the emotions I refuse to permit to intrude on the pleasantries. For once, I simply exist in the moment.

The camps on the beach are filled with the dissonant sounds of men, and a few women, cooking, gambling, joking, and relaxing before another lengthy voyage. I recognize a few members of our crew and give small waves of acknowledgment, but we keep to ourselves as we enjoy the beauty of this new place. The island is a beautiful contrast to where we originated: full of life and merriment compared to the solemn shores we left behind.

Together, we walk arm in arm down the sandy streets back to our boarding house as the sun finally dips into the sea. Upon entering the courtyard, Lyra retreats to her room immediately, while I take a moment to request a tray be brought for my evening meal. I pause at my door, glancing at the locked door next to it, wishing Lennox was back to spend the night with, but, instead, I slip into my empty quarters to spend the night alone with my thoughts.

CHAPTER 31

The next morning I awake yet again with no plans. Lyra informed me last night that she is visiting her grandmother for lunch and invited me to join her, but I politely declined as quickly as the invitation was extended. While I wait for my breakfast tray, I sit at the vanity, brushing through my loose hair.

Between the sea voyage and my time here on the island, the sun has added a pink hue to my cheeks. The once sharp planes of my face seem less severe than they appeared in the dark glass at the House, filling out after gaining some weight. I can almost see a glimpse of the young woman I was years ago looking back at me in the reflection, except my eyes are no longer bright and curious — I don't think the wary fierceness will ever depart them now. Like a wild beast held in captivity too long, I might tolerate my handler, but I will never fully trust them.

The door between my chamber and Lennox's remains firmly closed. No noise has reached me through the wall to indicate he has slept in his room since he departed my bed, except for the knock I refused to answer — something I now regret.

My eyes rake over the half-packed trunk and the pile of discarded sheer dresses I sorted through yesterday, a reminder that I must decide my plans, and soon. My stay in this room ends once the *Bartered Soul* departs, and I feel unmoored without knowing my next step.

Speaking with Siobhan yesterday gives me hope that the island's inhabitants and visitors will be open to having another former priestess as a healer in their midst. No one has accosted me here, and I feel relatively safe for the first time in a long while.

At the House of Starlight, I grew bold and haughty — protected by the secure walls of the brothel, the shadows I lurked in, and my fallen status. I carefully hid any signs that I might still honor the Goddess – my muted sigil and my past merely a novelty there. Men sought to bed a trained priestess for her notoriety, her beauty, her skills of the flesh – not for anything sacred like they would have paid for at the temple. Even so, I wielded my skills at seduction as a shield, pretending I was still the brave young woman I had been in Athene, someone that men bowed to and respected. But outside those walls, on the streets of Artemisia, I remained cloaked in fear — like a stag in a kingswood, always on the lookout for danger.

Having a friend — friends, if I include Siobhan — is novel to me. Sharing tea and pleasantries with these women cracked something within that had been locked away, and it feels easier to imagine a life for myself here. A life no longer hiding or running from my past, or quaking in fear and hiding my brow when soldiers walk past. Here, maybe the weight of these past years would finally lift from my shoulders and mind.

Choosing to focus solely on my choice in whether to stay or not, I don't examine the other feelings that torment me when I think of the future — the hope that Lennox won't leave me. That he won't go find another lonely refugee in an alley or brothel to carry to safety, forgetting about me here burning for him in the warm island sun.

No matter how badly my heart aches at the thought, it's something I can't bring myself to even say out loud, let alone bring up to him when I see him. It's bad enough that he's seen my tears as often as he has already — I won't beg him to love me — and the thought of being that vulnerable frightens me as much as my true identity. I cannot allow anyone to view me as a stray kitten in need of coddling, no matter how much I hope Marie is right about his feelings for me.

It also hasn't escaped my notice that he still hasn't paid me; the coins and credit I've used for my meals and new clothing have been from him, but nothing like the large sum that was promised. The more I sit and allow myself to sink into these thoughts, the more agitated I feel. The tapping of the servant at my door snaps me out of my spiral of emotions, and I rush to open the door for her to drop off the tea service as well as fruit and pastries.

"Excuse me," I stop the girl before she can scoot back out of the room.

"Yes, Missus?" she asks, eyes downcast.

"Do you know of any lodging for rent? Long term?" I ask. As a local, she will surely have an idea of places to go, and I want to be out from under Marie's scrutiny soon.

The girl blushes before asking, "Are you looking for lodging in exchange for...coin...? Or...?" She unobtrusively cuts her eyes to the pile of sheer dresses in the corner, and it dawns on me that the same servants deliver food and clean the rooms — between the sheer gowns on the floor and the state of disarray Lennox and I had left my room in, she must think I am looking for work in a brothel.

"You can look me in the eye, girl," I say firmly. She jerks her head up quickly as her blush deepens.

"I meant no offense, Missus, I just..." She stutters and stands there opening and closing her mouth, unsure what to say next.

"I'm not looking for a brothel — I need a place to live if I am going to stay here." I don't wish to frighten her, but if I am to start over I don't want rumors starting amongst the staff that I am looking for that kind of work again. "Do you know of any?"

"No, Missus...I can ask around though, if you please?"

"That's all right, I will look for myself. Thank you." I dismiss her with a wave of my hand.

Perhaps I haven't fully snapped out of the spiral I was descending after all if I can be so easily riled over someone assuming I am...well, exactly what I am.

———

AS BEFORE, THE DAY PASSES QUICKLY WHILE I TOUR THE TOWN on my own. The brightly painted buildings boost my mood, as do the flowers climbing the sides of the verandahs, which scent the entire town with their perfume instead of the stench of night soil and unwashed bodies so common in

Selennia now. A few signs written in the common tongue advertise rooms to rent and help wanted, beacons of hope for my independence once I make up my mind about what to do next.

While the island is a melting pot of cultures and languages, most of the people who permanently inhabit the island speak the common tongue, as well as a patois of the native language. The common tongue was a part of my studies at the temple, alongside the ancient language of the Goddess, and I'm thankful for the usefulness of those studies as I converse with most of the travelers and inhabitants with ease.

With no set plans for the day, I consider dropping by to chat with Siobhan without Lyra present to glean more about the woman. I pass by the coral building, but she stands at the counter with a customer, so I continue my walk toward the heart of town. The seamstress' door is propped open, and I restrain myself outside the door to keep from checking on my items — bothering her won't get the stitching done any quicker.

The sun begins to sink lower in the sky as I approach the boarding house again, and my pulse increases, sending a thrill through me. Tonight is the full moon. It's almost time to wear my robe and see Lennox again, all in one night. My excitement nearly bubbles over when I enter the courtyard and quickly make my way up the stairs to my room.

The sight of several boxes laying on my bed surprises me when I enter my chamber. The packages are all the same style and shape, but one has two different notes attached under a bow — one sealed in dark green wax, and the other in royal purple.

Lennox and Marie. On one item?

I decide to open these notes and the accompanying box last, pulling one of the others close to unwrap. The sight of several of the items from the seamstress pulls a delighted laugh from my mouth, as I run my fingers over the light, pretty fabric. The second box holds the remainder of my order, and I beam with delight, laying the items out to admire.

The last box sits on the bed, staring at me with the two notes on top. I pause for a moment, chewing on my lip in hesitation, before finally reaching for the notes.

I open Marie's first and find a generic invitation:

YOUR PRESENCE IS REQUESTED AT A HALLOW'S EVE *masquerade held at Madame Marie Benoit's home. Formal attire and masks are required.*

MY HEAD COCKS TO THE SIDE IN CONSIDERATION, BUT PERHAPS Marie will leave me in peace if I attend. I've missed celebrating Hallow's Eve, so the prospect of a celebration overrides my hesitation at being around Marie again.

The second note beckons. I crack the emerald wax to find:

I MADE SURE THIS CAME ALONGSIDE THE INVITE FROM MARIE. Please allow me to escort you to her home tomorrow. I hope you find the enclosed ensemble acceptable, my fierce one. —B

• • •

EXCITEMENT SENDS A SHIVER DOWN MY SPINE AT THE MENTION of an ensemble, and I ungracefully tear into the third box on my bed. Inside is a gown made of midnight and moonbeams.

Black lace mixes with sheer panels of chiffon and solid fine silks in the darkest blue shot with black. If the sun was not shining through the shutters, I would have mistaken the deep navy for solid black. Silver threads course through the fabrics, outlining constellations and moon phases, not unlike the ones that line the edges of my priestess robe.

Laying on top of the dress is a black lace mask to cover my eyes, igniting the memory of the rites I shared with Lennox. The mask is identical to the one I wore that night, and to the one the figurehead of the *Bartered Soul* bears. The outfit is as fierce as it is beautiful — Lennox knows me well. My hands glide over the fabric of the gown once more, heart swelling at the gift, before I set to work preparing myself for the ceremony on the beach this evening.

CHAPTER 32

J ust as the Goddess steps into her chariot to pull the full moon into the sky, I prepare to emerge from the dim interior of my room at twilight. My hand stills on the door handle while I force a steadying breath into my lungs, unsure how the inhabitants are going to react when I descend into the courtyard in my priestess raiment.

All of my nerves are eased when my eyes land on a positively casual Lennox waiting at the foot of the stairs. Wearing a plain linen shirt with the sleeves rolled to his elbows, his sinewy, inked forearms are bared for the world to admire. A full bottle of wine hangs by the neck in his long fingers as he looks upward at the sound of my door closing. The heat from his gaze makes me feel as if my blood is boiling in my veins.

Even relaxed like this, it's easy to see the dangerous pirate that lurks just beneath his skin, and he is waiting for me — the thought makes me eager to be within his grasp. My legs peek from the slit in my robe as I slowly descend the stairs, my eyes never leaving his as I languidly drag a finger over the banister.

"Good evening, my pretty priestess," he greets me, his voice smoky as he drags hungry eyes down my body and back to my face. Maybe he *has* missed me in the past few days.

"Good evening, Captain. Shall we go?" I place my hand in his outstretched palm and walk with my head high through the stares of the courtyard.

We stroll through town, eyes following our every step, as we make our way to the beach. The breath is sucked out of my lungs as we near our destination at the number of bonfires lining the shore between the camps of sailors. Cheers and laughter drift from the groups huddled around the fires. Drunken men and women dance while others sit cross-legged on the sand passing bottles between them. I haven't ventured to the water's edge alone at night to know if this is a usual occurrence, but the air of the evening seems charged with anticipation in a way I assume is special for tonight.

Looking to Lennox for guidance, I follow his direction when he nods toward a larger fire burning on its own. A large man stands off to the side, like a sentinel watching the beach, and I recognize Erik as we approach. I haven't seen him since our dinner at Marie's, so I can't hold back the smile that spreads across my face at the sight of the big man. He returns my smile and bobs his head, far above my own, in greeting.

"Hello, Mistress. I hope you have enjoyed the island so far," Erik says when I get within earshot, his light eyes and heavy torcs reflecting the flames of the bonfire.

"Erik." I nod my head in return. "Yes, it has been lovely so far, with so many beautiful plants and kind people here. I didn't realize men from the ship might come out for the ceremony this evening," I reply, shifting my focus from him to Lennox.

When I look back at Erik, his focus has drifted over my head. His looming height makes this an easy feat, but in the flickering firelight, I can see his cheeks are flushed, and a broad smile spreads across his normally stoic countenance. Lennox is also smiling slightly in the same direction, so I follow their gaze into the darkness to find what has pleased them both.

Where I am a silvered moonbeam, Siobhan is dressed like a ray of sunlight. Her gown is not as revealing as my robe, but it is made similarly – gracefully following her curves with flowing fabric in rich gold silk, the edges trimmed with dark embroidery that I know is a dark blue hue.

Her choice of colors confirms that while I, as one destined to become a high priestess, trained in sacred texts and the physical acts of love, Siobhan was trained in divination and reading the stars. Both of us were also schooled in healing and herblore, but that is not unusual additional knowledge for a priestess to possess.

The jolt of seeing another priestess in her ceremonial colors is nothing compared to the shock I feel at the delight that lights Siobhan's face, followed by Erik scooping her into his arms. He lifts her far from the ground in an embrace while he spins them around on the sand, and presses his mouth to hers. Lennox remains at my side, and a laugh escapes from him as he watches the joy radiating from the two.

"I take it they are acquainted?" I ask, raising my brows in amusement.

He chuckles again. "That they are. It makes Erik very happy to see her doing well after the voyage we spent together to get her here. He's madly in love with her, and she with him. But he knows she is happy with her life and shop here, so he visits when he can, and they live their lives in between."

I smile to cover the ache in my chest. Am I looking at my future? I may not have divination training, but I am a fool to think my future holds hope for anything other than brief visits from Lennox while he carries on with his piracy and life at sea. It's more than I could have hoped for two months ago, so why does it pain me now?

"Andromeda!" Another familiar face calls from the path down to the beach. Lyra races towards us dressed in a light flowing gown that streams behind her as she dashes to our sides by the fire. "I was so afraid I would miss the ceremony!" Flushed and giggling from her flight, she gives both myself and Lennox a hug when she reaches us. "Siobhan looks beautiful!"

"She does indeed," I reply as Siobhan and Erik approach us, their embrace finally broken.

"Good evening, Andromeda," Siobhan says, bowing slightly.

"Good evening, Siobhan," I return the gesture, feeling nostalgia wash over me. "Shall we begin?"

"Let's," Siobhan replies and takes my hand in her own.

Her hands are warm and dry compared to my sweaty palms; she doesn't tremble or falter.

"May I?" Lyra asks shyly, glancing between us.

"Of course, I would be delighted for my protégé to learn the Old Ways," Siobhan replies after I nod my head in consent. The number three is sacred, so the ceremony will feel more powerful with her addition, even though Lyra isn't trained or initiated. Lennox walks to my side and hands me the bottle of wine — an offering.

"For luck, if you please?" he whispers against my ear before he drifts away.

As we approach the fire, other crew members from the ship arrive to create a circle around us and the blaze, the same as they did on the deck a month ago. This feels right — a cycle is ending. Two moons ago, I began this journey when Lennox approached me at the House of Starlight. A month ago, he made me remember who I am. Now, I am preparing to leave that life behind for another rebirth.

With the fire burning, I do not need to light a candle, but I do pour some of the wine in the fire and on the sand — an offering to the Goddess in thanks and prayer. My voice rings out over the night as I begin the prayer chant, Siobhan echoing my words in the correct places, Lyra looking on. We hold hands tightly, and as the chant intensifies, a deep warmth spreads from my chest, through my arms, and into my hands. The same sensation was reawakened on the deck of the *Bartered Soul* at the last ceremony, but this time it's much stronger. Eyes closed, I hear Siobhan's voice stumble slightly before evening out again. Lyra gasps and tightens her grip.

At that, I open my eyes to see what has garnered such a response, and it takes all the power I possess to keep my knees from buckling. Where our hands are connected, a faint glow surrounds them, and Siobhan's brow is illuminated where her sigil rests. I know when her eyes meet mine that my brow looks the same. The only sound on the beach is the crackling fire, the soft lapping waves of the ocean, and our chant — the crew members standing around us are silent — some wide-eyed, some with tears on their cheeks. I shift from my chanting into our song and the entire crew's voices join us, the warmth in my chest intensifying as we sing.

The Goddess has returned to us.

————

SOMETIME LATER, THE CEREMONY ENDS, BUT THE FIRE continues to burn. Waves crash on the shore and bottles are passed around under the bright, white moonlight while I stand to the side, watching contently with Siobhan and Lyra.

"What *was* that?" Lyra asks, the fire illuminating the look of shock she still wears, its reflection on her eyes making them look golden instead of hazel.

"The Goddess, my dear," Siobhan replies with a happy sigh. "The *glow* was a sign an initiate was truly ready to begin her training. After living in the temple for a few years, at a reasonable age, she could go through the rites." Lyra's face is alight with excitement at Siobhan's words, listening raptly. The golden woman smiles as she continues, "Then she honed the skills she was most adept at, was taught general knowledge, and would train in the ability to wield the *glow*."

Siobhan's eyes swing to me at that. "It has been so, so long since I felt Her... truly felt Her. Thank you, Andromeda, for doing this, for reminding us all of our power." Her gaze doesn't settle on only Lyra and me, but also on the female members of the crew and the women who have drifted over from other fires to observe.

"I don't think I had anything to do with it," I reply, even though I admit it has been years for me as well. "It was the three of us together."

Memories of ceremonies in the temple flood my mind, feeling this power amplified so much more when we were all together. During Queen Adelaide's rule, and the rule of the queens who preceded her, the priestesses of the Goddess were not merely instruments of religious dogma — they trained and honed their divine feminine energy to channel magic gifted from the Goddess herself. Rarely was that magic used for sinister purposes — priestesses mainly accessed it to heal, promote growth, or for divination. But the most powerful, usually high priestesses, could use it for defensive purposes. However, all but the strongest of the high priestesses needed support from her sisters to access her maximum power.

All those years ago, I had been an initiate headed for a high priestess ranking. Before my mind can go down the memories of everything that stopped that path for me, Lyra's voice breaks through my thoughts.

"I remember Mother talking about my granny having special powers, but I don't remember seeing her actually *glow*." Lyra still looks awestruck as she inspects her hands.

"That would make sense since your grandmother was a priestess. You and your mother could likely have joined her to boost her power if history had gone differently," Siobhan says sadly, touching the girl on the shoulder gently.

My eyes snap up when I comprehend her words — Lennox told me his mother was a believer, not that she was a *priestess*. My lips part to comment, but Siobhan continues.

"Although the divine feminine energy was accessible to all, it has always been more powerful in females, especially within a family," Siobhan's voice takes on the tone of the many tutors of my past. "The power that a group of uninitiated women could command was minimal compared to the might a group of priestesses used to wield. But it still would have been fearsome for a village to have that much power residing in it."

Her words ring true, and bitterness for our plight fills my soul. That bitterness seeps into my words as I add, "The King knew exactly what he was doing when he ruined our temples and murdered our sisters, scattering us to the winds. Without each other, we are lessened. We can still heal, or divine, or worship on our own. But together, whether in ceremony or in action, we are stronger. We have power inside of each of us, but it is magnified when we work in conjunction."

Siobhan nods sadly, and the two continue to converse in quiet tones, speaking over plans for the future. But I am weighed down by my past.

The raucous laughter and merriment around me fades as I remember the horror that the soldiers inflicted when they invaded our temple. Standing with my bare feet in the soft white sand of Delosia, not overwhelmed with anxiety over a need to flee or cower in fear for the first time in years, is the first time I can fully acknowledge Blackwell's true sin against us. When he murdered my aunt and stole her throne, he dismantled centuries of work women in our country had done. He destroyed the religion that worshiped women as healers, mothers, caregivers, warriors, and scholars. He deemed us sinful for utilizing our sexual energies, whether as an act of love or in ceremony. He declared that we were only worthy if we were married and producing heirs for our husbands, or else earning money on our backs to pay sin taxes to his coffers.

I wonder if Blackwell and those who follow the new religion are even true believers of this new God, or if they merely see it as a source of manipulative power and controlling fear. The hatred and rage that has numbed me for the past eight years blazes within my soul, burning in my chest as hot as the bonfire that kisses my cheeks with its heat.

"Andromeda? Are you well?" Lennox joins me, interrupting my contemplation. The worry written on his face tells me this may not have been the first time he's attempted to pull me from my thoughts.

I shake myself and nod. "I'm fine."

"Would you like to go back to the boarding house?" Concern furrows his brow as he studies my face in the firelight. "Are you sure you're all right?"

"No, I am sure. I'm fine. Thank you."

"That was spectacular," he confides, "I haven't seen the *glow* in such a long time. Not since Celeste was still a maiden frolicking with mother."

"You didn't tell me your mother was a priestess. Why would you lie?" I murmur.

With a small smile, he cuts his eyes to me. "It was more of an omission. By the time Celeste and I came along, she *was* only a believer, not a priestess any longer. She left her temple to wed my father. I'll tell you the tale sometime."

The course of the evening has left me too overwhelmed to be upset with him over a technicality — I wasn't forthcoming about my past or family, either. For the remainder of the night, I remain unmoored and unfocused, intoxicated with the feeling of the Goddess' touch on my skin and the emotions swirling under my flesh.

The breeze is cool and salty on my flushed cheeks, mixing with the smell of the burning wood in the fire and the scent of the strong alcohol that's passed around. Siobhan informs me of a room for let above her shop before she is swept off her feet into Erik's arms again, and both the thought of the room and their love bring a small smile to my face, easing some of the tension that rode me so hard earlier. He kisses her deeply for all to see before they head into the darkness outside the line of the fire's glow. Tonight, they will share other energy besides that gifted by the moonlight.

Lyra laughs with some of the crew, and, as always, she impresses me with her ability to blend in with any group she is faced with. Lennox hovers near me where I sit in the sand, always within earshot, but I cannot bring myself to enjoy the celebratory atmosphere.

Before the ceremony, I felt like a lovesick creature worried over saying goodbye, but now I am reminded of what I truly am — a wrathful beast hidden in the attire of a priestess. My skin feels too tight, and I cannot relinquish my worries long enough to relish in the company of my friends.

Lennox's warm, rough palm slips into my hand as I gaze at the depths of the fire. "Let's go back. You don't look well," he whispers to me, pulling me to my feet. The fire glints off the chain trailing between my breasts as well as the shimmering powder dusting my décolletage and shoulders when I look down at myself.

"All right," I whisper back, and we turn toward the pathway back to town. "Should we retrieve Lyra?"

"No, she will be fine. No one in this town will hurt Marie's granddaughter or my niece, but even if she weren't our relative, they all love her. She is well-guarded." He points to the group where Lyra stands to show me that Pike is guarding her, the older man as watchful as if she were his own blood, while she talks with the other men and women.

CHAPTER 33

We stroll in silence through the streets, and noise drifting from one of the alleys draws my eye to the familiar sounds of pleasure.

"A brothel," Lennox answers my unasked question when he sees where I am looking.

"I hadn't realized there was one near here. I didn't see it when I wandered around earlier." I don't confess that I was hoping to avoid any Houses on the island — I can't bring myself to admit that might be one of my only options for work, should I need it.

"It's secreted away. But don't worry, the women who work there pay rent and keep all the coin they earn. It's run more like a hotel with well-paid security. Marie makes sure none of the women are coerced into working, and that they are all of a suitable age. It's not like back home," he explains. "They're respected for the service they provide and are protected here. If anyone should seek to harm one of them, they receive swift justice."

I shiver at the memory of the justice I served to Crewes, and to the soldier in the tent outside my temple. It wasn't swift.

Lennox wraps an arm around me as we continue our walk in silence, smelling of sea and smoke and wine. Despite the warm night, I find myself sinking into his comforting embrace. As we reach the boarding house he turns me toward him, studying my face in the light from a lamp hanging outside the entrance.

Delicate fingers brush a few loose strands of hair from my forehead as he carefully grazes his thumb over my brow. His touch travels down my face, tracing my cheekbones and my lip, then my neck and collarbone. Each caress sends heat coursing through me straight to my core as I stand still and allow him to survey me. I hold in a smile, comparing the anger I felt the first night he touched and inspected me in the office at the House of Starlight to how differently I feel now.

He rubs his thumb over my lower lip once more, leaning closer to whisper his question. "May I join you in your bed tonight, my pretty priestess?"

"Yes, Captain," I respond, my voice ragged as I restrain myself from groping him on the streets.

We walk through the courtyard, Lennox stopping at the bar to retrieve another bottle of wine on the way, and up the stairs. Propriety is left downstairs as we enter my room together. Two goblets sit on the low table in the center of the room, and he pours sweet wine for each of us, passing me a glass as he sips his own. I drink deeply from the goblet, the warm red liquid soothing the fire in my soul from earlier.

Lennox moves to stand near the armoire where the gown and mask hang for tomorrow's party, inspecting the embroidered trim as he sips his wine. "Do you like the gown? I hoped it wasn't presumptuous to send it to you. I wasn't sure you would accept the invitation to Marie's, but I wanted you to have something just in case."

"It's perfect, thank you. I appreciate the offer to escort me."

I brush past him and surreptitiously close the lid to my trunk where my new pieces from the seamstress are stashed. I don't wish to discuss my uncertain plans for the future just yet, and I fear that looking at them will open the door to questions.

"It's my honor to escort you."

When he turns to face me, his deep green eyes are alight with wine and emotion. The space between us disappears as Lennox strides toward me, and I tremble with the anticipation of his touch. His warm hand wraps behind my head, placing the wine glass he holds in the other on my vanity before slanting his mouth against mine. I ache with desire as he presses my lower back, pushing our bodies flush together while he runs his tongue against mine.

I still comically cling to my wine, unsure what to do with the goblet, while my free hand grips the front of his shirt. I feel him smile against my mouth before looking at my hand. He takes the glass from me and drinks it down, placing the empty glass next to his, and returns to me. Before he can encircle me in his arms again, I slip free of his grasp, dancing delicately across the floor like a bird flitting from a cat, a smirk on my mouth at his look of confusion.

In the middle of the room, I freeze where I stand and meet his eyes before I slowly, teasingly, lower one shoulder of my robe off my arm. His eyes watch my hands, and he begins to prowl toward me, a sensual predator stalking his prey. The other shoulder drops and my robe slips down, exposing my peaked breasts and flat stomach. He reaches me as the garment falls to the floor, a puddle of moonbeams made cloth at my feet, standing on display for him in nothing but my jewelry and gold shimmer as he walks around me.

When he returns to face me, he gently rubs the pad of his thumb over my hard nipple, and I exhale sharply at the touch. Wetness pools between my thighs with the anticipation of his touch, and my legs feel loose beneath me. My fingers dig into the fabric of his waistband and slowly unbutton his pants, the tension between us luxuriously thick. Glancing up through my lashes, I watch as he bites his lower lip, eyes focused on my hands working on his buttons. When they're freed, I pull his shirt over his head, then push his pants down. His eyes are hungry, taking in all of my nakedness in front of him as he steps from his boots and pants while I explore his firm chest and stomach with my hands and mouth.

Placing my palm flat on his chest, I push him gently to one of the chairs near the low table until he sits. His mouth closes over one of my nipples as I stand between his thighs, and a gasp of pleasure leaves me of its own volition. His mouth leaves my skin momentarily as he smiles up at me, rewarding the breathy sound by running his hand up my thigh, slipping a finger into the wetness he finds there, before capturing my moan with a fevered kiss.

Impatient, I crave the distraction his body offers me. Removing his hand from me, I step back, push his legs together, then sit astride his lap. With a shift of my hips, I raise up slightly before sliding over his hard length, gripping the back of the chair as I sink down fully.

"Oh, *fuck*," he whispers huskily into my loose hair as I settle on him and begin to move, whimpering at the fullness of our joining.

My hips rock, the friction between us delicious, as I capture his mouth with mine. Our tongues brush against one another, the sweet wine still lingering on our mouths, sending heat pulsing through my core. Release tightens in my belly with every move while Lennox's hands clutch my hips.

"Look at me," he whispers, breaking our kiss, dark eyes searching my face.

Emotion overflows in his gaze, and my heart skips a beat while I wonder what truth is reflecting in my own. It only takes a few more moments before I reach the edge and tumble over, pleasure pulsing through me as I stifle my cry against his shoulder. With a satisfied growl, he grips my hips harder, grinding me against him before finishing soon after me.

Chests heaving in tandem, Lennox curls over me, his arms laced around my waist as he holds me to his bare chest, tenderly kissing my forehead. With a sigh, I pull back slightly so I can look at him, kissing his soft mouth gently before resting my forehead against his.

"To the Goddess," I whisper.

Lennox smiles as he runs his hands down my hair and

back a few times. "To the Goddess," he replies softly before I pull away and stand.

As I walk toward the basin of clean water and the clean shift laid out on my vanity stool, I turn to glance at him over my shoulder.

"Will you stay with me tonight?"

His smile is sweet as he nods his agreement.

CHAPTER 34

Taking advantage of the cooler morning temperatures, I meander down the gritty streets toward the apothecary shop in the early morning glow. The milder temperature means I'm not soaked with sweat like I will be in a few hours, and I am grateful for the respite — it has become increasingly clear to me that getting used to the strong sun and humid heat will take longer than the week I have been here.

I'd hastily dressed and readied myself, leaving Lennox at the boarding house to attend to his own affairs, and slipped out the front door before Lyra came poking around. I will see them both this evening for Marie's event, but I need to be alone with my thoughts for a bit.

Hopefully, I can catch Siobhan alone before customers start trickling through her doors as I am eager to discuss the ceremony from last night. I was surprised this morning to find that my sigil was still slightly darker than it was before the ceremony — a remnant of the *glow* — and curiosity has me wondering if Siobhan has experienced the same effect.

For eight years, it has only seemed to fade into my skin — the crescent-shaped mark dimming significantly once I fled the temple and ceased worshiping with others, even though I continued to do so quietly alone.

Disappointment greets me when I reach the shop and find a note tacked to the cheerful green door:

WILL OPEN AROUND NOON — *I AM HARVESTING IN THE GARDEN. If you require urgent attention, please visit me there. – Siobhan*

THE GARDEN. I HAVE NO IDEA WHERE TO BEGIN TO FIND A garden, but if she has instructed customers to find her there, I assume it must be well known and not terribly far. A woman walks past me on her way to the market, so I stop her to inquire after Siobhan.

"Oh yes, Mistress! Miss Siobhan grows a lovely garden just outside of town. If you follow the road straight, you can't miss it. It's just to the right once you pass the last buildings," the woman instructs me, pointing her finger in the correct direction.

"Thank you for your guidance," I say, looking in the direction she's pointed.

"Of course, Mistress." She dips into a small curtsey and continues in the opposite direction from me. The courtesy takes me aback briefly, and I blink at her retreating form a few times before continuing on my way.

The instructions are easy to follow, and I would have stumbled upon the garden on my own if I had continued my exploration down the road. A neat wooden fence wraps around the perimeter, more to denote the edges than to keep things out since it isn't solid. The gaps in the fencing allow me to see all of the plants within, regardless of their varying heights.

Vegetables, as well as medicinal plants and herbs, flourish in the tilled soil. Nearby trees are covered in whimsical pink puffballs that sway in the gentle morning breeze. A vining plant with delicate purple flowers covers one side of the fence, wrapping me in the sweetest scent when I bend to inspect their unique blooms. My eyes rove over the greenery and pops of color as I look for Siobhan, landing on a tall, handsome sentry who stands distracted near the far fence line. Erik.

"My, what an interesting scarecrow," I tease as I approach the fence. Erik's head jerks up from where it was directed and two rows of plants rustle before Siobhan's copper head pops up above them, bearing fruit in hand. Her smile is genuine and warm as her gaze settles on me.

"Hello, Sister!" Siobhan calls, handing the fruit to Erik to wipe her hands on the apron she wears over her linen skirt.

"Good morning! I hope I'm not interrupting," I respond before I step through the little gate into the lush and tidy space.

"Of course not. I am pleased to see you! Welcome to my garden," she says as she holds her hands out gesturing around at the space.

"It's lovely. I have never had much luck growing my own herbs, but it seems the climate here agrees with it." My eyes continue to soak up the different plants and flowers as I approach the couple through the rows.

While I'd always relished my time in the hothouse with

my aunt, nurturing gardens had not been a part of my training at the temple. My herbal knowledge was focused on their uses in healing, not bringing them forth. By the time I made it to the House of Starlight, where skills in the cultivation of healing plants would have greatly benefitted me and the other women living there, it was too late to learn. The soil outside of Artemisia was too rocky to sustain tender plants, and the city was so crowded with cobble-stones and sooty buildings that there was no place to attempt their growth.

"It's wonderful to be able to nurture the medicine from the start, but I am lucky to get what I can't grow from the Captain when he stops on Delosia. Erik usually takes a list for me, and if they come across it on ships or at ports, they get it for me." Siobhan beams at the large man, who still holds the fruit she handed him. His stern face is soft in her presence and he returns the expression.

"Will the two of you be attending the Hallow's Eve party at Marie's this evening?" I venture to ask. It would be nice to have someone to talk to so I can avoid Marie's clutches.

"No." Siobhan's happy expression only falters for a moment, but in that moment, I feel her sadness at being separated from him. "Unfortunately, Erik must ready the ship for their departure. He's going to have dinner with me first, then complete his duties in the late hours."

Erik casts his eyes to his feet, sparing a glance at Siobhan, his disappointment palpable. The reminder of the men's impending departure sits heavy on my heart and I wonder if my own countenance reflects the same feelings. I've been avoiding the reality that my time with Lennox is nearing an end and don't want to look too closely at my emotions while I am with Erik and Siobhan. Fearing my sadness may be etched on my face, I bite the inside of my cheek to distract myself, tucking the feeling into the same space I have been storing them for years. A space that might not be able to hold many more hurts.

"I see. Well, at least you will have a final meal together in private. Is there anything I can assist you with here or at the shop?" I change the subject, moving to the topic that brought me to visit in the first place.

"Yes! That would be wonderful." Siobhan grins, pulling an extra pair of leather gloves from her apron and passing them to me. "Erik needs to meet with the shipwright in town and check in with the crew soon, so he was about to leave. An extra set of hands is always appreciated. I can show you some of the native species and explain their uses while you are here since they will be unfamiliar to you."

As I pull the soft gloves on, she takes the fruit from Erik and places them in a basket before pulling him down for a kiss, his long dark braid mingling with her red curls. He cups her face gently as they break apart, and turns to walk back into the town with a quiet wave to me.

"A man of few words, that one," I mutter to Siobhan.

"He has lots of words, he just uses them wisely." She wistfully smiles at his back, then takes my gloved hands in her own. "Last night was amazing, I haven't felt Goddess energy like that since before the King came to my temple. Thank you for inviting me to join you."

"I feel the same way. I can't help but wonder what would happen if we were able to gather more lost sisters, or find new ones, like Lyra. What power would we hold then?"

"At the rate Lennox brings them, it might not take long to find more," Siobhan responds, releasing me and turning to pick up a pair of shears.

"What do you mean?" I ask. I know Lennox has saved some girls from the Houses and taught them sailing or dropped them off at safe ports, but we haven't discussed his operation in detail.

"Has he not told you? I thought you would know everything after seeing the two of you together." Siobhan hesitates as if she doesn't know whether this is her story to tell, her smooth brow pulling together in a slight furrow, but continues, "As you heard yesterday, Captain Lennox's mother was a priestess. She left the temple when she fell in love with his father so she could marry him.

"When William and his sister were growing up, she taught them both to worship the Goddess. His father passed away when William was young, but I can tell his mother was always a strong force in their family based on how he spoke about her. Apparently, his sister was destined for the temple, but she fell in love early with Lyra's father and married young instead.

"William told me he participated in the rites when he was a young man..." Her voice trails off while her eyes flicker over my face in recognition and mild surprise. "With...you...?" she breathes.

I can only nod in answer, my cheeks unexpectedly burning.

"Now I know why you're familiar!" she exclaims. "I spent days standing at the bow of the *Bartered Soul* in prayer with that figurehead. She was a kindred spirit for me when I was lost."

Her confession makes me swallow the bitter tears that threaten to fall at her words — I know about being lost. I spent what seems like an eternity lost myself, before making my way to the House of Starlight and then pulling myself back into the form I exist in now. Although it is a sad memory, it brings me joy to know I was able to soothe Siobhan during her time on the ship, even if it was merely my likeness doing so.

"I don't understand what this has to do with other priestesses?" I admit. I am eager to know more about Lennox, but cannot understand what his backstory has to do with others like me.

"Oh, yes, well... I'm sure he told you he was pressed into service on one of Blackwell's ships when he was away from his village? It was shortly after the fighting started, and he wasn't able to escape them. They forced him to labor on their ship while other men fighting for the King murdered his family just because of his mother's past.

"Lyra's father sent Celeste and Lyra away when he heard the King's army was on the move. His mother, Marie, had fled earlier to set up a home for them all, but things didn't work out as planned. Lyra's father and Lennox's mother never made it to Artemisia. When he found out, William went wild.

"He killed the Captain of the ship while it was under attack by pirates, then joined them until he could get back home. That's how he met Erik. When he got to his village, he saw what they did to his mother and the nearby temple, and it drove him mad. Erik told me Lennox was a beast afterward.

"Any man wearing Blackwell's colors, or preaching the new religion, was cut down. From that point on, he sought out former priestesses to rescue, and spirited them away. After a few years, our number dwindled, so many of us were..."

"I know..." I won't make her speak the words: *burned, beaten, broken.*

"He began working with Celeste to find young girls in the Houses that wanted to escape. I'm sure you know they're targeted for their purity — these men who preach about women being sinful sure seem interested in ruining that which they see as pure," Siobhan snarls the last words and my stomach churns. I have seen how so-called "Godly men" act in the presence of beautiful girls, and I know why she is bitter.

She continues, "He would *buy* them, make it seem like he was deranged and evil. That he planned to use them for his twisted pleasure and then discard them. It solidified people's fear of him, making them believe in his cruelty while allowing him to smuggle the girls to safe places across the sea, or to teach them to sail on his ship dressed as men.

"I think a few may have wanted to go back home, but they knew they had to remain silent about their experience, to protect the others, so Lennox could continue his work. The opportunities for young women are endless if they are offered an escape from bondage, but no one would fear a pirate who was saving women, would they?"

"No, they would see him as weak," I nod in understanding. "He needs to be a fearful legend, a true monster of the depths." His ruse had worked well. Almost too well. Had I, myself, not expected him and his crew to use me and discard me the day he *purchased* me?

"And he is, to those who deserve his wrath. I saw what he is capable of on my voyage here." She shudders at the memory. "He isn't someone I would want to trifle with, even though I trust him with my own safety."

Siobhan's eyes are haunted. I am certain she witnessed something similar to the attack I was present for, but where she was appalled, I was entranced by Lennox's brutality. It matches my own.

"I'm glad he found you finally," she says, glancing at me from the side of her eye.

"What do you mean?"

"He spoke to me of a priestess from the Western coast with coal-black hair, sapphire eyes, and flesh as white as a pearl. It was one of the first things he asked me about when he rescued me and saw what I was. Whether I was from the temple nearby; if I had a sister such as you. He has looked for you since the beginning," Siobhan confides quietly, cutting her eyes to look at me again. "His heart has been yours since you took it at the rites years ago."

My heart stutters in my chest and my eyes burn. I look up toward the sun, hoping I can blame the moisture in my eyes on the bright rays.

"I told him he would find you. I saw it when I pulled cards for him. I hope you don't mind that I did a reading for you as well?" she cautiously adds.

"Excuse me?" I look up from pulling a stray weed from the bed I stand over.

"I did a reading — well, I scried for a sign actually," she admits. "I'm trained in divination, I'm sure you knew that?"

"I did, but I confess I didn't learn much about the art beyond the very basics," I confide.

"I saw such sadness in you when you came to the shop with Lyra. I know you have suffered great loss, but I could feel that you have so much spirit. I just had to pry a bit." She twists her hands together as though she is embarrassed at having inquired about me from the universe.

"I usually get feelings about people, and since you were asking about work, I wanted to see if I could glean anything from my crystal. I see such great things for you, but so much hardship.

"It isn't clear pictures or anything, but I saw blood and a crown, a dagger striking out, flowers falling. So much power. I'm not sure if it was your past or a glimpse of your future. But, if you stay here with me I can't imagine it is your future... unless war is brought here."

She swallows hard at the admission, and I can understand her nervousness — but a crown, and blood, and flowers? That sounds like my aunt, not me. Plus, I couldn't possibly bring war here. No one knows who I am.

Except they do.

"Are you all right?" Siobhan asks, pausing in her work to study my face. "I know some people are leery of what I see."

"Yes, I'm fine. I just... well, I hoped that I could live out a quiet life here. That this was the end of my journeying. Helping in your shop, living in a room of my own, that's all

I want now. I have no power. No grand plans, or intention of causing a war," I explain.

"Sometimes the universe doesn't care about our plans, Andromeda," she mutters gently before returning to her weeding.

The conversation turns to lighter topics after her confession. We pull wayward weeds in companionable silence for a while, Siobhan inserting commentary on plants and their uses as we move along the rows. The vegetables she grows for herself and her neighbors, in addition to many of the herbs for her remedies. On our walk back to town, she points out a path that leads to the jungle beyond where she forages for other useful plants and tropical fruit.

"Will you be staying, then?" Siobhan asks as we unpack the full baskets from the garden in her small kitchen workspace.

"I should get back," I answer. "I'll have tea at the boarding house before I have to ready myself for Marie's tonight."

"No. I mean on the island. I'm happy to have you share my home, but I wasn't sure if you would be staying?"

"I don't see many other options. I can't just sail off on my own. If I'm to make a life for myself, this seems like the place to do so. I have at least two people I can call friends here and an opportunity that doesn't require me to lay on my back for a living." I clench my jaw as I trail off. *This is what I came here to discuss, why am I distressed at the change in topic?*

"Of course." Siobhan gives me a knowing look. My guard has fallen by the wayside and my inner turmoil is evident. "We can confirm everything tomorrow after the men set sail. I can help you get everything over here from your room. Lyra can help and it will keep us both occupied."

I bid farewell to Siobhan as she begins hanging herbs and bundling food for her neighbors, stepping out onto the bustling sidewalk. The streets are crowded with foot traffic and a few small wagons of people purchasing supplies and food from the marketplace, but they are all empty faces as I walk back to the boarding house engulfed in my thoughts, finally facing the reality that this is my final night with Lennox.

CHAPTER 35

The servants filled the tub in my bathing chamber with water that's so hot my flesh turns pink as soon as I step in it. It's been a long time since I attended anything as grand as I am anticipating this evening to be, so I add oils and herbs to perfume my skin, and soap my body and hair in preparation for the night.

The ripple of excitement coursing through me at the opportunity to celebrate Hallow's Eve publicly again can't be stifled by the fact that this is my last night with Lennox. Perhaps I can let myself imagine, just for one night, that I am a noblewoman again, and that we have some sort of normal future to enjoy together. Any feeling akin to hope has been smothered for so long that it makes me slightly anxious to even pretend. Nevertheless, I scrub until my skin is tender — due in equal parts to the harsh texture of the sponge and the scalding water. My breath catches as I sluice cool clean water over me to rinse any remaining soap from my body, gooseflesh pebbling across me.

The soft linen towel waiting for me soothes the sting

from the sponge and I dry quickly, wrapping my long hair in the fabric to squeeze any lingering liquid from the strands. The gown Lennox sent me stills hangs on the front of the armoire. I stand bare in the briny breeze admiring it, touching the embroidery delicately in admiration of the seamstress' skill — this must have taken weeks to create. I have no idea how he had it made in such a short time.

My hands still in their exploration — *when had he had this made?* I wonder. Siobhan's tale earlier made it seem like he has been searching for me for years, and I find myself sifting through my memories for the first time I saw him sweep through the doors of the House of Starlight.

It must have been a few years ago that he first entered the salon, when a prickle of knowing had crept up my spine at the sight of him. At that time, rumors of his cruel exploits preceded him, so I made sure to stay far away from the man, afraid of anyone known to trade in flesh on the sea. Now, I understand that he was visiting his sister, checking on his niece, and maybe, just maybe, checking in on me, too.

I let the thought simmer in my mind, but can't understand why he wouldn't have approached me immediately if he knew me then. There are still so many unanswered questions about him, and we only have tonight, at least until he returns to Delosia again.

Sitting at my vanity, I sip a cup of tea while my hair dries, adding a small ring of kohl around my eyes and lightly staining my lips. The lace mask will hide most of my face for the night, so heavy cosmetics aren't needed — a relief after wearing them so often in the House of Starlight. I pin my clean tresses into a braided chignon to better show off my neck and the deep-vee at the front and back of the gown, then add my ceremonial body chain which will show in the front vee. Carefully, I slip into my finery, savoring the glide of the silk on my skin, and the glint of the embroidery in the golden light that seeps through my open shutters.

I look like royalty with my full skirts of sheer fabric. The silver embroidery makes me think of shooting stars as the fabric rustles with my movements. All I am missing is a crown, but I am not presumptuous enough to wear my golden ceremonial circlet. The bodice is snug enough to keep my breasts held in place despite its low neckline, but I will need to be mindful of my movements just to be certain. It's elegant, but risqué enough for me to feel like a dark goddess — not a princess. Dangerous and free, like the she-wolf Lennox always names me.

As I tie the black lace mask over my eyes to complete my ensemble, there is a tap at my door.

"Yes?" I call out, looking in the long mirror on the front of the armoire to admire a full view of myself.

"Are you ready?" the Captain's deep voice rumbles through the wooden door. My heart rate increases and a flush of color blooms on my chest at the sound of him.

I open the door a moment later, "Yes, I am."

His eyes travel from my face, gliding down the length of my body. Slowly, he returns them to meet my eyes, and suddenly, it's he who is the feral one. A devastating grin turns up the corners of his mouth, and heat pools in my belly at that look, making me want to forget about the party and let that wicked mouth do whatever it wills for our last night together. Instead, I simply raise a brow and return his smile.

Tonight, he is finely attired in a black coat trimmed in silver embroidery so similar to that on my dress that there is no mistaking we are a matched set. A masculine version of the mask I wear is secured to his face, causing the memory of the rites to flash in my mind at the sight. I can't believe I hadn't recognized him immediately. There is no mistaking his identity now, and the memory of those gentle caresses in the moonlight only fuels my need for him.

"Andromeda, you look... delicious," he whispers to me as I step from my room and lock the door.

"Thank you, Captain. Perhaps you can have me for dessert," I respond, brushing against him lightly as I head to the stairs.

He chuckles darkly behind me as he follows me down the stairs into the courtyard. At the base of the stairs, Lyra waits in a gold gown and mask, dark curls in a halo around her pretty face. Lennox takes one of us on each arm to escort us to Marie's.

OTHER GUESTS WAIT TO FILE IN THE OPEN DOOR AT MARIE'S when we arrive, so we stand in line to walk up the stairs to the verandah in silence. While everyone is beautifully attired in their finery, the masks chill me, despite the heat of the night. Hallow's Eve is a night of magic and mystery, when the veil to the afterlife is thin. After all the memories of my aunt resurfacing, the thought of being closer to the dead makes me shudder; I do not want to find any more surprises awaiting me in this house.

As we enter the parlor, my eyes are immediately pulled

to Marie, garbed in a violent purple gown fit for a queen — which, on this island, she is close to being. She greets Lyra with a tight hug and grips my hand with both of hers before kissing my knuckles. I swallow both my nerves and the bile rising in my throat to gracefully accept the greeting instead of pulling away; surely she doesn't plan to reveal me tonight.

"Good evening, my dear," Marie says to me. "You look beautiful."

"Thank you, Marie. You look lovely tonight as well. Everything looks so festive. Are your events always so grand?" I ask, my eyes searching her face for any indication of betrayal.

"We usually celebrate a bit more quietly, but it isn't every day that my granddaughter is returned to me. I have missed her while we were apart for so long." Marie doesn't show any signs that she has any other purpose for this party than the holiday and Lyra's debut to the island, but I am still wary and unable to take her at her word enough to relax fully.

I accept a glass of wine from a servant, hoping it will soothe my nerves. Lyra and Lennox follow my lead, each plucking a glass from the tray as the servant passes. Lyra is quickly swept into conversation with a lovely couple in matching white masks as she stands with her grandmother, while Lennox and I escape to a dim corner.

"Would it be rude if we slipped away and just spent the evening in bed?" the Captain breathes against my ear as we stand close together.

"Probably — but you're a pirate. Aren't you allowed to have poor manners?" I rasp back, running my hand over his dark coat, feeling his hard chest beneath as he presses closer.

I can't resist standing on my tiptoes to brush a kiss against his neck and his throaty gasp sends a tingle through me, making my heart flutter and my belly heat. He presses a hand against my lower back and pulls me toward him, causing me to melt into him in the darkness. I pull back slightly so I can meet his eyes, and it feels like time has stopped as we stare at one another. His dark eyes flicker down to my mouth, but as we lean toward one another, a voice cuts through the din of the revelers.

"Lennox! Captain Lennox! William, where the hell are you, man?" a deep voice echoes over the din of the party.

We pull apart, and Lennox steps from our dim sanctuary, sighing in irritation as he straightens the front of his coat. "Yes, Jackson," he calls out. Only the faintest hint of annoyance tinges his tone, making me smile at his restraint as I hold in a laugh. The flamboyantly dressed Captain Jackson is searching the crowd, clearly the one who is calling for Lennox.

"Ah, William, there you are! A moment if you can spare it?" Jackson looks between Lennox and me in our dark corner, a slow smile spreading across his ruddy face. I haven't had much need to speak with the gaudy man, but his jovial tone and bright clothing put me at ease as they mask the violence he no doubt administers and condones in his role as Captain of the *Selkie's Tears*.

"I'll be back in a moment," Lennox leans over and whispers close, sending a shiver over my heated skin. I simply incline my head in understanding, and linger, observing the partygoers. It isn't long before music begins playing, encouraging some of the couples to move to the center of the cleared room to dance. I sip my wine and watch wistfully, remembering nights hidden away in alcoves watching courtiers dance at the palace for holidays when I was at the castle with my aunt. I was always too young to partake in the balls and had departed for the temple by the time I was old enough to join.

"Mistress, would you care to dance?"

I'm so lost in my memories, and the wine, that I didn't pay attention to the man approaching me in my dark corner. His sensual voice startles me at its close proximity. I recognize him from the dinner at Marie's, but cannot immediately remember his name.

Giving a pleasant smile to mask my uncertainty, I hastily shuffle through the names of the men from that night as he stands looking at me expectantly. A gold tooth glints from beneath his gold mask when he smiles and extends his hand to take mine. The mask and the tooth coordinate with the heavy red and gold brocade coat he wears despite the warmth of the night. Eyes so dark they're almost black rake over my body and I remember — Mario di Micios.

"Captain... di Micios?" I ask, testing the name in case I have remembered wrong.

"Ah, you remember me! Wonderful." He smiles broadly again, kissing my knuckles as Marie did. While her gesture felt like respect, his sends a tingle of unease through my hand, and I have to fight the urge to snatch it back from him too quickly.

"I do, Captain. How are you this evening?" I ask

politely, sipping from my goblet and looking for Lennox in the crowd.

"Please, call me Mario, Mistress Andromeda. I ask again — will you dance with me?" he persists, extending his hand to me once again.

I have no excuse readied to deny him. Lennox mentioned that most of the captains have some form of truce. I don't wish to upset the balance by being discourteous, nor should I have anything to fear. So, despite my hesitance, I set my glass down and place my hand lightly in his, allowing him to lead me onto the dance floor. The band is playing a slow song, and we fall in step easily with the other dancers. Di Micios places his hand at a respectful place on my waist, while I manage to keep our bodies at a reasonable distance apart as we sway to the song.

"So, Mistress, will you be staying on the island, or are you returning to Lennox's service?" Mario asks after a few moments of silence.

"His *service*?" I ask, taken aback at the phrasing, my feet falling out of step for a moment before I catch back up to the tempo.

"Yes. I wasn't sure if you would be joining the women at the local House or if you were returning to service him on his ship. You were purchased for his bed, correct?" he asks with another golden smile. "I hoped you might be staying on the island longer, as I would... *very much* enjoy your company myself," he explains, leering down at me.

My blood chills at the insinuation. Di Micios isn't wrong in his assumption about my relationship with Lennox — at least not in the way it started — but the reminder of the life I am escaping makes my stomach churn. I pull away from his grip and bump into another couple. They grumble their displeasure at my clumsiness, but I don't move back toward my partner — I want to keep space between the Tomcat and myself.

"I'm not certain of my plans yet, but none of them include bedding *you*, Captain," I hiss at him as he reaches for me again.

"I meant no offense! I merely find you to be extremely attractive and I only thought — " he continues, as if he cannot understand how I could be upset at the suggestion.

"Whatever you meant, I am not just a whore to be passed around between captains," I interrupt coldly, trying to keep my voice low.

Despite my attempt to keep our conversation quiet, mutters and curious stares from the other guests surround us. Di Micios reaches for my arm again, and as I step back in another retreat, trying to avoid the other bodies floating around me, a black-clad arm appears from the crowd to grip the Captain's wrist. He blanches at the contact and steps away from me in haste, trying to pull away from the fingers digging into his arm and the man they belong to.

"What the fuck did you do to her?" Lennox's voice is a low growl as he pulls di Micios near, tightening his grasp.

"I only asked her of her plans after you leave!" di Micios hastily explains. "I wasn't sure if you'd bought her for the next voyage, or — "

He never finishes his statement. Lennox jerks him off the ground by the front of his shirt and slams him into the wall of the darkened corner where we shared soft whispers and gentle caresses earlier.

"She isn't bought or owned by anyone, you piece of shit.

She isn't some whore for you to sniff after like a fucking cat in heat. Touch her again in my presence and I'll cut off your hands." Lennox trembles with fury as he continues to grip di Micios' shirtfront. "Try anything when I'm gone and I won't have to intervene. She can take care of it herself. Surely you heard what she did to Crewes on the way here?" Lennox snarls. Di Micios' olive skin pales as his eyes rake over me, the fear in his eyes clear.

"Now apologize, and get the fuck out of our sight." Lennox releases the man roughly. Di Micios stumbles as he grabs at his rumpled shirtfront to straighten it, all hint of attraction drowned by Lennox's threats. Other guests openly stare at us now as di Micios bows curtly to me.

"Apologies, Mistress. I meant no harm to you," di Micios mutters before retreating from us. He pushes through the crowd angrily and out the door before Marie can speak to him. She cuts her eyes at Lennox and shakes her head with a frown, but Lennox doesn't seem to pay any heed to her disapproval. He takes my hand in his and roughly pulls me through the crowd.

As we pass Marie and Lyra, he asks, "Your office?"

Marie nods her head in response, a ghost of a smile on her full lips.

CHAPTER 36

I stumble slightly as Lennox tugs me through the door to Marie's office, the same books and shelves lining the space as before. He releases my hand as he turns to lock the door behind us, and the propulsion of our movements makes me stagger. Pausing for a moment, he still faces the door, one hand on the lock, the other flat against the wooden surface next to where he rests his forehead. I watch as he fights to collect himself, but when he turns to look at me, he is still breathing rapidly, and his eyes are stormy.

"Did he hurt you?" he asks, running his gaze over my body.

"No, I'm fine." I, too, am breathing hard at the intensity of the emotions radiating between us and can barely whisper my response. "What *was* that back there?"

Even if it makes my cheeks flush with pleasure at Lennox's response to di Micios' unwanted attention, I am slightly taken aback at the fierceness in his attitude toward the other captain.

"I just —" he starts, then takes a shuddering breath. "I

can't stand the thought of anyone else touching you, or hurting you again." His voice is a harsh rasp in the quiet of the office, like a confession to the Goddess.

"I can't either," I murmur back, taking a few tentative steps toward him. His breath still comes in rapid pants, so I approach like I would a wounded beast, nervous I might scare him away. This is the first time I have seen him show any true emotion in public. He is usually unreadable and relaxed in a crowd; seeing him drop the carefully cultivated facade makes me want to soothe him.

I reach my hand up to cup his cheek, and he covers my hand with his own before meeting my gaze through our masks and leaning his face deeper into my palm. The tension between us is as thick as the harbor fogs back home, the familiar flutter in my chest evolves into wild beats as we study one another. Lennox brings his other arm around my back and pulls me closer, holding me firmly against him while I rest my cheek and free hand on his chest. For a few moments, we simply stand there, motionless in each other's arms, our breaths slowing to match one another's as I listen to the steady thump of his heart.

When I glance back up at him, desire burns in his eyes, and, even though we are at a party, standing in the private office of the leader of the island, I raise my mouth to brush against his. That small touch ignites the spark that always dances between us. His hand clutches the fabric at my lower back and the other clasps the back of my neck as he deepens our kiss. I throw caution to the wind and melt against his body, cupping the other side of his face with my hand. He makes a noise in the back of his throat and nips at my lip while we kiss, causing a gasp to escape from me in the quiet.

That gasp is all it takes for him to back me against the wall of bookshelves that line the office, pinning me against them as he brushes his tongue against mine. Suddenly, his hands are at my hips, and he lifts me against the shelving, my dress pushed up and my legs exposed. I wrap them around his waist and grab his shoulders, digging my fingers into the fabric of his coat as he kisses my neck and throat. I can feel his hardness pressing against me and I rub against him, groaning as he grips my bare skin.

"Billy," I breathe as his mouth grazes my throat. I can feel his lips quirk into a smile at his name.

Balanced there between him and the shelving, he releases me with one hand and pulls at the top of my dress, freeing one of my breasts from the low bodice. He pulls my nipple into his mouth, sucking and biting while I bite my lip to keep from moaning — I don't think either of us necessarily wants *this* entire house to hear what we are doing. When he returns to my mouth, I run my hands down his chest and stomach to the buttons of his breeches and quickly unbutton them, freeing him without pushing the fabric down to his knees. He still supports my weight as he kisses me, and I pull up the rest of my dress to expose myself to him.

Quickly, I guide him to my entrance and we slide together, kissing to mask the sounds of our shared pleasure. The wooden shelves bite into my back, likely leaving red marks on my skin from the pressure, and the smell of leather and parchment surrounds me, but I don't care where I am, or what priceless books or artwork I might be pressed against. All I can focus on is my last night with Lennox as he rests his face against the space where my neck and shoulder meet, each thrust bringing me closer to release as he kisses my flushed skin.

I press my mouth against his shoulder, biting on the material of his coat as I tumble over the edge, trying to quiet my cry of pleasure. He presses his mouth against mine, stifling his own moan as he comes soon after. We stand there, locked in our embrace, savoring the moment of closeness before he lowers me to my feet.

WE RETURN TO THE PARTY AFTER TAKING TEN MINUTES OR SO to straighten ourselves, allowing the flush on my chest and neck to fade from where his stubble and kisses graced them. Most of the guests haven't taken note of our absence, too entranced by the ambiance of Marie's hospitality, but Marie's sharp gaze finds us, and her mouth quirks as she rolls her eyes to the heavens. I don't know why my face burns at her acknowledgment, but I smile demurely down at my hands as we walk past.

"I hope I haven't caused any problems between you and the other captains," I murmur to Lennox when I notice some of the other men from the dinner that first night glancing at us and speaking quietly to one another.

"No, the Tomcat couldn't resist trying. The others all understand the boundaries. They aren't as prone to whip their dicks out as di Micios. He thought he was being sly since he knows I'm leaving tomorrow. I've heard rumors in town of his desire for *Lennox's Priestess*," he says, irritation coloring his words. Especially the final ones.

"Even so, I know you mentioned you are all sometimes allies. I don't want to get in the way of business."

"Fuck di Micios. You're more important than any business I might have with him, or any of the others," he soothes me with his pretty words, rubbing his thumb against my hand where we clasp them together. "My business here is done tonight, I think. May I escort you to the boarding house, or do you wish to stay?"

"No, I'm ready to leave," I answer with relief, and we quietly make our way to bid farewell to our hostess. I assume I will see Lyra and Marie tomorrow, but we stop to speak with the two women before we leave out of courtesy. They're backlit by a banquet of candles lining the hallway and are luminous in the warm glow.

"Thank you for a lovely evening, Marie." Lennox bows as he kisses the older woman's hand. Her warm brown eyes dance with amusement at his statement.

"Oh, you're quite welcome. I hope you two didn't leave any messes for me in my office," she replies looking between us pointedly. "It sounded like a bit of a commotion." I blush under her scrutiny — when did I become a blushing flower?

"I will see you both tomorrow," I say glancing between the two women.

Marie nods in agreement, and I curtsey slightly to her in respect, receiving a slight dip of her chin in response. Lyra hugs me goodnight before Lennox and I turn to head into the night. Glancing over my shoulder as we reach the door, I hope Lyra will allow herself to have a bit of fun tonight, even though I'm sure the memory of Charlie's loss is likely on her mind, both because tonight is a night to remember the dead, and as she is forced to watch lovers twirl on the dancefloor, sneaking kisses in darkened corners.

Hand in hand, Lennox and I stroll silently along the streets back to the boarding house. His grip on me is tight, but I don't mind it at all, it's as if we both fear the other will float away on the dark breeze. A lump in my throat makes it hard to swallow when I think of him sailing away in the morning, but when I try to string words together to explain my feelings, they slip away like white sand through my fingers. When we reach the boarding house, we continue our quiet walk up the stairs to our rooms.

"Will you stay with me tonight?" I ask hesitantly, looking up through my lashes with uncertainty. I'm past caring whether I sound desperate; I only want him close for our last night.

"Of course. I will always stay with you if you ask me to," he replies, brushing a loose strand of my hair back from my cheek, his thumb lingering on my cheekbone under my mask.

But I know his words are pretty lies. If I ask him to stay forever, he will refuse me. His life is aboard his ship and mine is... uncertain.

"I have something for you," he continues, jogging me back to the conversation. "I'll bring it through the adjoining door in just a moment." We each go into our separate rooms, but a few moments later the adjoining door opens and he walks in with a small chest.

"This is for you," he says, placing it on the low table in between the chairs where I usually have tea. He hands me a skeleton key for the lock and sits down to wait for me to open it. I look between the key and his face, furrowing my brow in confusion, but kneel down to unlock the box. When I lift the lid, a tremor of emotions rolls through me: sorrow, revulsion, heartbreak, fury.

It is full of gold — the final payment for my time with him. Payment for services rendered, and time that is at an end. I swallow the bile and tears that threaten to drown me. To keep from knocking the chest over in rage, I push the anger I always keep leashed back down where it burns in my chest so hot I could melt the entire chest of gold. The feelings I have for him crack into pieces at the knowledge that this was all just a business transaction. When I look at him, uncertainty lines his face, his brow furrowed to mimic my own, obviously unsure why I look unhappy instead of pleased with my bounty.

"What's wrong?" he asks, sliding from the chair to kneel beside me.

"I just..." I start, gripping my hands together so hard my knuckles are white. *Am I truly going to tell him how I feel?* I steel myself, trying to quiet the tremors running over me from the raging sea in my breast. He will be gone tomorrow, it doesn't matter — I need this to be said.

The words come out in a shaky whisper, "I thought that since the deal with Lyra was false, perhaps the one between us would turn out to be as well. That you might want me the same way I want you. But I see now that I was just another line on the ledger for this trip."

I swallow again, trying to keep the tears threatening to fall contained within their banks, hoping the lace mask I still wear will hide how hurt I am.

He gasps at my words. "Andromeda," Lennox starts, but pauses, "No. Fuck it! *Nerissa*." He pulls my face up to look at him, using my true name for the first time since I told him to forget it after Marie's disastrous dinner that first night on the island.

"Nerissa, don't think this," he gestures between us, his voice almost a plea, "isn't real. It's always been real for me. This is your money. *Yours*. Every coin you paid to Celeste for the past years has been set aside, except for the bare minimum to pay for your food and other necessities. She keeps it safe for when women want to escape.

"This is *yours*. I am not paying for you. You are not owned by anyone but yourself. Do you understand? I may want you to be mine, but you do not belong to anyone unless you choose to."

Ripping the mask from his eyes, I see the truth of his words on his handsome face, emerald eyes flicking across mine as if he is trying to read my thoughts. He reaches up slowly to untie my mask, letting it fall to the floor beside us.

My stomach somersaults in my body as I hold his hands in mine, glancing again at the chest of gold. It is enough to buy a life anywhere — a freedom I could have never antici-pated. But the only thing I want is him, and he will be gone tomorrow. I finally release the sob that has been threatening to break free and fall into his arms, gripping him tightly to me as we kneel on the hardwood floor.

CHAPTER 37

I lay awake into the early hours of the next morning, staring at the darkness of my room while Lennox breathes evenly next to me. After our confessions, we made love sweetly, like we did that first night so many years ago in the grove. But I cannot find a peaceful sleep as he has.

I turn my options over in my mind as the hours tick by. I know he has to leave today. I have the opportunity to stay here with my friends, or to depart on my own to make an entirely new life for myself. If I stay, I will have sisters in Siobhan and Lyra, as well as a place I am understood and welcomed. But, will I be forever haunted by my true identity with Marie always watching me here?

If I wish to flee to a completely new place, I now have the funds to start over. I can have a reputable business like Siobhan in a place where I will command respect and no one knows my past. If I choose that option, though, I will likely never see Lennox again, and I don't know if my heart, or his, can take another fracture. One more heartbreak may be the end of me, but I can't bring myself to beg him to take me with him. If he wanted me to come, he would have asked already, especially after last night. Plus, life at sea is dangerous for the best of sailors, moreso for a fleeing priestess without seafaring knowledge if the men protecting her are killed.

Another option tickles my thoughts — an ember that has smoldered since the night of the full moon. The night my smoored wrath was rekindled by the recognition of the King's sins. Despite my best efforts, Marie's words have sunken under my skin, just like she knew they would. They now swirl along with the repressed anger and near-constant guilt at the memories of my aunt and sister priestesses.

What if I could topple Blackwell's reign?

It would be my right — to seek vengeance against the man responsible for the destruction of my family, my home, and my entire way of existence. But what can one woman do on her own? I would have Marie's help, but would it align with my own goals, or further hers? I roll over with frustration as I mull over these thoughts.

I do not wish to be a queen. I never have. I don't want to be responsible for ruling a country, but if Marie is right and I could rally those who *could* rule, perhaps it would be enough. I tuck the thought away, more kindling for my sleeplessness, and continue to toss under the coverlet. Rolling over to view Lennox's dark outline, I wish sleep would overtake my wild thoughts and allow me some peace. Finally, I lay still in the darkness, willing my mind blank until I drift into nothingness.

SUNLIGHT BARELY TRICKLES THROUGH THE SHEER CURTAINS when I open my eyes. When I roll over to snuggle against Lennox, I'm greeted by an empty space, and I jolt upright looking around for a sign of him. His clothing is gone, and the door to his room stands open between our chambers. Throwing the coverlet from my body, I dash to the open door, hoping he is readying his belongings for his departure.

A folded piece of parchment rests prominently on the small table in his room, dark green wax sealing it. The outside simply has the letter *N* sketched on its creamy surface. When I pick up the note, something small and metallic hits the ground, but I'm so anxious to read the words that I ignore it, opting to crack the wax instead.

NERISSA —

I know you said not to call you that, but it is part of who you are. The girl I fell for in the firelight all those years ago. A queen in bearing, if not in name. The queen of my heart for eternity.

You may remove your bracelet at any time. I left the key for you with this note. It was never your soul that was bartered, it has always been mine. When I found the Western Temple destroyed upon my return to land, I promised the Goddess that I would seek vengeance for those who honored Her, for you, if She would only grant me the ability to find you again. She has honored Her part of the bargain. I will continue to honor mine.

I'm sorry to have left without telling you. Sailors are a superstitious lot, we believe it is bad luck to say "goodbye," so I wish you good fortune and hope that when I return, I will see you again. It's not fair to ask you to wait for me, but I hope you will. Perhaps you will say a prayer to Her for my safe return.

Even though leaving you means leaving a part of myself behind, I can not ask you to come with me. I will not be an influence on your choices — you deserve to make a life of your own choosing for once, here, or anywhere you desire. Do not be influenced by me, Marie, or who your aunt was. You deserve to be happy, whatever that means. I promise you I will be back. I will always come back for you. I hope you will be here for me to return to.

You own my heart and soul. You have since I first laid eyes on you, and you always will. I love you, Nerissa.

Forever yours, with all my heart,

Billy

MY HEART SHATTERS COMPLETELY, POUNDING ERRATICALLY IN my chest, as I rapidly read and reread the words. A sob escapes my lips, even though I hold a hand across my mouth, as I sink to my knees on the hard floorboards, clutching the parchment in my fist. As I kneel, I cast my eyes around to seek out the source of the metallic sound I heard when I picked up the note. A glint catches my eye across the floor, and I crawl to find the tiny screwdriver that unlocks the gold bangle at my wrist. In my anger, I throw it farther across the room.

If he felt this way, why didn't he just tell me last night? Why didn't he ask me to come with him? To at least see him off at the docks?

But I know.

It would have been too hard for us to say goodbye this

morning; neither of us would want the crew to see our emotions like that. We are two of a kind, our masks firmly in place and emotions reined in when we are in the public eye. He thinks he is honoring me by giving me choices, but he took away my choice to come with him by leaving me like this.

I hurry to the window and rip open the curtains before pushing open the shutters. It's still early morning; the sun has barely risen, and warm pink and orange light paints the buildings as it continues its ascent. It might not be too late.

I rush back through the door between our rooms and throw open my trunk, grabbing some of the new garments. I dress quickly, dash out the door, and down the stairs to the courtyard.

A few of the servants are milling about already, preparing for the day, and one girl has to jump out of my way as I storm out the door into the street. I can only hope the ship is leaving from the docks, and not from the small bay we originally dropped anchor in. If I choose wrong, I will miss them. Knowing they had to load new supplies and offload others, I assume the docks are the most logical choice, so I turn in that direction, running with the rising sun in my eyes.

Panting, I reach the docks and look around, placing my hands on my knees as I try to catch my breath. A painful stitch burns in my ribs from the sprint, and my heart has still not slowed since Lennox's letter ratcheted it into a frenzy. My eyes desperately rove over each body that comes into my line of sight, searching for anyone from the crew of the *Bartered Soul* still on land. Sailors mill around, a few giving me surprised looks at my harried appearance, but none are familiar.

A few ships already move through the water toward the open sea, while several others are anchored in berths with crates and barrels being loaded, but the sun is still in my eyes, so it isn't easy to tell which they are. I run up a set of stairs for a better vantage point over the crates and barrels, scanning the ships still anchored. None of them have a familiar crew, and I do not see the priestess figurehead I am so well acquainted with.

My heart stutters as I look closer at the ships already sailing away. The *Bartered Soul* is gone. From this view, I can tell she is one of the ships cutting through the turquoise sea. For a moment I fear my knees may give out.

To prevent myself from collapsing, I slowly lower myself to my knees and try to catch my breath. I wrap my arms around my chest to try to hold myself together and to push down the rising panic.

This isn't the end.

He will come back.

I can begin planning while he is gone, and when he returns, I will have an idea of how we move forward. Together. I can tell him how I feel, and I can avoid being parted from him again. I keep breathing, trying to hold in my emotions, to draw the mask back over my face before I go back to pack up my belongings. As I breathe and turn in on myself, I vaguely hear the swift step of approaching boots.

"So, it seems that we'll take turns chasing each other through the streets, then?" a deep rumble says at my side.

I choke on a breathless sob as I look up — eyes trailing

up boots, breeches, a fine lightweight coat in emerald green — before meeting a matching green gaze as Lennox stands over me with the sun at his back.

"I won't deny it. I had hoped you might try to catch us." Lennox gives a small smile, extending his hand to help me off my knees. He trembles slightly at my touch, riding the emotions I am trying to tamp down myself.

"You left me," I breathe into his chest as he pulls me into a firm embrace, "Without saying anything."

"I didn't want you to make a decision based on me. You deserve to be free," he says into my hair, caressing the back of my head with his large hand as he still holds me against him. He then holds me away from him and scans my clothing.

"Interesting new wardrobe," he smirks.

Dressed almost identically to him, my tall leather boots fit over slim-fitting breeches, topped with a linen tunic, and a midnight blue lightweight coat similar in style to his emerald one, but in a more feminine size. I have also commissioned a belt with a sheath for my dagger — I no longer plan to keep it hidden in a pocket.

"I figured if I plan on becoming a pirate, I should take clothing inspiration from a fashionable expert," I explain, raising my brows and pursing my lips, waiting for his reply.

"A pirate? You want to come with us then?" His eyes light up as he studies my face for an explanation, his grin stretching across his face.

"I do. I want to come with you. *You* are my choice. You and this crew are my family now, along with Siobhan and Lyra. I want to help take care of them, and everyone like us.

I don't want to be apart from you," I whisper. I look up at him, waiting for his response.

"I was hoping you would say something like that." His smile turns wicked as he picks me up and spins me around in excitement. When he places me back down, we face the ships at the dock. One looks familiar, but the figurehead is no longer the griffin of King Dargan. I take a step forward, looking at the woodwork and paint of the new figurehead – it's a black wolf, carved with a vicious snarl on its lips. Its white teeth gleam in the sunlight, the sigil of the Goddess glowing at its brow.

"The *Archangel*?" I question, looking between the ship and Lennox.

"Indeed. We made some necessary adjustments for our purposes. It *is* bad luck to change the name of a ship, but I thought perhaps a blessing from a priestess might negate that," he replies, gesturing for me to walk to the back to view the name, newly painted across the stern.

Andromeda's Vengeance.

"Oh, I think that is something I can definitely help with," I reply before kissing him firmly on the mouth.

EPILOGUE

The *Bartered Soul* waits in the bay while we ready the newly-named *Andromeda's Vengeance* for departure. I asked Siobhan and Lyra to join me in blessing her to ward off any bad luck. Of course, they were happy to help.

Siobhan brought a supply of herbs and tinctures for me to use in my surgery, enough for both the sloop and the brigantine to be stocked. I know she is sad to not have a second send-off with Erik, but he is acting as Captain for the *Bartered Soul* now that we have two vessels in our fleet, and is already adrift.

Siobhan squeezes my hand once, a tight smile on her lips, before saying, "I will miss you and I'm sad to see you leave. I hoped to have a sister at the apothecary, but I understand why you are sailing with him. You've been separated for far too long, and it brings me such joy for both of you to have found each other. Stay safe, Sister. I hope to see you when the ships return."

Even though it is unlike me to be so demonstrative, I pull her to me for a hug. I am so thankful to have found another kindred soul, and I can't depart without showing my feelings. She holds me tightly for a moment, smiling brightly when she pulls away, her eyes brilliant blue under the shine of unshed tears.

"I'll be back, Siobhan. We all will. I promise."

"May the Goddess bless you all," she says before walking down the steps of the dock.

As I stand with Lennox watching the crew load the final crates on the sloop, Marie joins Lyra to bid us farewell. The older woman pulls me aside for a quick word before we weigh anchor.

"I know you don't wish to speak about it, but you need to know that you and Lennox have the full support of this entire island, my dear. Do not fear the knowledge I possess. Feel free to call on me if you need to."

She squeezes my hand and presses a small, firm oval into my palm before she turns away. When I unwrap my fingers, the miniature of my Aunt Adelaide, the one that she confronted me with in her study, stares back at me from my palm.

"Thank you," I call out to her, stopping her withdrawal. "Thank you for reminding me of who I am, and for arranging for me to bring Lyra here."

"Thank you. For humoring me. For listening. Even if you aren't ready to hear what I have to say. I know that you have endured so much already, but you are not alone, child. You never were. Remember that."

She continues on her way to wait for Lyra farther up the beach, giving us a moment of privacy. The younger woman wraps me in an embrace so full of warmth, it feels like being hugged by the sun. She has a bright future here with her grandmother and Siobhan. I can only hope I am able to return to see her soon.

"I'll see you soon, Lyra," I whisper, remembering what Lennox said about *goodbye* being bad luck, holding her tightly in our embrace.

"I love you, Andromeda. Please be safe," she whispers back.

When she steps away, tears spill out of her hazel eyes, but she smiles brightly and dashes them away. Turning to her uncle, she wraps Lennox in a tight hug and kisses his cheek, then joins Marie where they can wave from the sand beside the dock. He laughs at his niece, smiling broadly at both women, before taking my hand in his to return to the *Vengeance*.

Lennox and I walk up the gangplank together and stand on the deck as the crew prepares for our departure; we will join Erik and the *Bartered Soul* along with Captain Jackson and the *Selkie's Tears* soon. Other captains are readying to depart in the next day or two, and our fleet will soon prowl the ocean hunting the King's ships, his men, and perhaps, even Blackwell himself.

Lennox told me we will stop in the city of New Aphros before returning to the open waters, and excitement swells in my chest at the anticipation of exploring another new city. I take a deep breath of the ocean air mingling with the sweet fragrance of the tropical flowers, then lean into Lennox where he holds me at his side.

"I love you, Billy," I whisper to him.

"I love you too, Nerissa," he replies, tilting my chin up with his finger to look into my eyes. Then, with a gentle squeeze and a kiss on the brow, he releases me and turns to the crew awaiting their orders.

"All right everyone, anchors aweigh!" He shouts to the crew. His orders are met with a howl rising into the air.

The wolves of *Vengeance* are ready to hunt.

ACKNOWLEDGMENTS

OMG – I wrote a book! And if you are reading this, you read it! It was a bit of a whirlwind once Andromeda and Lennox made their way into my mind, and I am so thankful you joined us on the adventure!

Of course, a huge thank you to my husband, Matt. You held things down while I obsessed and wrote for hours on end, you read my super rough draft (even though I know that's not your thing), and you always remind me when I am being my own worst critic and spiraling into self-sabotage. I love you, and can't wait to give you the rundown for the next book ad nauseum.

To Anne, thanks for taking a chance on reading a friend of a friend's rough draft and helping me flesh things out, offering great critiques, and even better reassurance. Your eyes were the first to read this story, and your words gave me the confidence to keep going. Thanks to Michelle for introducing us, even if just through the internet, and for inspiring and encouraging me to get my words down on paper, and for being such an accepting friend all around. Brooke, you are always a book bestie and I hope you like the final product.

Jess, my number one hype woman, I am so glad I found you on Instagram and shared this with you. You have been a ray of sunshine and a total babe from start to finish.

Thank you for always being in my corner and boosting me up when I am feeling unsure.

Aimee, you are an angel. Not only are you an amazing author, but you have been such a wonderful friend and editor. I answer the phone when you call, so you know we are real-life besties! You also made me force myself to understand Discord so I could link up with our amazing group there!

To the ladies of *The Daily Discord* (wink to Aimee and Bethany for that one) — Bethany, Elle, Ray, Sarah, and Aimee, herself — I am so happy to have found y'all. I can't wait until we can have a real-life meet-up, but until then I will cackle at our convos and can't wait to soak up more of your knowledge and read all your WIPs. You are the best support group and I couldn't do this without your humor and love.

Lex, thanks for taking the time to check out some of the spice for me to make sure it was on the right track. Hopefully, the rest of the scenes don't disappoint.

To all my alpha, beta, ARC readers, and the amazing friends I have been supported by on Instagram/Bookstagram — you have no idea how much you have helped in making this dream a reality. You have all been so kind and welcoming, and really made me feel confident in sharing my words with the world. I hope you love this story as much as I do, and that you will stick around for the next part of Andromeda's story.

About the Author

L.B. Benson is a lifelong reader with eclectic taste. She even formally documented her love of books by earning a Bachelor of Arts in English from the University of Texas. If a book has a good plot, she will give it a chance – you can find her engrossed in anything from Dickens to dark romance, but she's a fantasy girl at heart and adores a dash of romance.

She spends her spare time dreaming up stories in the Texas countryside where she lives with her husband and daughter, growing veggies and snuggling with their animals. *The Bartered Soul* marks Benson's first foray to the other side of the page as her debut novel, and is the first book in the *Andromeda's Account* series.

Stay up to date on upcoming releases by following along at https://lbtheauthor.com or on Instagram @lb_the_author